DEFIANT ISLAND

Books by Robert Rayner

Colorland

The Atlantic Trilogy

The Ragged Believers
Defiant Island
Second Wind

DEFIANT ISLAND

Robert Rayner

SPEAKING VOLUMES, LLC
NAPLES, FLORIDA
2015

Defiant Island

ISBN 978-1-62815-322-4

For Nancy and Sue, old friends

Acknowledgments

Thanks to Carrie Mac, David Goss, and Terry Seguin for reading and responding to the manuscript, and to Dr. Stephen Smith for his 'medical reading'.

And thanks, as always, to Nancy, for her support, and for putting up with the inherent unsociability of writing. Most of the time.

Chapter One

It was that step just before the bend in the stairs that did it.

Carol-Ann would be mad at her for falling because she would be the one, she always said, who'd be stuck looking after her if she had an accident. She should have been more careful, Heaven knows, having lived in the house all her life.

Her friend, Gladys, had commented on it just a day or two before. "Cornelia Morse, this step is dangerous. It's so worn and slippery, it's inviting me to slip on it and fall downstairs."

Gladys had arrived mid-morning and found Cornelia still in bed. "What are you doing there with half the day gone, old girl?"

"I think I forgot to get up."

"Well get your arse out of bed now."

Gladys had led the way down the stairs, grumbling about their narrowness. "You can tell these steps were made by a young man."

"That'd be my father."

"I know—and I wish he'd remembered that old folks, like your ma and us, might have to use them one day, and made them bigger."

"Ma was always grumbling about them, but she still managed them, even when she was in her eighties."

"I remember."

"And she was always telling us to slow down on them when we were girls and running round the house like wild things."

" 'Magine—running around like wild things. I'd like to see us running around like wild things now, at our age."

Gladys had giggled, and in her giggle Cornelia had caught a vestige of the wild things they'd once been.

"How old are we, Gladys?"

Gladys had stopped, carefully, on the stairs in order to look around at her old friend.

"What do you mean how old are we? It's your birthday. Don't tell me you've forgotten. You're eighty-three today. That's why I'm here—because it's your birthday and we're going out to celebrate. That's if you're ever ready. Now get your arse down these stairs."

They'd advanced a few more cautious steps before Gladys had paused again to make the observation about the dangerous step and about falling downstairs.

And that was exactly what had happened to Cornelia now.

At least, she thought that was what had happened. She couldn't remember, but she guessed it. She was lying at the foot of the stairs, one leg bent under her, the other splayed at an awkward angle. She couldn't move, and her hip hurt badly.

Maybe if she could sleep a little it would ease her discomfort.

Her birthday—yes. Gladys was right. She had forgotten. They went to the big island to celebrate with a walk on the cliffs, followed by supper, and a night at the Wharf Inn.

They called at the store on the way to the ferry, and Dale said, "So you girls are out on the town again, eh?"

Carol-Ann grumbled, "I don't think you two should be driving around. You're not safe behind the wheel, Gladys. And why do you have to stay overnight, anyway?"

Gladys said, "Because your ma and me are going to get pissed."

Dale said, "You're a couple of wild things."

Carol-Ann pursed her lips. "I'll be the one who has to look after Cornelia if she's injured."

After their walk, they had a gin and tonic before supper, then clam chowder with a glass of white wine.

Gladys said, lifting her glass, "Happy birthday, old thing."

Cornelia responded, "Bottoms up."

Gladys retorted, "More like bottoms down at our age. My bum's hanging lower every day. I swear my cheeks will be dragging on the ground soon."

Cornelia giggled. "The things you say, Gladys."

Coming back to White Rock Island on the ferry the next morning, they got out of the car and stood side by side on the deck. Gladys put her arm around Cornelia and said, "I suppose you'll be bossing me around now."

Cornelia said, "I wouldn't boss you around, Gladys."

"You always have done as soon as you're older than me."

"But we're the same age."

"Not until I have my birthday next week. You're eighty-three now, and I'm still a spring chicken of eighty-two." Gladys looked at her old friend and added, "It was your birthday yesterday, remember?"

Cornelia thought for a moment. "We had supper at the Wharf Inn."

Gladys said, "Right."

Gladys said …

She must have been sleeping. It was around noon because the sunlight, streaming dustily through the coloured panes above the front door, shone into the parlour.

Perhaps she should wait in there. Perhaps crawl there. No—her aching legs would not respond.

But—wait?

Why did she think 'wait'?

Wait—for what; for whom?

Yes—for Gladys, of course, for Gladys and Tom. They were going to Saint John because Tom was getting a business award and had invited them to see the presentation, and she was to wait for them to pick her up at her house. That was why Dale hadn't called in first thing this morning to check on her, like he usually did, because she'd told him she was going to Saint John with Gladys.

She remembered Gladys saying, "We'll be celebrating with Tom next week. Don't forget—like you forgot your birthday."

Don't forget…

But, oh dear, yes, she had forgotten. They arrived and were in a hurry and she wasn't ready and she said, flapping her hands at them, "Go without me. Go on." She felt she'd let them down; that they were disappointed with her.

Gladys said, "We'll wait."

But she was too flustered—her vague days seemed to be getting vaguer and more frequent—and said, "Go on."

Gladys said, "Are you sure, ducky?"

"Yes. Go on. But get me the knitting pattern, the one we were going to look for in town. I can't remember what it's called…" Getting flustered again.

Gladys said, "Call and tell me. Call me at Tom's house. Dale's got the number if you can't find it."

"I'll call from the store. I've got to go down this afternoon. I'm out of bread."

"Tell Dale to call in and check on you tomorrow morning, otherwise he'll think you're away with me and he won't come by."

That was why Dale hadn't come to check on her this morning. She was supposed to be away with Gladys and Tom, but she'd forgotten about the trip. She should have written it down. Carol-Ann told her to write things down. She told her to make a sign to read in the morning: Brush hair. She didn't like it when Cornelia went to the store and her hair wasn't done. Gladys told her to do her hair, too. But she didn't grumble about it. She just said, "Brush your bloody hair, Cornelia. You look like a goddam hippie." Gladys said she looked like a hippie not just because of her hair, but because of the long, loose dresses, in rich, dark colours, she liked to wear with her blouses. When Cornelia took the trouble to twist her grey hair into a careful, tight bun, instead of leaving it hanging loosely behind her,

Gladys appraised her and said, "That's better. Chicks like us should never leave the house without getting dolled up. We can't disappoint the guys."

Cornelia imagined Gladys dressed to the nines for Tom's award. Would they be in Saint John yet, or still in Tom's helicopter? Well—not his helicopter. It belonged to Brunswick Oil, but he seemed to be able to use it whenever he wanted. When Cornelia asked Gladys what Tom did at the company, she said, "He's a big shot. He thinks he's important." But you could tell she was proud of her son. He bought her a cellular telephone and a computer and he telephoned and sent her e-mails every day. He'd programmed her cellular telephone, she said, so that all she had to do was press one button and it rang to his, and he'd answer it wherever he was and whatever he was doing. Even if it was an emergency and she couldn't talk, he'd know it was her and he'd send the helicopter, with a doctor.

When he set up the computer after Gladys had that little attack a few years ago, he said, "Now you're wired."

Gladys said, "I've been wired all my life." She crossed her eyes and ran her hands through her hair so that it stood up straight all around her head. Cornelia, who was visiting while Dale helped Tom set everything up, crossed her eyes, too, and stuck her tongue out the side of her mouth, and wiggled her fingers on each side of her head.

Tom looked at Dale and said, "We've got a couple of wild things here."

Wild things, they were, she and Gladys. That was what their mothers used to call them when they were growing up on the island. It had started when they were little girls—little madams, that was another of her mother's phrases for them—and had carried on when they were teenagers. They made a club room in the attic of Gladys's house, with a sign on the door: Cornelia Mullen and Gladys Cronk. Wild Things. Private. Once they barricaded themselves in, when they were in trouble for something, and stayed there so long it grew dark—there were no lamps up there, and they weren't allowed to take candles to the attic—and they lay down and clung to one another.

5

Cornelia opened her eyes. She'd been dreaming—of herself and Gladys, wild things in the attic, on the floor. Was she awake? Or was this the dream—her lying helpless on the floor at the bottom of the stairs in the dark? She thought she'd opened her eyes but now she wasn't sure. She closed them—yes, they must have been open—and opened them again. It was still dark. It must be evening. Would Dale come when the store closed? No—he thought she was away, otherwise he'd come, like Tom promised to come if ever Gladys was in trouble.

She was as proud of Dale as Gladys was of Tom. She was proud of how he'd gone away to Fredericton to get his degree and how he'd returned to teach at the island school, just as she used to, even if Carol-Ann was scornful of his teaching the little kids, saying if he had to teach, he could at least teach at the high school on the big island, Deer Isle, where the older students from both Deer Isle and White Rock went. Cornelia had been doubtful about his giving up teaching to work at the store when Carol-Ann inherited it from her parents, but he supplemented their income with a few hours at the fish plant, and they seemed to be doing all right, and she thought Dale was happy.

Cornelia was proud, too, that Dale took care of her, like Tom did Gladys. He called in every day—every morning, and most evenings when the store closed at eight thirty.

But today he wouldn't come, hadn't come this morning and wouldn't come tonight, because she'd told him she was going to the mainland with Gladys and Tom to stay the night, and, yes, she was supposed to go down to the store to buy bread and to telephone Gladys about the knitting pattern.

Yes.

But her hip hurt, and she couldn't move her legs, and in any case she felt too tired to try.

She needed to sleep.

Chapter Two

The helicopter rose like a prehistoric bird over the city. It hovered above the squat functionalism of the Brunswick Oil head offices before heading past the refineries toward the docks, where fishing boats mingled with oil tankers and container ships from around the world. Following the island ferry route, it headed out over Passamaquoddy Sound to Deer Isle, passing over the ferries as they plied between the city and this largest of the islands in the Sound. For a while it followed the shore road that wound past the shingled beaches and sprinkled settlements of the benign eastern shore, then turned away from the coast and headed over the barrens of the interior until the unfolding carpet of Labrador tea and wild rhododendron gave way to the cliffs of the rugged and unpopulated western shore.

Tearing his eyes from the tumult of surging eddies, ephemeral whirlpools and jagged rocks, Tom looked to the horizon, knowing that the eponymous white rocks of his childhood home, White Rock Island, would be dancing there, a siren mirage beckoning the traveller's eyes from the bleak ferocity of Deer Isle's western shore to the improbable idyll wavering on the horizon.

Tom's vision of White Rock Island was ambivalent. The businessman in him saw its extraordinary untapped cottage and tourist potential, at the same time as something in him, the remnants of his upbringing, made him dread the exploitation which would destroy the very elements that made it so attractive. He knew the value his colleagues and acquaintances placed on waterfront and seclusion. He knew he could buy up acres of the island cheaply and, for at least three times the price he'd pay the innocent owners, sell it to his city bound friends for whom waterfront and seclusion meant thirty feet of garbage strewn mud on a polluted lake teeming with power boats and ringed with well-appointed cabins. For them, White Rock Island would be a breathtaking, pristine paradise. In his desire to keep that potential a secret he spoke disparagingly to his business friends of his childhood home. At parties and coffee breaks, when they expressed envious disbelief at his birthplace—*Tell us again where you're from, Tom*—envisaging a romantic childhood environment not far from the reality of White Rock's geography, he scoffed that it was just a cold and windswept rock in the Atlantic, with bugs in the spring, fog in the summer, freezing rain and ice in the winter. *What about the fall*, they asked. Fall was nice, he conceded. When the fog lifted in October you had a week to enjoy it before the freezing rain hit in November. It was hardly the desert island they were imagining. And genes were a problem. In response to their raised eyebrows, he'd add, deadpan, genes—lack of variety. As they spluttered over their coffee or their gins and tonics, he elaborated on the interconnectedness of the island population. He'd muse quietly that the only place you got to meet girls was at family reunions. Perhaps that was why he'd stayed single. He had nightmares of finding himself married to a first cousin. They slapped him on the back and poured him another coffee or bought another round while he thought ashamedly of his betrayal of his mother and her friends, and guiltily of Adrian, at home in the town house in Saint John. He wondered why he felt so outcast when he thought of the island, pondering how he embodied the reversal of a romantic cliché: not the city dweller cast away on an island, but the islander exiled in the city. Was it his mother's fierce and proud independence in keeping her illegitimate and only child despite the censure of a community bound by tradition? Did that defiance linger in him, causing him to shun his home at the same time as he treasured its uniqueness? Was it, simply, his solitariness, the feeling of somehow always being apart from the island children he grew up with, although he played on the rocks and among the tidepools with them as an infant; started school with eight of them in the kindergarten class of 1960; suffered with them, but couldn't share, their burgeoning awareness of sexuality at high school; graduated with them, although his feeling of apartness

8

drove him to shun the graduation ceremonies, despite being the winner of the Maritime Foods and Beverages Inc. award for top academic marks. His mother understood, she said. He was glad, then, to forsake the island world of fishing and fish plant that his schoolmates entered, and to accept the offer of Maritime Foods to take him on at their head office in Saint John, from where within two years Brunswick Oil enticed him to their junior executive training programme. Now his world was Saint John, Halifax, Montreal, Boston, Toronto, Calgary—and White Rock Island was a relic of his past, bound to him only by his mother.

He glanced at her, sitting beside him, noting the excitement in her face as she bobbed her head to see the island in the distance. She caught his eye and said, "There she is." He marvelled at her love for the island, his own ambivalence underscored anew by it, and he realized again that he could never act on his business instincts. Through his mother's eyes, he saw and valued the island's peace and independence, and the strength of its community, and even when she was no longer there to embody that appreciation (and how much longer, he wondered, would she be there, already aged eight-two), he knew he would be incapable of that ultimate betrayal of her memory. When she was gone, he would simply forget the island and bind himself solely to his city life. Meanwhile he admired and loved her zest and independence.

She sat beside him, erect, shoulders back, chin high, glasses—goldrimmed, round, delicate—perched on her small nose. Her sharp features, he thought, would make her look ill-tempered if they didn't contain a constant readiness to laugh. He knew she'd had her hair done especially for this trip—it looked like grey frosting—although it was always immaculate in a tight wavy perm. He could never tell whether she'd just been to, or was due for, her weekly visit to *Holly's Cuts 'n' Styles* on the island. He looked more closely. Yes, as he expected, her lipstick matched her linen pant suit, one of several she wore for 'best', which seemed to him to encompass anything that took her from her house. Today's suit was scarlet, the lipstick a frosty pink.

"What's the lipstick today, Ma?"

"*Passion in the Snow.*"

He shook his head. "Good God."

She grinned.

She was feisty. He hated the word but couldn't think of a better one. She was looking at the island again. Watching her excitement, he wondered: How much longer will you draw me back here?

*****

Gladys sneaked a look at her son, her precious boy, admiring him, his athletic build, his tawny hair. She liked how he wore it fringed at the front and long at the back. It was ironic, she thought, that in face and form he exemplified what many admired as the archetypal athlete when he so despised the character and actions and attitudes associated with what he called the jock set. He looked the same in his forties as he did in his twenties, even wore the same clothes, the ones he was wearing now, the cords and the sweater, always a sweater, never a sports jacket or suit. Even when he entered the business world of Brunswick Oil he quietly resisted the pressure to adopt the executive uniform of grey or dark blue suit, and was good enough at his job to get away with it. He said it was stupid for him to wear a jacket he took off as soon as he arrived at work. He preferred something utilitarian to wear outside the office, like the canvas field coat he wore now.

He saw her looking at him and said, "What?"

"Nothing, precious boy."

"Ma, I'm forty-two."

"You're still my precious boy."

She always called him her precious boy. He feigned exasperation at it, but she knew he liked it.

She was aware of, and understood, Tom's ambivalent feelings toward the island, not the guilty thoughts of exploiting it, but his apartness from it, the same apartness that had made him wary of closeness with his peers on the island, that fomented his dislike of any group activity. She was glad to take advantage of what she called his dual citizenship, city and island. She loved the occasional business trips she shared with him. She liked staying with him and Adrian in Saint John, strolling through the city market, taking coffee at The Harbour Café in the city centre, having lunch on the boardwalk watching the harbour traffic. Although this had been just an overnight trip, to see Tom receive another business award, she was returning, as she always did, with joy and excitement to the island, whose long ago censure of Tom's birth she'd accepted, even as she'd defied it, as simply an inevitable part of the culture she belonged to. She loved not just the island's solitary beauty and the interdependence of neighbours and friends that sustained its independence, but also its daily life, the quilting evenings, the church suppers, the single island store, the lifelong friendships, like hers with Cornelia.

Cornelia!

She shouted to Tom above the clatter of the helicopter, "Cornelia was supposed to telephone me in Saint John."

"She probably forgot. You know how scatty she's getting, like forgetting she was coming with us."

"But I told her to phone because she needed a knitting pattern. We were going to get it in town, and when she wasn't ready, I said I'd get it for her. I said call me and tell me the pattern you want. She had to go down to the store to get bread—she'd run out—and I said to call me from there. She forgets lots of things, I know, but she wouldn't forget that. She can't knit any more until she gets it, and she knits every day, so she'd have remembered. I know she would."

"I'll pick it up for her and send it out."

"That's sweet of you, precious boy—but I'm still worried. I'm afraid something's happened to her."

They were nearly over the island. The ferry, a scow alongside a fishing boat, which made the fifty minute crossing between Deer Isle and White Rock Island three times a day, with extra crossings on the whim of the operators and in emergencies, was arriving too. Gladys, her joy clouded by worry for her old friend, looked down as the helicopter flew over the ferry, past the wharf, and circled cautiously beyond the harbour.

Tom, also looking down, noted with interest the sole passenger on the ferry. He was leaning against the rail, jotting something in a notebook. Even from a distance, Tom sensed a kind of subtle, arresting presence about the stranger. His dark suit posited him as one of the politicians or bureaucrats who sometimes visited the island, rather than a tourist, but the russet sweat shirt suggested a freedom from dress code of the kind Tom himself had successfully won. Tom wondered idly whether that freedom had been earned, like his, through defiance, or whether it came from simply having the authority to dress as he pleased. The latter, Tom guessed. He wasn't sure why. It was something to do with the stance—casual, but ex- uding confidence and a quiet authority ready to be exercised; and with the age—forties, Tom surmised, perhaps a little older than himself; and even with the appearance—the weather worn complexion, the grey streaking the cinnamon coloured hair; the compact build.

Chapter Three

The stranger on the ferry looked up at the helicopter, returned briefly to his notebook, then directed his gaze at the island unfolding before him.

Patrick Given had been here once before as a child of eight holidaying with his parents. His vague memory of the island was not so much of scene and deed as of feelings—of peace, security, and serenity. His search to regain those same feelings had drawn him to the island now. It was an elusive and romantic quest, he admitted to himself, half ashamed of his quixotic adventure. But, he told himself, he had nothing to lose. He lived in a state of such emotional torment that the travel itself—the drive from his Ottawa apartment to the airport, the flight in his light aircraft to the tiny Deer Isle air field, the hitching of a ride to the ferry terminal, the ferry ride—was a kind of balm, and the present destination, while it remained a destination, offered at least the hope of the kind of peace he remembered from his childhood visit. His parents, avid birdwatchers, had come once to Deer Isle, attracted by its reputation as a haven for rare bird life with its dramatic and unassailable cliffs and inlets. The only child, he had followed his parents as they tramped the clifftop footpaths scouring the rocks for unusual sightings. He remembered his binoculars bumping against his knees as he walked. They had spent one day on White Rock Island, where they had followed directions from the ferry to the trail through the woods of the interior that led to the white sand beaches of the western shore. He recalled the wonder of emerging from the forest and seeing the beach, sensationally empty, stretching to a distant headland. While his parents explored the shore and the edge of the woods for birds, he played in the sand, watched the movement of the tide, paddled in the shallows, discovered varieties of seaweed and schools of tiny fish. Exhausted by his play, he fell asleep at the top of the beach, with the fragrance of the woods on one side and the salt laden air on the other. When he woke, he was enthralled by the peace and safety of his surroundings. He was conscious of having slept in an environment entirely foreign to his home in suburban Toronto, yet with no fear of its strangeness, and no suspicion of vulnerability, despite the dense woods harbouring unimaginable creatures on one side, and on the other the sea, which he'd discovered devoured the beach with astonishing speed. He found his parents sleeping nearby and when they woke, they too, were awed by the tranquility and security of their surroundings. They spoke in hushed voices, as if in church, until they disembarked from the ferry back on Deer Isle. As he grew older, he thought of that day, that awakening, as a kind of mystical experience. Now, nearly forty years later, he craved the profound peace and security he remembered from that visit as solace not from the world of work, deals and negotiations and risks, but from the business of everyday living amid a confusion of emotions that threatened to overwhelm him.

The scow ground against the ramp at the wharf. Stepping carefully through seaweed strewn by the retreating tide, he climbed the ramp. He hesitated at the top—he remembered nothing of this—but with the ferry landing forming one end of the island's single road there was only one way to go. Two children, a boy and a girl, pedaled their bicycles past him and raced recklessly down the slippery ramp onto the ferry's deck, from where they were chased by the ferry hand, roaring a feigned anger. As they pedaled furiously past him again, he thought—there we are, Penelope and I, on our bicycles, except that we explored not the wharf and ferry ramp of a remote island, but the suburban network of tidy roads and driveways around our homes.

The little girl and boy in whom Patrick had seen Penelope and himself abandoned their bicycles and sat in front of the island store, a hundred yards along the coast road. It occurred to Patrick that he'd need somewhere to stay, and that would be a good place to enquire.

It was shift change time at the fish plant just beyond the wharf where the road ended and the store was busy with workers, the women in light blue smocks, their hair in nets, the men in dark blue shirts. Patrick opened the door onto voices raised in raucous protest.

"They'll close it down. That's what they'll do."

"They say they'll keep it open."

"Right—like they kept the plant on Grass Island open. Less than a year it lasted after they took it over."

"If the plant's going to be shut down you might as well shut down the island."

"There'll still be the fishing. Only change would be the boys having to take the catch over to the plant on Deer Isle."

"That won't work. They're at full capacity over there now, with the catch from the Deer Isle boats. They'd have to take the fish to Blacks Harbour. That'd add three hours to every trip. It just wouldn't pay."

"You know what'll happen. The fishers'll take themselves over there to live."

"That's what I'm telling you—it'll be the end of the island."

"That's what they want. It's more efficient."

"That's what who wants?"

"The fish companies, the provincial government ..."

"And the island be buggered."

"That's about it."

"I guess if they close the plant down at least the federal government might throw some money at us to keep something going on the island."

"Yeah—and how long will that last?"

"Is that how you want to live, anyway—on government handouts?"

"I don't want anyone's charity."

While the fish workers grumbled around the counter, Patrick browsed along the aisles of the store. The shelves held a mixture of food, clothing, hardware and souvenirs. He stopped to examine an oversized plastic lobster claw bearing a picture of White Rock Island harbour, and a gold rimmed plate with the same scene. Further along he found a few post-cards—of fishing boats at the wharf, and of the ferry, and of the craggy shoreline. He chose one. He'd send it to Peggy. He knew she had a collection of his postcards from all over the world.

Among the souvenirs was a pile of brochures, the front page of which proclaimed: *Uncrowded … Unspoiled … Unbelievable … White Rock Island.*

Patrick opened one of the brochures and read: *White Rock Island is a sliver of rock in Passamaquoddy Sound. Five miles long and one mile wide, it lies ten miles west of Deer Isle, the famous tourist destination. The islanders, one hundred and fifty of them, live along the Shore Road, White Rock Island's only road, their houses perched on the white rocks which give the island its name. If you venture to the western shore, you will find the hidden treasure of the island—a three mile stretch of beach, the open sea on one side, the woods of the interior on the other. The white sands are bounded at one end by the forbidding and impassable Northern Head cliffs, and at the other by the equally forbidding Southern Point cliffs, through and around which, nevertheless, a difficult trail meanders. Stay and enjoy the amenities of the island, centred around the main wharf where the ferry docks.*

Patrick turned to the back page and read: *A Brief History of the Island. Legend has it that White Rock Island was originally a prosperous farming community in the late nineteenth century, but no evidence for this exists, and almost certainly the legend can be consigned to folklore. We can surmise that it perhaps reflected the wish of the original settlers, as they struggled for survival at the turn of the century, that the terrain on which they found themselves offered at least a little soil among the unproductive rocks. We are satisfied—and proud—that the history of the island has always been one of a thriving fishing community.*

Patrick tucked the brochure in his pocket and wandered to the back of the store, where picture windows looked out onto the harbour and the fishing boats tied up along the wharf. Below the windows a shelf offered a selection of magazines. Penelope stared at him from the cover of one, an old edition of *La Vie*. He picked it up and examined the flawless, famous face. He looked from Penelope to the island scene beyond the windows,

16

wondering where she was now; whether she might be wondering where he was.

As the fish plant workers straggled out, he approached the counter with his postcard.

The man behind it, who wore the same dark blue shirt as the plant workers, said, "*Welcome* to White Rock Island. I hope you didn't mind getting caught up in the *protest*." His thinning sandy hair flopped across the brow of his ruddy face, which was distinguished by a full-lipped mouth. He spoke in an affected laconic drawl, emphasizing certain words with self-conscious irony, perhaps mocking his own words, perhaps simply betraying uncertainty.

"Of course not. What's going on?"

"The fish plant *workers* got the word this morning. The present owners are selling up and they're afraid the new *owners* will close the plant."

"Who are the buyers?"

"Some *outfit* called I.C.E."

"International Consolidated Enterprises?"

"I *suppose*. Heard of them?"

"Yup. Will they close it, do you think?"

"It's what has happened to other *plants* we know on the *mainland* that have been bought *out*, but that was by other companies. No-one seems to *know* anything about International Consolidated."

"Would it mean the end of the island, like the workers were saying, if the plant closed?"

"Not in the *short* term—but in the *long* term …" He shrugged. "Well, I give it ten years *tops*. If there's no work the youngsters will move away—plenty of them do that already—and that means no young *families*. Then the school will close, and I doubt we'd be able to *hang on* here at the store for long. We *barely* make ends meet as it is."

"That's tough."

"It's *business*."

"Well …"

"There's a *meeting* next week, at the community hall. The present owner is supposed to be coming, and someone from I.C.E., to make some sort of *announcement*. If you're still here and you're finding island life too quiet and you want some *entertainment* you should look in."

"I won't find island life too quiet."

"Have you been here before?"

"Once—a long time ago."

"Come to enjoy the *scenery*, have you? That's what the *tourists* usually like. It's about all we've got to offer on the island."

"Something like that. I'm hoping to find somewhere to stay."

As Patrick spoke, a woman, short, dark, bristling with energy and impatience, entered the store.

The man behind the counter said, "This is my *wife*, Carol-Ann. She runs the store. I just *help out* here. My real *work* is at the plant."

"Your real work is here, my boy, not playing with your buddies at the plant for the few hours you get over there. Did you get the shelves restocked?"

"Yes, *ma'm*." He turned back to Patrick. "I should have introduced myself. I'm *Dale*—Dale *Morse*."

"Patrick Given."

"From?"

"Ottawa."

"*Wow*. You certainly like a change of pace for your *holiday*, don't you? How did you get here? You don't have a *car*. I saw you *walk* off the ferry…"

Carol-Ann Morse, extracting a pile of papers from a clipboard and slamming them on the counter as she tipped her head at her husband, muttered to Patrick, "He claims he's busy, but he's got time to watch the ferry unload."

"I flew to Deer Isle."

18

"*Charter* flight?"

"My own plane, actually. I flew myself."

"*Wow.*" Patrick shook hands with them both as Dale Morse continued to his wife, "This *gentleman* is looking for *somewhere* to stay."

Carol-Ann Morse, making for the aisles with clipboard in hand, said, "There's a bed and breakfast just up the road. I know they've got a vacancy."

"That would be ideal."

"I'll call and say you're on the way. How long are you staying?"

"I'm not sure. Say a week."

The door burst open. Gladys entered and bustled to the counter. Tom followed.

Dale Morse said, "What's *up*, Gladys?"

"Where's Cornelia?"

"With *you*—isn't she?"

Gladys turned to Tom. "I told you something was wrong." Turned back to Dale. "She changed her mind at the last minute. She didn't come with us."

"I didn't *check in* on mother because I thought she was with *you*."

"She was coming down to the store because she'd run out of bread. That was yesterday morning. She wouldn't go a day without bread. Something's happened to her. I know it."

Chapter Four

Something pushing against her, digging into her back. Dale Senior trying to wake her.

She said—she thought she said—"Is it time to get up already?"

Her eyes were open.

Dale Senior still pushing. She closed her eyes. Dear Dale Senior, waking her in the early morning, as she insisted he did, before he went down to the wharf.

Pushing again.

She opened her eyes.

Light from the wrong direction. It lit the wall opposite her bed in the morning, not behind it.

Wait.

Not her bedroom. She was at the bottom of the stairs. Why was she sleeping at the bottom of the stairs?

More pushing.

No—not Dale Senior, of course not. Not for many years.

She'd fallen downstairs. She remembered.

It must be Dale, at last. She tried to move out of the way but her body would not respond. She settled back. Never mind. Dale was here. She'd be all right now. The door pushed against her again.

She never locked the door, not since Carol-Ann had told her not to. "Supposing something happens to you and we need to get in. You must leave your door open."

"Supposing someone comes in—to rob me, or attack me … or … or rape me?"

That was the sort of thing Gladys would say.

Carol-Ann rolled her eyes, and Dale said, "I *don't* think so. *Not* on White Rock Island."

Gladys said, when Cornelia told her of the exchange, "You should be so lucky, daft old thing like you. But if you do get assaulted, send the mad rapist down to me when he's done with you. I'll show him a trick or two."

The door pushing.

She called, "Dale."

A voice, not Dale. "Whatever …"

Carol-Ann squeezed sideways through the door. Dale followed her.

Carol-Ann, hands on her hips: "Oh my God. How long have you been lying here?" Kneeling beside her. "Can you move? No. Don't move. Oh my God." Feeling her pulse. Touching her leg. "Can you feel that?"

"I don't know. Feel what?"

"Can you feel my hand?"

"Where are you touching me?"

"Lie still."

Dale squeezed past Carol-Ann, stepped over Cornelia, and ran upstairs. He returned with a blanket and pillow. Carol-Ann lifted Cornelia's head deftly, gently, and slid the pillow beneath it. She tucked the blanket around her. All the time she and Dale asked questions, not giving her time to answer.

"What happened?"

"Did you fall?"

"Why didn't you yell and scream for help?"

"Do you hurt badly?"

Carol-Ann called through the front door, "Tom, got your cell? Ambulance—pronto. She's fallen."

Now Gladys was squeezing through the door. "Poor ducky. I knew something had happened."

Dale was bending over Cornelia, adjusting the pillow needlessly. She took his hand. He was crying.

"You always look in on me in the morning."

"*Not* when you tell us you're going to be *away*. I thought you were *away* with Gladys and Tom, otherwise I would have been *here* as usual. I should have *known*. I should have *guessed*."

Cornelia heard Tom say, "Air ambulance is on the way."

Carol-Ann put a hand on Cornelia's forehead. Patted her arm. "You poor old thing. You can't go on living here alone like this, you know. We can't risk having something like this happen again. You'll have to move into the old folks' home on the big island."

Cornelia closed her eyes. The last thing she saw was Gladys, frowning.

Chapter Five

The White Rock Island Community Hall stood opposite the ferry ramp, so that the first thing islanders and visitors saw as they drove up from the ferry was the bulletin board in front of the hall listing forthcoming events. Patrick, out for a stroll that morning, had stopped to read the announcements: a church supper next Tuesday from four until six, the quilting club meeting on Wednesday, aerobic exercise with Patti at two on Tuesday and Thursday (*men* especially welcome), darts and cards on Friday nights. And a meeting at five o' clock on Tuesday for Island Fisheries plant workers and their families, to be addressed by the owner, Mr. Gerard Clinch. (A Representative from International Consolidated Enterprises may be in attendance.) Someone had taped a banner across the sign, stating, 'Tonight. All Welcome.'

Patrick's bed and breakfast accommodation was less than a quarter of a mile from the island centre. It was set back from the Shore Road and its garden was a few yards of rough grass fringed by wild flowers and giving way to the white rocks that stretched the length of the eastern shore. He was sitting on the rocks after supper, gazing across the channel towards the distant coast of Deer Isle, when he became aware of an increase in traffic and pedestrians on the normally quiet road on the other side of the house. Recalling the announcement about the meeting, and the fish plant workers' outrage, he walked down to the community hall. He hesitated at the door, anxious not to intrude, wondering whether the All Welcome invitation extended to visitors who had no involvement with the island. His bed and breakfast hosts, Fran and Peter Miller, were already seated and waved him in, at the same time as Dale Morse appeared behind him.

"Coming *in*?"

"I'm afraid of intruding. I'm not sure I have the right …"

"The meeting's open to all. You're a *businessman* of some kind I'd guess—right? You'll find it *interesting*. See how we conduct meetings down east. It'll be a change from your *meetings* in Ottawa. There's nothing else to do—unless you're going to sit and watch the *sea* all evening."

Patrick was dressed in his old jeans, the ones Peggy had forbidden him to wear to the office, even on casual Fridays, and a White Rock Island sweat shirt he'd bought from Carol-Ann at the store. On the chest it bore a picture of the striking white rocks at the entrance to the harbour, with the legend, It's *all white* on White Rock Island! He'd held it up in disbelief while browsing through the store, and seeing Carol-Ann watching him had bought it out of guilt. Now he'd grown fond of it and wore it all the time, the sleeves pushed back and a tear in the side where he'd snagged it on the rocks.

It was his eighth day on the island, eight days of walking, reading, watching the sea, and thinking about Penelope.

*****

She was the little girl who trailed after the adored, patient older boy next door. For a few years, when he was a teenager and she was in primary school, he was her cautious babysitter. As she entered high school and he began work on the neighbourhood newspaper, they discovered shared interests—bicycle rides, long walks, late Romantic music, nineteenth century novels—which eased them into friendship. After that, it never occurred to them that they would ever be apart, and it was a shock to them both when Patrick discovered he had to go away to study in Ottawa if he was going to be serious about his journalism. It was an even bigger shock when they discovered what separation wrought in them. Patrick, always shy and reticent, shunned all social life at college. Penelope was listless at home. At Christmas, when Patrick returned from his first term, he put his bags in his room and set off to say hello to Penelope. Meanwhile she'd seen the taxi arrive and was also heading next door. They met in the snow on the sidewalk between their houses. Neither had thought of a greeting. They'd never had to greet one another before; they'd always been just *there*. They stopped six feet apart, stunned. Before, their platonic and profound friendship had precluded the awakening of the kind of frantic desire they'd witnessed among their friends. Now, without warning, they were transfixed. They couldn't speak, didn't dare touch. She was sixteen.

*****

"Shouldn't I wear something more formal for the meeting?" he asked Dale, who had come straight from the store and was wearing the gray jacket and black slacks he habitually wore there when not in his fish plant work clothes.

"Nah," he said. "Anything *goes*." He looked Patrick up and down, his eyes coming to rest on his sweat shirt. "That's one of our more *tasteful* souvenirs. You look like a *tourist*."

"I am a tourist."

Dale raised his eyebrows. "*Are* you?"

Caught off guard by Dale's question, by its strangeness and by the sudden seriousness with which it was delivered, Patrick changed the subject. "How's Mrs. Morse Senior?"

Patrick had been back to the store several times following Gladys and Tom's dramatic arrival on the island. Dale, Carol-Ann, Gladys and Tom had hurried from the store, leaving him alone, Dale calling back, "Anything *else* you need—just leave the money on the counter, or drop in *later*." Since then he had learned, while buying postcards and newspapers, and trying unsuccessfully to avoid looking at *La Vie*, of the events which had followed—the air ambulance taking Cornelia to hospital in Saint John, her overnight stay, her present convalescence on Deer Isle.

Now Dale pursed his lips, held up his hand, tilted it back and forth. At the same time a car passed and he changed the doubting gesture into a wave. Patrick turned in time to see Gladys, whom he remembered from the brief encounter on the day of his arrival, pass and turn down to the ferry. Hunched over the wheel and leaning forward in her seat, she seemed unaware of Dale's wave.

They entered the hall, where Dale was immediately drawn into conversation with a crowd of plant workers, while Patrick took the opportunity of moving away to sit by himself at the back of the hall, anticipating an unobtrusive departure if he felt too out of place. The people crowding the hall seemed to have divided themselves into three groups—the fishers, the plant workers, distinguishable by their blue work clothes, and island residents not directly affected by any changes at the plant. Among the latter group Patrick included the children playing tag at the rear of the hall, running backwards and forwards, twisting, dodging and spinning behind him. With a pang, he saw that the bicycling friends, the boy and girl who reminded him of Penelope and himself, were among them. Patrick supposed he himself formed a fourth group—the uninvolved, the disinterested. It would be pleasant, he thought, to witness what promised to be tense business proceedings without having to feel any responsibility for the outcome.

A squat, fleshy man, red faced, Patrick guessed in his sixties, who had been in the middle of a noisy crowd of plant workers at the front of the hall, climbed the stairs at the side of the stage. He seemed uncomfortable in a blue suit, pulling at the sleeves of the jacket and adjusting the collar as he walked to centre stage and held up his hands, looking at the crowd with the fawning eyes of a retriever. The noise in the hall slowly subsided as he spoke.

"Ladies and gentlemen, friends, fellow islanders. I know for a number of years I haven't lived on the island ..."

"Not since we ran you off," someone called from the audience.

The speaker laughed nervously. "... But I still think of myself as an islander—and it's as an islander that I want to speak to you tonight. I don't need to introduce myself ..."

Another call from the audience: "Don't then."

The speaker fingered his tie, and pressed on, "... But I will. I am Gerard Clinch, owner of the plant where we've worked together for many years ..."

More shouted interruptions.

"You haven't worked there since your pa passed away and left it to you."

"You've never worked in your life."

Gerard Clinch swallowed and laughed again. He tugged at the sleeves of his jacket, then clasped his hands in front of him, as if about to pray, and went on in a quieter voice.

"When my daddy started the plant in 1910, times were very different, yes, they were very different. It was a different time altogether. Times have changed, as you know, and things aren't the same as they were. These are very different times and very difficult times, very different and very difficult ..."

An old man sitting at the end of the front row—a former fisherman, Patrick guessed from his weathered face—called out, "And I suppose times weren't difficult when we started the plant with your pa."

"No, no. I'm not saying that. I'm saying that times now are different, very different, and difficult, not necessarily harder, oh no, but different, and harder in a different way."

"Does anybody know what he's talking about?" someone called.

"Now you know he wants to go into politics," a plant worker responded. "He's just practicing his politician talk."

Gerard Clinch laughed and shook his finger at the heckler. "It's nothing to do with politics. I'm just saying that times are different now, very different, and very difficult, yes, very, very difficult and different ..."

"Gerard Clinch, will you shut up about how times are different and difficult and say what you've got to say," a woman shouted.

"Yes, yes, of course. What I want to say is ..." He paused and drew a deep breath. "What I need to say is ... Times are ... difficult and different now."

There was a chorus of groans and boos.

"... And that means we have to make some changes, some big changes ..." The heckling stopped as Gerard Clinch moved his hands from their prayer like position and wrung them as he continued, "... To the plant, changes to the plant. It's time for me to get out of the business. I don't want to, but I'm getting too old to be catching and gutting and packing fish ..."

A plant worker snarled, "You haven't been in the plant for five years or more, and when you were there you certainly weren't packing fish."

There were shouts of agreement and Gerard Clinch had to pause until the muttering of scorn and contempt had passed. "... And I'm pleased to announce that a major company—and I mean a *major* company—has expressed an interest in taking over the business."

"What major company?" someone called.

"I'm coming to that." He paused again, spread his hands wide as if to bless the audience, took a deep breath, and announced, "I.C.E."

"I.C. what?"

"I don't know about I see; more like I smell—and what I smell is sell-out."

A chorus of support for the hecklers followed.

"Yeah—sell-out ..."

"Sell out the island ..."

"Workers be buggered ..."

"To hell with those that worked for you all these years ..."

Gerard Clinch struggled on, shouting above the uproar. "I.C.E. is a highly respected international—yes, *international*—company which has a high regard and concern for the island and for the plant workers. On that I give you my personal—yes, my *personal*—assurance, as a fellow islander. You know you can trust me."

The hall filled with instantaneous, uproarious laughter, through which shouts penetrated.

"Your personal assurance is worth about as much as you pay us for the fish we catch."

"… And that's piss all."

"We might as well sink the island now."

"I'll trade your personal assurance for the tropical beach I've got for sale on the island."

Patrick rose amid the uproar. People were standing, shouting and stabbing accusing fingers at Gerard Clinch. Many were talking amongst themselves. The children, who had grown quiet and still, sensing the seriousness and tension of the adults' exchanges, resumed their chasing, laughing hilariously, infected by the commotion. Patrick was embarrassed for the speaker, for his ineffectuality and for the contempt in which he—their supposed boss—was held, which Patrick knew the man must realize, and he was upset by the helplessness of the islanders, by their inability effectively to articulate their protest. He walked to the door and was about to slip quietly out when the hall suddenly became silent. He turned and looked back at the stage. Gerard Clinch still stood, helpless and impotent, at centre stage, while from the wings three men emerged. Dressed in identical dark suits, with white shirts and ties of different striped patterns which nevertheless blended perfectly, they advanced in a v-shaped phalanx, a tall, sleek haired man at their head. Patrick caught himself comparing, in a kind of bizarre admiration, the appearance of the newcomers to that of the hapless Gerard Clinch, thinking, "Now that, Gerard Clinch, is how you wear a suit."

The leader of the newcomers took centre stage, folded his arms, and surveyed the audience. "Thank you for your attention. I do appreciate your courteous silence." He stressed the last word so that it became a menacing imperative. His eyes continued to travel the room like a challenge.

Patrick leaned back against the door jamb, curious.

The newcomer repeated, "Thank you for your attention. I am Conrad Wise, chairman and chief executive officer of International Consolidated Enterprises. These are my executive assistants." He indicated his companions, who took up positions on either side of their leader. "I am here to announce that I.C.E., International Consolidated Enterprises, intends to buy Clinch and *Son* Fisheries."

He emphasized *Son*, as he did so making a small, mocking bow in the direction of Gerard Clinch, who had retired to the side of the stage, where he looked down and fiddled with the buttons of his jacket.

The speaker continued, "We are currently at the bidding stage, but in the absence of another potential buyer, and with all of the operations of Clinch and *Son*"—the mocking bow again—"in their present precarious financial situation, and with the limited prospects offered by fish plants in locations such as …" He looked around as if seeing, through the walls of the hall, not only the island beyond, but also its struggles through generations to wrench a living from the sea, contemptuous of them, and repeated, "… In locations such as … *this*, the emergence of a rival bidder I would suggest is highly unlikely."

Something was nagging at Patrick's memory, eclipsing his intended stance of uninvolvement. He moved outside onto the front steps of the hall and tapped a number into his cell phone.

"Peggy? I was hoping I might catch you."

"Patrick, where are you?"

"On a little island in Passamaquoddy Sound."

"Are you all right?"

"Yes. Yes—thank you. I'm doing fine. Listen. I need some information."

"I thought you were on holiday."

"I am. I'm just curious about something. Can you get me figures for supply and demand of fish products for eastern Canada and the eastern States?"

"You'll have to give me a moment."

"I'll wait."

He heard the rustle of papers, and the tap of Peggy's fingers on her keyboard, and she delivered some figures.

"Okay—thank you. One more thing. What can you give me on I.C.E?"

"International Consolidated? Give me another moment."

He heard Peggy's fingers on the keyboard again before she relayed more information.

"I thought so. Thanks, Peggy."

"How's the journal?"

"The journal? Oh—the journal. Yes—it's going well. It's been useful."

"You forgot all about it, didn't you?"

He confessed, "Only in the last few days. I wrote in it until then. The island seems to have calmed me down."

"Well that's good."

"Yes. Thanks again, Peggy. Go home now. It's getting late. Hey—there's a postcard on the way. See you soon."

As he folded away the cell phone he pictured Peggy at her desk in the office on Queen Street, her head bent over her computer, her glasses slipping to the end of her nose as she concentrated on the screen, her dark hair falling across her face, hiding it. Around her, darkness, with everyone else gone for the day; a solitary pool of light at her desk. He thought guiltily of the journal she had given him before he left, suggesting he write in it as a kind of therapy, knowing his restless emotions. It was in his pocket now, untouched after his first few days on the island. He withdrew it and skimmed through the few pages he'd written.

Chapter Six

Ottawa Airport: October 12th

I'll write this for you, Penelope, although you'll never see it. I'm not even sure what it will turn out to be—a journal of holiday travel, some kind of self-indulgent emotional catharsis, a celebration of our long friendship, or a mourning for the death of love. I'm taking this trip not to forget you (how could I forget you?), but to try and exorcise the grip you have on my emotions, which you have invaded so comprehensively that without you I live in disarray. I want my independence back—the independence I enjoyed when we were friends, not lovers. And I want emotional peace.

My destination was to have been first London, then Paris, Rome, Milan. I thought these cities would order my disheveled feelings with their excitement and spectacle. Well— like a woman companion bought for the evening, they might have offered a tawdry distraction and an ephemeral excitement, but no balm for my restlessness; no peace.

So I'm changing my plans, and I'm heading not to the U.K., but to another, much smaller, island.

Deer Isle Airfield: October 12th (afternoon)

I'm sitting on a fish crate (empty) beside the tiny airstrip on Deer Isle, the biggest and best known of the Passamaquoddy Sound islands. I flew in this afternoon and, as soon as the airfield manager has finished preparing his own plane to fly some tourists out later today, he'll give me a ride across Deer Isle so that I can get the ferry to White Rock Island.

I hear you saying, incredulously—Where? White Rock Island? Why?

Here's why: As I sat in Ottawa thinking about this search for emotional independence and peace, I remembered having once, a long time ago, discovered a profound serenity on White Rock Island, and I thought: If I returned, could I rediscover it?

Passamaquoddy Sound (on the White Rock Island ferry): October 12th (late afternoon)

The world is littered with your image, on television, on magazine covers, on bill-boards. I want to see your face without my emotions reeling, without my rationality splintering into giddy distraction. I want to be able to meet you without my throat constricting, my hands sweating, my legs trembling—yes, trembling.

This is what I mean by emotional independence.

The ferry is approaching White Rock Island. A helicopter flies over, also heading for the island, and I wonder who is arriving by that more efficient means, and what business they have on the island.

White Rock Island—on the wharf: October 13th

As I wander idly between my lodging and the wharf, I watch a little boy and girl playing on their bicycles.

Do you remember our bicycle rides? And do you remember once when, trailing behind me, as usual, you were confronted by some men who were working on the road? They stopped you and asked whether a pretty young miss like you would like to keep them company. By the time I realized you were no longer behind me and looked back, you were surrounded. They meant no harm, but their playfulness seemed threatening. I remember thinking, gallantly, I would rescue you, even as I wondered how I could take them all on. When they saw me turn they said, 'Here comes your boyfriend,' and, smiling, sent you on your way. I think at that moment I began to be aware of you as more than my friend, although it took me—us—years to discover it.

White Rock Island—on the rocks behind my lodging: October 14th

I went out in a fishing boat today, with a fisherman called Samuel, and his young partner, Jeffrey, through a kind arrangement made by Dale, the gentleman from the store.

I thought—I am a world away from your world. Am I finding emotional peace? Am I coming to terms with whatever our new relationship is? What are we now, Penelope? Old friends? Old lovers? Nothing? I don't think I could bear the latter. I'd like us to be friends, old and special friends, as we used to be. I wish now that old and special friendship had never become love. Could it have been avoided, or were we fixed on an inexorable, inevitable drive to love? If a certain eye contact had been missed, a serendipitous touch unacknowledged, a sudden intrusion of circumstances avoided (the men joking with you), could we have avoided love? Would we have been better off without it?

When did it start, anyway?

White Rock Island—on the rocks (again): October 15th

A long walk today, from my lodging to the Southern Point cliffs. On the way I passed the trail through the woods of the interior to the western shore, where I experienced the extraordinary peace of mind I came here to rediscover. I'm afraid of taking that trail. I'm enjoying this quiet time on the island, and fear the nirvana I'm imagining will turn out to be as chimerical as love.

I've been thinking about the start of love. Was there one moment when we were friends, the next when we loved? Was it a lightning strike tempering friendship into love, or was it a gradual encroachment, a tide of love creeping silently over the sands of our long friendship? I don't know. I think all we can do is look back and say—there, at that moment, I know I loved you then.

That moment in the snow between our houses—I know I loved you then! I knew— we knew—at that moment things would never be the same again in our lives. As we looked at one another then, we knew, no matter what happened thereafter, whether our destinies entwined or diverged, we knew love would always be between us. There was nothing we could do to undo it.

White Rock Island—early morning on the wharf: October 16th

Neither do we know the moment when love dies—lightning strike of contempt or creeping tide of indifference; only that it has died.

We had a ritual, whenever we got out of bed during the night, leaving the other, of touching when we returned—a stroke of the hip, a pat on the arm, something. Did you know that? When we met in Monaco last year, you got out of bed in the night and sat by the window for half an hour. You didn't realize I was awake, too. When you came back to bed that night, you didn't touch me, so I didn't touch you.

Today I plan to walk to the western shore.

Chapter Seven

The little girl in whom Patrick saw Penelope sidled from the hall. She looked up at him curiously. He smiled and said, "Where's your friend?" She shrugged and skipped away, alone. Patrick tucked the journal into his pocket and stepped quietly back into the hall. Conrad Wise was still talking.

"Therefore, in a matter of days, Clinch and Son Fisheries will fall under the control of International Consolidated Enterprises. Are there any questions?"

It was a challenge, not an invitation, and was followed by silence, until a voice said, hesitantly, "*Changes*. Will there be *changes*?"

Patrick recognised Dale's voice with surprise. He realized he had been insensitive to the concern masked by Dale's flippancy.

Conrad Wise said quietly, "Of course there will be changes."

Another voice, truculence hiding fear: "What sort of changes? Enough changes to close us down?"

"No, my friend. Believe me—and I speak for the company—there will be changes, but the plant will not be closed down. However"—he held up a warning finger—"there are concerns with the plant as it is. You will be aware that there is a transport problem when you live on an island. You know all about that; you live with it. You know, and I know, how frustrating—and expensive—it can be. We at I.C.E. will have the same problem with transport where the fish plant is concerned; a problem of shipping and distribution. My managers calculate the cost of shipping from an island to be ten times—yes, ten times—that of shipping from a plant on the mainland, and they say to me—this is not economical. If you buy the plant, you will have to close it down in the end. You will have to cut your losses and close it down. That's what they tell me. You will have to *close it down*."

A chorus of protest rose from the audience. Conrad Wise held up his hands and thundered, "But I tell them no way—*no way*—will I close it down, even if it costs twenty times more than mainland plants." The boos and catcalls turned to applause. Wise leaned forward, as if confiding in the audience. "They tell me I'm crazy." The audience laughed as Wise shrugged and held his arms wide, inviting them to share with him the absurdity of the accusation, to admire his tolerance of their misunderstanding, and repeated, "Crazy! But I say to them—I don't care what you tell me. I will not close the plant down." He went on quickly, "But—in order to accomplish this, something has to give, I'm afraid, and that something will be a reduction either in the number of workers or in the number of shifts. I'm sorry. I will do my darndest—my darndest, I promise—to keep this to an absolute minimum, and I hope we can take care of it through attrition, through retirement and through people moving naturally away, and so on. But you must—we must—be prepared for some hardship."

Like chastised children now allowed to return to the loving fold, forgiven, the audience warmed to Conrad Wise's stern benevolence.

Chapter Eight

While Conrad Wise addressed the islanders, Gladys was visiting Cornelia at the Sunny Haven Seniors' Complex in North Head, on Deer Isle. Carol-Ann had pressed the home, which offered some medical care, to let Cornelia complete her convalescence there, after a stay at the island's cottage hospital on her return from Saint John, and then to become a permanent resident. It was a week since Cornelia had been transported from the cottage hospital to Sunny Haven. Dale and Carol-Ann had met her there, to install her, with a few of her clothes, and three photographs—one of Dale Senior at the wheel of his boat with little Dale beside him, one of Cornelia's parents, and one of Cornelia and Gladys the year they left high school.

Later the same day, they telephoned to see how she was settling in and Carol-Ann said, "Why don't we make some improvements to your house while you're away? We could put a telephone in, and a satellite for the television. We could modernise the kitchen a bit, and the house needs a new septic system. Why don't we get all that done?"

Gladys found Cornelia sitting in a wicker chair in the common room. Other residents were sitting nearby, some sleeping, some gazing around as if searching for someone or something, some looking vacantly at someone or something unknown.

Gladys said, "This place is bloody awful."

"It's not so bad," Cornelia protested. "They look after you and make your meals. And look—I'm learning needlepoint."

Gladys said, "Whoopee-friggin'-doo."

"The supervisor says she's glad I've moved in."

"You didn't move in," Gladys said darkly. "You were moved in."

Cornelia had a bed sitting room, with bathroom, half way along the east hallway of the complex. The east hallway was for semi-independent living, the west hallway was for full care residents, and between the wings lay the dining room and common room, where residents watched television and were organised by the activity director.

Peering from the common room as a resident was helped out by one of the attendants, Gladys warned, "Watch they don't try and drag you down that west hallway."

"That's for people who can't manage," Cornelia asserted. "I'm independent."

"You're semi-independent," Gladys corrected her. "You've gone from independent in your own house on White Rock to semi-independent in Sunny Haven within the space of a few weeks. How long before Carol-Ann pushes you one step further?"

"It's for the best," Cornelia protested. "And it's not just Carol-Ann. Dale says I need looking after. He says I deserve to be cosseted at my age. And I do have trouble remembering things sometimes."

"I know you do, Cornelia. But who doesn't? I can't remember what year it is—hell, I can't remember what *day* it is—half the time. We may be forgetful, but that doesn't mean we can't manage."

"Well I'm here now."

"I guess so."

"Shall we have some tea? They bring it round at six o' clock."

"Tea be buggered. Where's the bar?" said Gladys. "I need a drink while I tell you the news."

"What news?"

"There's a big meeting—it's going on right now—about the plant being sold."

"Mr. Clinch wouldn't sell the plant."

"Old Mr. Clinch wouldn't. Young Mr. Clinch would sell his mother if he thought he could get a half decent price for the old girl, and if he thought he could get someone else to cook and clean for him, preferably someone younger and better looking than his ma. There's a bunch of suits on the island come from some big company that wants to buy the plant. Right now they're probably putting the boot to poor Gerry Clinch. Then they'll put the boot to the island."

Chapter Nine

Patrick had been trying to preserve his disinterested stance, but sensing the onset of the audience's complacency, fearing it would render them even more helpless, he abandoned it. When Conrad Wise said were there any more questions, Patrick asked, leaning casually against the rear door, "What's the problem with shipping?"

Dale looked around. He thought he recognised Patrick's voice, but there was something different about it. Discovering Patrick, Dale thought—it's not just his voice; his posture is different, too, although he's leaning so casually against the door. Who is he?

"What do you mean, my friend?" Conrad Wise demanded.

"I mean why is it so expensive to ship from White Rock Island?"

The chairman shook his head, indulging the question, despite its naïveté. "It's simple, isn't it? We have to ship by ferry from here to Deer Isle, by ferry from Deer Isle to the mainland, and only then can we start trucking our product into eastern Canada, which itself is a limited market."

"Why not ship to the States?"

"My dear sir, you don't understand. You cannot simply ship to the States. The States won't allow it."

"Yes, they will. Last year the Maine Senate passed the Memorandum of Understanding Concerning Shipping as an addendum to the Fisheries Products Reciprocal Agreement. That means you can ship from White Rock Island direct to Maine—it's only an hour by sea—and from there you have easy access to the eastern States and beyond."

"But, my dear sir, the duty…"

"There is none. That's why it's called a Reciprocal Agreement. Maine can ship to the Maritime Provinces in the same way. White Rock's shipping costs would be lower, not higher, than that of mainland plants, and the island's proximity to the States gives it a distinct marketing advantage. I say you should consider expanding the plant, not contracting it."

Above the swell of support which greeted Patrick, and as heads turned curiously at the stranger's intervention, Conrad Wise raised his voice. "I assure you, sir, it's more complex than you realize." He rushed on before Patrick could respond, "It would be unrealistic to expand the plant when there's the problem of supply. Simply put, we have too many fish plants serving too small a market. That means reductions—in working hours or in staff. It could mean closure—except that, as I have already explained, I *will not* close this plant."

He paused for the audience to again buzz its approval of his benevolence. Patrick was pleased when they failed to do so.

Wise repeated, "I will not close—but if we are to stay open and be viable, we have to reduce the workforce or the number of shifts."

"Not necessarily. The supply of fish products is, as you accurately state, in a surplus position—sometimes. It is also notoriously inconsistent and unpredictable, depending on weather conditions, fish stocks, provincial and federal regulations, seasons, and so on. What I would suggest you do, then, is increase your storage capacity, using state of the art equipment, so that you can maintain a constant supply when your competitors are struggling to do so."

As Patrick spoke, he saw Wise nod discreetly to one of the executive assistants, who moved to the side of the stage, where he stood with his arms folded, staring at Patrick, as a chorus rose from the audience: "Constant supply … Right on … He's right … Increase storage … Stranger's right … Probably need to hire more, not lay off …"

When Conrad Wise tried to respond, he was greeted with calls of, "We've heard enough … Get your facts right, Mr. Wise … Leave our plant the way it is …" He tried to raise his voice above the uproar, but when it persisted, he gave up and stood, silent, glaring at his inquisitor.

Patrick asked, stilling the chorus, "Does International Consolidated have any other interests in the fishing industry?"

Conrad Wise assumed a rueful smile. "I confess this will be our first venture into fishing, and I hope it's one we won't regret. I'm sure it won't be—with the help of the good people, and good workers, of White Rock Island."

There was a scatter of applause for the compliments before Patrick went on, "When I say International Consolidated, I mean its subsidiary companies as well as the parent company. So I ask again—does I.C.E. have any interest already in the fishing industry?"

The second executive assistant, at a nod from Conrad Wise, took up a position on the other side of the stage and stood like his colleague, with his arms folded, staring at the questioner, while the chairman explained, "I.C.E. is a very big company—bigger, I would suggest, with respect—than anything in your experience, sir. As its name suggests, it is an international company with multi-faceted interests, some large, some small, some even smaller than Clinch and Son Fisheries. But, if I may say so, size has nothing to do with our concern for the continued viability of all our interests, large and small. In fact …"—he leaned towards the audience, as if to confide in them, raising a hand and beckoning them towards him—"… I have a special weakness for the smaller companies. I always say—the smaller the company, the better it is, like Clinch and Son, and the more precious it is to me."

There was more applause, as men and women in the audience turned to one another, nodding in agreement; turned back to Conrad Wise, smiling.

Patrick waited for the applause to subside, then pressed on. "You haven't answered my question."

Conrad Wise held his arms wide, inviting the audience into his further confidence, as he nodded in Patrick's direction. "The question is obviously very important to this gentleman, for him to ask it so persistently and to take up so much of the limited time—limited and *precious* time—we have to get to know one another. You'll have to let me know whether you want me to go into even more detail about the inner workings—the *boring* inner workings—of International Consolidated in order to appease his curiosity, or whether we should continue with other, perhaps more relevant and important, questions from the floor."

Some members of the audience were now looking back at Patrick, frowning and shaking their heads at his stubborn, persistent questioning, questions that seemed to offend the patient Conrad Wise.

Patrick spoke above the growing murmur. "Perhaps I can ask some further questions, which might shed some light on your reluctance to answer my first question." He noticed the chairman's henchmen leave the stage and begin to make their way towards the back of the hall, weaving through the audience crowded in the aisles. Patrick walked as far as the back row of seats and raised his voice, silencing the audience. "Isn't it true that I.C.E. owns Upper Canada Foods and Beverages Incorporated, a subsidiary of which is Fisherman's Finest Foods, which owns the largest fish packing plant in North America?"

Conrad Wise snapped, shielding his eyes as he stared down at his questioner, "Do you mind telling us who would like to know?"

"A friend of the island. And isn't it also true that in the last two years the same Fisherman's Finest Foods has bought out twelve operations similar to Clinch and Son Fisheries—bought them and closed them within a few months, so creating a near monopoly on frozen fish products?"

The chairman's associates had moved to each side of Patrick.

Conrad Wise said, "These are complex questions. My colleagues will be happy to discuss them with you outside."

"I'll discuss them in here."

One of the executive assistants took Patrick by the arm.

Patrick, shaking himself free, said, "Get your hands off me."

"Come with us, please, sir," the other said, taking Patrick's other arm.

A voice behind them said, "The visitor said he'd like to stay," and another voice, "So do like he says. Get your hands off him."

Turning, Patrick discovered Samuel and Jeffrey, and two other fishermen, standing close behind him. Dale was there, too. He nodded encouragingly. The I.C.E. executives hesitated. Samuel leaned close to them and muttered, "Get lost, boys."

Dale called to Conrad Wise, "We're waiting for an *answer*. Is what *he* says true?"

Conrad Wise looked long and hard at Patrick, then amid the growing demand from the audience for answers, stalked from the stage. Gerard Clinch scuttled after him. The executive assistants, with an equally long and hard stare at Patrick, retreated to the stage and followed the chairman.

Patrick said to the fishermen around him, "Thanks."

Samuel patted him on the shoulder. "You might want to look out for yourself. Let us know if you need some help."

Patrick caught Dale's eye.

Dale nodded once, slowly.

Chapter Ten

At Sunny Haven, Cornelia woke from a happy, vital dream which she couldn't remember. She closed her eyes and tried to sleep again, to recall it, but the dream was tucked behind the veil of consciousness which had invaded her. She opened her eyes and looked around her room. It was early morning but already she could hear distant noises from the kitchen where the staff were preparing breakfast. The dream she strove to recall seemed to contain an image and a message of some kind. Her eyes, roving the room, reached the bedside table, landed on the photograph of Dale Senior. Of course—he was the image in the dream. She often dreamed about Dale Senior, but this time his dream image seemed to convey something more. It wasn't a dream of fancy and invention; it was a dream of a memory.

Dale Senior and she were together, somewhere important.

Yes: They were on the western shore, on the immense, white, sandy beach. They were very young, not yet married, before Dale became Dale Senior, although she couldn't think of him as anything but Dale Senior. He was saying …

The image faded as her memory faltered.

She concentrated.

The beach was wide because the tide was low. Yes—it was spring, when the tides were at their highest and lowest, and now the tide was at its lowest point of the year. Dale Senior was saying, "I'll show you a secret." He was leading her towards the wall of solid rock that bordered the southern end of the beach. Although the tide was low, waves still washed viciously against the foot of the rocks. Dale Senior was saying, "Wait. Wait. Now—quick." He was holding her by the hand, running at the rock face, dragging her behind him, veering around it at the last second, just as she thought he was going to run into it, timing his run so that they rounded the rock face between the retreat of one wave and the tumbling forward of the next. As the wave crashed into the rock behind them, they stopped, foam swirling around their feet.

Cornelia drew her breath in sharply, her eyes wide. She whispered, "It's a wonderland."

Dale Senior, gazing around, said, "Yes."

The beach stretched before them until it came up against another solid wall of rock, this one reaching into deep water, far beyond where the waves were breaking. Inland, between the two forbidding walls of rock, the beach extended to a line of grassy dunes. Beyond them, sun drenched meadows rose gently to the foot of a sheer cliff.

Dale Senior said, "We've only got a half hour to explore before the tide is too high to get back to the other beach."

"What happens if we don't make it back?"

"We're trapped—until the next equinox." He grinned as Cornelia looked sharply at him and added, "There is a way out through the cliff up there, but it's hard and dangerous and I don't want to take you that way."

Still holding her by the hand, but gently now, he led her up the beach, through the dunes, and into the meadows. Cornelia saw with surprise that rock walls divided them, and Dale Senior explained, "As they cleared the land, they piled the rocks into walls."

"Who cleared the land? When?"

"My family—three generations ago, in the eighteen hundreds. This is called Morse Cove. The Morses were the original settlers. They farmed here until the turn of the century."

"I thought White Rock Island had always been a fishing community."

"The settlers turned to fishing when they left here."

"But why did they leave?"

"Because it's such a difficult place to get to." He pointed to where the low tide revealed a jagged line of rocks at the entrance to the cove. "Coming in by sea was mighty dangerous. There is a channel through the rocks, but it's hard to navigate, and they lost a few boats to it. And by land, you either had to climb through a fissure in the cliffs up there ..."—he nodded towards the apparently solid wall of rock beyond the meadows—"... or scramble around from the other beach, like we did, on the one or two days a year when the tide might be just low enough to make it possible. But there was another reason."

They had walked to the upper limit of the meadows. He pointed at the long grass moving gently in the breeze.

"Look."

"I don't see anything."

Kneeling and carefully parting the grass, he repeated, "Look."

Cornelia sighed, "Oh." Through the grass pushed aside by Dale Senior she could see a tiny headstone. Looking further, she made out three more. "What happened?"

"Smallpox. It wiped out a generation. They decided—this would be my grandfather's time—it was too hard to continue, with the loss of the children and with the difficulty of getting in and out. The island was settled on the eastern shore by then, and some wanted easier contact with the others." He winked. "Family's all well and good, but there's some things family can't provide. So they upped and left the cove, and it's been deserted ever since. It's a sort of secret. The old timers know it's here, but they don't talk about it, out of respect for my grandfather. He wanted it left as a memorial to the kids. So—this is my secret place."

"But why did they settle somewhere so hard to reach?"

"Because of all this..." Dale Senior released her hand and stretched his arms wide to indicate the beach and the meadows and the sun. "This is where they landed—not by design; they were driven ashore here and were lucky to get through the rocks. But they thought they were in paradise. They had fresh water from springs up there ..."—he pointed to where the meadows gave way to tumbled rocks—"... and a warm, sheltered spot to build, and farm land with a south western exposure. It was heaven. Still is, eh? My great-grandfather always said this place is the key to the island's prosperity and survival." Dale Senior nodded emphatically. "Morse Cove is the key."

Cornelia closed her eyes and turned on her side to try and sleep some more, still picturing Dale Senior. He was the image in the dream. That was the precious part of it. The message, that Morse Cove was the key, seemed unimportant beside his memory. She didn't understand it, anyway, and by the time she woke again had forgotten it.

*****

Peggy called Patrick a few days later. He was sprawled on the rocks behind the house where he was staying.

"Patrick, I thought you were on vacation down there."

"I am. Why do you ask?"

"Because I've had the Chairman of the International Manufacturing and Marketing Council on the phone this morning asking for clarification of your involvement in the buyout of Clinch Fisheries."

Patrick laughed. "I suspect he's a friend of Conrad Wise, who must have found out who I am. What's he saying?"

"He says International Consolidated has laid a complaint of unethical conduct against you, claiming you had no right to attend an information session they'd planned in good faith on White Rock Island with the Clinch and Son Fisheries workers, and that, still without revealing your identity or your business interests, you undermined their presentation. He wants an explanation of your conduct."

"Tell him to go and you-know-what himself."

"I told him that already."

"You used the f- word?"

"Well—yes."

"Good for you."

"But that's not all, Patrick. Now there are two gentlemen from I.C.E. sitting in the hallway outside the office here. They say they're Conrad Wise's executive assistants and they have to talk to you. They don't look very friendly."

"I met them here on the island."

"I said you were on vacation and I didn't know when you'd be back."

"Leave them sitting there and have building security keep an eye on them."

After saying goodbye, Patrick reflected for a moment before pressing another preset number on his phone. A recorded message announced, "Soames's Investigation and Security. Leave a message, whoever you are."

"Hello, Mike. Patrick Given here. Do something for me, will you, please? Have someone keep an eye on Peggy—discreetly, of course—twenty four hours a day for the next few days. Don't intervene unless she's threatened. I'll be in touch as soon as I'm back in Ottawa. Let me know if anything happens."

*****

The next time Gladys visited Cornelia, a week later, Cornelia said, "What's power of attorney?"

Gladys looked sharply at her friend. "It's for crazies who've lost their marbles and don't know what's best for them. Why?"

"Well—Dale and Carol-Ann were here yesterday, and they said they needed power of attorney to do things to my house. They said it would be useful because then they wouldn't have to keep coming to me to get my signature for the improvements, having the telephone put in, and the new septic system, and the satellite, and all that."

Gladys said, "Hmmm."

*****

Patrick decided to slip away quietly from the island. Since the meeting he found himself a kind of celebrity. Islanders driving past him as he walked sounded their horns and gave him a thumbs up. Customers at the store, where he called every morning to buy a newspaper when the early ferry brought them in, greeted him familiarly—everyone seemed to know his name—and often shook his hand. He didn't mind, but found he'd lost the tranquility that anonymity had bestowed. Besides, Peggy had called again to say there were a few business matters needing his attention in Ottawa. He walked down to the ferry ramp to catch the first crossing. Plant workers arriving for the six o' clock shift passed him, hands raised in greeting. Although the store wasn't open, Dale was already behind the counter. He looked up as Patrick passed. Patrick pointed to the ferry, held up his bag, and waved.

Dale mouthed, "See you again."

Patrick shrugged.

Dale nodded once, slowly, and saluted.

As the ferry maneuvered through the harbour, fishermen preparing for the day waved to Patrick. With one hand he waved back, with the other pulled his cell phone from a pocket.

"Hi, Peggy. I know you're not there yet—it's early Tuesday morning—but I want to leave a message now before I get in the air. I'm on my way. I'll be there tonight, or tomorrow morning latest. Find something out for me in the meantime, will you, please? I want to know how much International Consolidated is offering for Clinch and Son Fisheries."

Chapter Eleven

A month after Patrick's visit to White Rock Island, a forty-two year old Fredericton lawyer, Bernard Appleby, was elected leader of the Progressive Democratic Alliance, a new party formed by the amalgamation of two minority parties. With an election only three months away, and without a seat in the legislature himself, he made reckless promises which even he saw no prospect of having to keep. He would require schools to guarantee that all children would be able to read by the age of seven. He would end all bridge tolls—indeed, all road tolls—in the province. He would increase the minimum wage. His simpering smile appeared more and more on television and in newspapers, and his nasal voice issued more and more from radio and television, resorting to sorrowful hurt at any hint of criticism. Carried away by his fondness for the image the media created for him, and the title they accorded him—Champion of the Ordinary People—he promised, after listening to warnings from the other leaders about the need for an increase in the provincial sales tax, to cut it to five per cent. Not only that. He would also cut personal income taxes. The media trumpeted the promises, and after the election Bernard Appleby found himself not only leader of a party with a huge majority, but also premier of the province.

When the opposition and the media started asking how he intended to fulfil his promises, he prevaricated for a few weeks before declaring that the answer was embodied in an innovative way of financing the various government departments. With the implementation of H.O.B.—Hands Off Budgeting—departments would receive a non-designated amount which they would *administer as they saw fit, free of any government interference.* This financial reform would confer *freedom, responsibility and accountability* on all departments. The only requirement was that they stay within their budget, thereby also keeping the government within its budget, which would take into account the promised five per cent provincial sales tax and reduced personal taxes. The allotted budgets, in their global sums, sounded impressive: nearly nine hundred million dollars for education; thirteen hundred million dollars for health; fifteen hundred million for highways. When the hospital and education authorities complained that they would be unable to operate on their allotted budgets, the premier told them to be creative in the application of their funding, and lectured them on the necessity of having the moral courage to make unpopular decisions where necessary without trying to hand off that responsibility to someone else, namely, himself. When hospitals closed beds and the school boards closed schools, the frustration of patients and parents was directed at the hospital and school boards, while Bernard Appleby expressed regret and disappointment at their actions. When criticism was directed at him, he stated sorrowfully that he was personally hurt—yes, *hurt*—when his efforts to improve the lot of the ordinary people of the province were called into question. He was doing his best—his *very best*—to deal with the problems left behind by the previous incumbent party. The problems were so complex that he did not expect the opposition or the media to understand them. But—let him say this—he considered it personally insulting to have his actions and decisions called into question when he was devoting his every waking hour of every day working for the betterment of the province. He pointed out the considerable sum the education department was receiving, and postulated that surely, with investment of this magnitude, parents could expect their children to read by the age of seven. If schools let the children down, by failing to teach them to read, their funding would be reduced. The government *would not pay for inefficiency and for a job not done, any more than ordinary people would expect to pay—say—the plumber for inefficiency and for a job not done.* Similarly, was it not reasonable to expect hospitals and doctors to produce an increasingly healthy population in return for the huge budget allotted to them? The number of admissions to hospital, and the number of people being treated at clinics, was expected to decrease. If it did not—the medical profession, like the schools, could expect funding to be reduced. The premier liked accountability criteria *that the ordinary people could understand; that were no more than simple common sense.* The only government department unaffected by the parsimony was highways. New roads and four lane highways abounded, while the children struggled in ever larger classes with ever more demoralized teachers, and the whimpering, hacking, bleeding line ups in the doctors' waiting rooms and in the hospital emergency rooms grew ever longer. But these things were hidden from most of the ordinary people, and even when, shocked, they discovered them, they were a small, inarticulate minority whose voices found it difficult to be heard.

Bernard Appleby came from a long established Fredericton family. His father was senior partner in a prosperous law firm. At school and at Brunswick University, on a scholarship awarded by his father's firm, he was the quintessential good student, docile, receptive, and willing to regurgitate without question or challenge whatever his teachers poured into him. After graduating with distinction, he married the daughter of one of his father's colleagues, another senior partner, and joined his father's law firm, where he was no more able to understand the dismay of clients when presented with his legal bills than he had been to sympathise with the financial struggles of his friends at university. He told his clients what he had told his friends: *You must expect to pay your way in this world.* He grew to despise the small amount of legal aid work he was required to do as a neophyte lawyer, and it was a small step from there to a profound conviction that self-sufficiency was paramount, that charity was a misguided incentive to perpetuate dependence, and that people were better off paying minimal taxes to a government that undertook to interfere as little as possible in their lives, the very convictions that made him so attractive a candidate to voters tired of paying high taxes and with no present need of society's help or support.

He was a slight, stooped man with a youthful face and black, sheeny hair that in moments of hurt surprise, when his actions were questioned, he allowed to fall over his forehead, from where, with a languid hand, he thrust it back, the temporary hirsute unruliness mirroring his anguish. His dark, close set eyes would half close as he hung and shook his head at the weight of his responsibility, and at the insensitivity of the questioner, so lacking in appreciation of his efforts. He did this so successfully that the media no longer asked questions he would regard as inappropriate.

As he sat in his Kings' Square office, the premier received a telephone call from his father.

"I was just talking to an old friend from my law school days in Toronto. I used to play racquetball with him at the Empire Club. He's C.E.O. of a big international company. He likes what you're doing for the province and he wants to support you—you, personally, as well as the Alliance. Play your cards right, do a little back scratching—you know what I mean—and he could be a big help to you."

"Who is it?"

"Conrad Wise."

Chapter Twelve

Tom took Gladys to Calgary, Toronto and Montreal. While he attended meetings, she shopped and visited tourist spots. They were gone for two weeks, and then she stayed at Tom's town house in Saint John for another week before he flew her to White Rock in the helicopter. He stayed two nights to make sure she was settled back in her house. The following morning he checked her cell phone, made sure her e-mail was working properly, called for the helicopter, and returned to Saint John. When he left, Gladys was tired, so for two days she slept late and stayed home reading and watching television and e-mailing Tom.

Then she took the ferry to Deer Isle.

It was an unusually warm November afternoon, and many of the residents of Sunny Haven had ventured into the grounds, where Gladys looked in vain for Cornelia. She went inside to the reception desk and asked where she might be.

The attendant said, "She's probably resting in her room. She's been staying in a lot lately. She says she feels tired and run down."

Gladys knocked at the door of Cornelia's room. There was no answer. When she knocked again, and there was still no response, she opened the door and peered in. The curtains were drawn, but through the gloom she could see a shape huddled in bed. The air smelled of stale breath and sweat and urine. She crossed the room and laid her hand gently on the sleeping form's shoulder. Cornelia was lying on her side, facing the wall. Her eyes were open.

"Feeling under the weather, old girl?" Gladys asked.

"I told you a moment ago I'm all right. I'm just a little tired."

"I don't know who you told but it wasn't me. I've just arrived."

Cornelia looked briefly at Gladys, then returned her gaze to the wall.

Gladys frowned and placed her hand on her friend's shoulder again. This time she shook it. "It's me, dummy."

Cornelia looked up again. "Who?"

"Me. Gladys."

"Gladys?"

"Shit, Cornelia. Get with it, will you? Gladys who you've known all your life."

Cornelia raised herself on one elbow and repeated, "Gladys," as if stating the conclusion of a long argument.

"Now we're getting somewhere. What are you doing in bed?"

"I was feeling tired."

"Feeling lazy is what you mean. Come on—move your arse."

"Where are we going?"

"I don't know. Anywhere. Tahiti. Istanbul. Honolulu. Or perhaps just for a walk around the grounds of Sunny Haven. Tell you what: We'll drive to the Wharf Inn."

"I've never been to Tahiti."

"And you won't be going there today. Maybe next week."

"It'd be expensive."

Cornelia had pulled herself to a sitting position. She moved her legs carefully off the bed and planted her hands on either side of herself.

"How's your hip, old girl?" Gladys asked.

"My hip?"

"The hip you hurt when you fell downstairs."

Cornelia thought for a moment. "It must have been that step. You were always warning me about it."

"You bet."

"You never missed a chance to say something about it."

"And I was right. You slipped on it and fell and hurt your hip. Remember? How is it?"

Cornelia reflected.

Gladys waited a few seconds before prompting, "Well—how is it?"

After a few more seconds of silence, Cornelia said slowly, "My hip?"

"No, your fanny. Jesus Christ, Cornelia. Your hip may be screwed but your brain isn't. Of course your hip. The doctor said you'd fractured it—remember? How is it?"

Cornelia stood, testing her hip. "It's much better. There's no need to be mad at me because I hurt my hip."

Gladys put her hands on Cornelia's shoulders and stared into her eyes. She hugged her suddenly and fiercely. "I'm not mad because you hurt your hip. I'm mad because … Well never mind. Can you walk?"

"I have a walking stick."

"Come on then. Get your stick and let's boogie."

"Where are we going?"

Gladys rolled her eyes and sighed. Then she grinned, put her arm around Cornelia, and hugged her again. "Oh, Cornelia."

Cornelia grinned. "Oh, Gladys."

"We'll drive to the Wharf Inn. We'll have tea there."

"Tea? At the Wharf Inn?" Cornelia frowned. "Is it my birthday?"

Gladys groaned. "Quick march, old girl. To the car."

As they drove, Gladys said, "It's quite the scene at your house on White Rock." Cornelia looked blankly at her, and she added, "The improvements Carol-Ann and Dale are doing—remember?"

"Oh. Yes. They talked to me about them. They're putting in a telephone, and a television with a satellite." She added, triumphantly, "The house will be wired—like you."

Gladys smiled. "That's more like it, ducky."

"They're putting a new septic system in, too. They said it was long overdue."

"They're right. You were always having trouble with it backing up so you had to get Moses Miller round with the honey wagon to flush it out. They're drilling a new well, too."

"I did have trouble with the well, didn't I?"

"Right. It'll be quite the restored mansion when they're done."

They were silent while Gladys backed the car into a parking space beside the Wharf Inn, which stood at the top of the busy road leading down to the North Head harbour.

Gladys paused with her hand on the door handle. "Do you miss it?"

"Miss it?"

"Your house—do you miss it?"

Cornelia didn't answer. She opened the door and hauled herself out on the fourth attempt. She stood still, gazing at the fishing boats lined up along the wharf.

Gladys climbed from the car. "Cornelia ..?"

Cornelia said slowly, "I don't miss the house too much. At least, I don't think I do. It's very convenient and easy at Sunny Haven. I don't have to worry about getting food in, and leaving the lights on, and forgetting I've put the kettle on …"

"You were always good at that."

"… And putting the garbage out, and letting Carol-Ann know where I am. I don't have anything to worry about at Sunny Haven."

"You don't have anything to think about is what you mean."

Gladys set off towards the Inn. Cornelia still gazed at the boats.

Gladys stopped, looking back. "What are you doing, Cornelia?"

"I'm thinking."

"That's good. What are you thinking about?"

Cornelia frowned. "I was thinking about having nothing to think about, like you said. Then I thought about cogito ergo sum. And that made me think—if I have nothing to think about … does that mean I stop existing?"

Gladys, hands on hips, said, "Oh Lordy. You're getting too deep for me." Then: "Come over here, Cornelia."

"Why?"

"Never mind why. Just come over here."

Cornelia obeyed.

"Now—turn around."

"What?"

"Turn yourself around. Face the harbour."

Cornelia obeyed again. Gladys, maintaining a careful and precarious balance, swung her foot and kicked her gently on the bum.

"Did you feel that?" she demanded.

Cornelia turned back, eyes wide. "Why yes. You kicked me on the bum."

"Right. As long as you know when you're being kicked up the bum, you're still existing. Come on. Never mind cogito ergo sum. Let's … let's …" In vain, she searched back in her mind to the year of Latin they'd studied at teacher's college. "Dammit. I was going to show off and say 'let's eat' in Latin."

"Voramus," Cornelia supplied, triumphant again.

"You're getting sharper by the minute, old girl," said Gladys. "Any sharper and you'll be dangerous. Where shall we sit?"

They chose a table overlooking the harbour. As they studied menus, Cornelia said, "I don't think I miss the house, not too much, but I do miss White Rock. And I miss you, Gladys."

"I bloody well miss you, too, Cornelia."

Gladys reached across the table and placed her hand on Cornelia's. She squeezed gently and winked.

Cornelia looked down at her menu. "What shall we eat?"

"Let's have something special."

"Why? Is it my birthday?"

Gladys looked up sharply.

Cornelia grinned. "Just kidding."

Chapter Thirteen

Patrick Given returned to the island. It was a one day visit, sandwiched between a meeting in Bangor, Maine, and another in Montreal. He'd called Gerard Clinch and asked him to arrange for him to talk to the plant workers—and, no, he didn't want Gerard Clinch there. The meeting had been set for lunch time, in the plant cafeteria. Jimmy Guptill, the plant manager, greeted Patrick.

"Welcome back. Can I ask what this mystery meeting is about?" he asked, as they shook hands.

"I've bought Clinch Fisheries," Patrick explained.

"What about—what was that outfit—International Consolidated?"

"I bid more."

"Lucky."

"Luck—and a colleague with connections."

Patrick thought gratefully of Peggy. Her network of contacts in the business and financial world consistently surprised him. She seemed to be on first name terms with countless chief executive officers, chairs of the board, company accountants and finance ministers.

"I meant lucky for us."

"Thank you. I hope so."

"Are you visiting all the Clinch plants?"

"No. I'm selling them off—all except this one."

"Why not this one?"

"I think it's got possibilities."

"So have the others. They're doing better than us—as I'm sure you know. We're running at a loss here. But of course you know that, too."

"Yes."

"So?"

Patrick shrugged.

Jimmy Guptill said, looking at Patrick, "Like I said—lucky for us. And lucky you like the island, eh?"

He led Patrick to the cafeteria. Together they mounted a small raised dais at one end of the room. The workers, some eating, fell silent after a buzz of recognition at Patrick's entry.

Jimmy Guptill held a welcoming arm toward Patrick and announced, "Guys and gals, here's your new boss. He's bought the plant."

There was a beat of surprised silence, then the workers broke into applause. Some stood.

Patrick held up his hand for silence. "Thank you for your welcome. And thank you, Mr. Guptill, for naming me the new boss—but it's a title I'm going to decline. It's true I've bought the plant, but I'm not the boss. You are the bosses—all of you. It's the job of the boss—the bosses—to make things work, and you're the ones who'll do that, by which I mean—make the plant profitable, which it is not now, as you know. It's been losing money for the last five years. It can't continue like that."

Someone called, "The government will put money in to keep us open."

"Maybe—but I don't believe that's the answer. That won't make the plant viable in the long term, and it's long term—permanent—viability I want to see, for your sake, and for the sake of the island; for the sake of its independence. I want us to make the plant profitable."

"I suppose you're talking lay-offs," someone grumbled.

"No. Production—unloading, cleaning, packing, freezing and shipping—has to be more efficient. I'll bring in some people I know to help us do that. Marketing must be more aggressive, and reach a wider area. My company can do that. Storage capacity needs to be increased. If we do these things, the people who work for me tell me that Clinch Fisheries can be profitable. You won't get rich—but you'll do all right, and you won't need government money to keep going."

"Clinch Fisheries? Is that what we'll still be called?" someone asked.

"What would you like to be called?"

"Not Clinch Fisheries," someone else shouted from the back. "Old Mr. Clinch was a gentleman and a worker. Master Gerard spoiled the name."

"What's the name of your outfit?" another plant worker asked Patrick. "Could we use that?"

"My business is Given and Associates," said Patrick. "It's too dry to make a good name for the plant."

"What then?" one of the women packers persisted.

Patrick thought of the independence he wanted for the island, so that it could remain the idyll of peace and security he felt it to be. He thought of the hardship generations had endured in maintaining a community on the island for the last hundred years.

"Well—you're an island, and you've refused to give up living here, you and your parents and grandparents and great-grandparents, even when times have been hard. It doesn't make sense that you're still here, but you've defied the odds, hung on, and, well, you're still here. You're defiant—a defiant island. Why don't we boast about that? Why don't we market ourselves—our products—as Defiant Island Products?"

"Will that be the name that goes on the plant, then, when we take the old one down?" the packer asked.

Patrick considered. "Let's put, just—*Defiant Island.*"

The fish plant workers settled back, grinning at one another.

Chapter Fourteen

Dale straightened himself in the chair, put his hands on his knees, and said, "Well."

Cornelia knew this was his signal that it was time for him to leave. He always did it, every time he came to visit, which he did, faithfully, twice during the week, and at least once at the weekend. Carol-Ann rarely came with him. She couldn't get away from the store during the week, he said, and on Sunday she needed to rest. She found it hard with him away from the store visiting Deer Isle two or three times a week, not to mention all the times he put in a shift at the plant.

It was six months later, and they were sitting in Cornelia's apartment at Sunny Haven, watching the news on the little television that Dale had persuaded her to have installed. Bernard Appleby was announcing the construction of the four lane Coastal Superhighway that would hug the south and east coast of the province, giving spectacular views, at one hundred twenty kilometers an hour, of the Bay of Fundy and the Northumberland Strait. Cornelia enjoyed watching the news, as well as golf and snooker. She didn't approve of Bernard Appleby, who seemed the epitome of all the spiritless 'good students' she'd taught, whose smug confidence in their blessedness had always so infuriated her, even as she strove to hide her dislike.

"You have to be going," Cornelia, smiling, supplied for Dale.

He rose. "I'm glad *things* have worked out so well for you here. I was worried, when you moved in, that you'd miss your house, and your *independence*."

"I'm truly happy here," Cornelia asserted.

And she was. The doctor said her hip had mended well, and she was walking more easily every week, sometimes even discarding her stick. She enjoyed the easy routine of life at Sunny Haven, the leisurely breakfast and undemanding chatter with a few residents she favoured, the stroll back to the east hallway for the morning news on her television, the scheduled morning rides in the Sunny Haven van to the North Head shops and post office, her slow lunch with a magazine or, once a week, the Island Gazette, afternoons of watching snooker or golf, or, now the weather was getting warmer, sitting in the grounds which looked down on the busy road into North Head and to the harbour beyond. She'd even enjoyed Christmas, which she'd spent at the home. Dale had planned to take her to White Rock for the holiday, but a storm blew in on Christmas Eve making the trip impossible, and then they were busy at the store, and the holiday had passed anyway, so she never did go to the island.

"I'm happy," she repeated, seeing Dale's raised eyebrows.

He hugged her, kissed the top of her head, said, "*See* you at the weekend," and left.

Gladys's visits were more demanding than Dale's, and there had been times when, secretly and guiltily, Cornelia had wished she would not come. She visited at least once a week, bearing all the news of White Rock Island, of the fish plant, of Dale and Carol-Ann, of Tom. She bombarded Cornelia with questions about the provincial and national news (Had she heard about the closure of the old St. Bartholomew's Hospital in Saint John? Did she think the teachers would go on strike? What did she think of the Progressive Democratic Alliance?), and sought a detailed account of all the goings on at Sunny Haven.

Cornelia protested once, "Why are you interrogating me?"

Gladys said bluntly, "To stop your brain going to mush."

"I follow the news."

"Do you *think* about the news?"

She was always urging Cornelia to take little trips away from Sunny Haven. They often went to the Wharf Inn for lunch or tea. They drove to the southern tip of the island to look at the lighthouse. They stopped in

Seal Harbour on the way back and inspected the new hardware store. Gladys urged her to go further afield.

Once she said, "Tom's taking me to Fredericton on Wednesday, in the helicopter. Why don't you come too? We'll pick you up. We'll land on the lawn at Sunny Haven! That'll shake the old folk up."

"But Wednesday's the day I get the van to North Head."

Gladys exploded. "Are you telling me you'd rather take a ramshackle van into North Head with a bunch of boring old girls than a helicopter to the city with your oldest friend and a cool stud like Tom?"

Cornelia really did not want her routine disturbed, but she amended her excuse to make it more acceptable to Gladys. "I'd be imposing too much on Tom."

Gladys scoffed. "Imposing? We'd be doing that boy a favour, keeping him company. Anybody'd jump at the chance of going to the capital with a couple of chicks like us."

Often Gladys suggested going to White Rock Island, but there never seemed to be time. Gladys wanted her to stay a night or two on the island, but Cornelia was afraid it would be too unsettling, now that she was comfortable on Deer Isle.

One evening Gladys marched into the common room of Sunny Haven, interrupting a yoga class. "Cornelia, get your arse out here."

Cornelia looked around at the surprised residents and said, "It's just Gladys."

Outside the common room, Gladys thrust a newspaper into Cornelia's hands. It was folded to an inside page.

"What's this?" Cornelia asked.

"It's a newspaper, for krissakes. What do you think it is?"

"The Island Gazette?"

"Of course not the Island Gazette. It's the Boston Citizen. Read." Gladys stabbed a finger at a circled portion of text. "Tom spotted it when he was big-wigging in Boston last week. He thought we'd be interested."

Cornelia read: *Highly attractive island property. Ideal summer and/or weekend executive getaway home, offering peace and seclusion in the unique fishing community of White Rock Island in Passamaquoddy Sound.*

Underneath the text was a picture of the advertised property. Cornelia peered at it, looked up at Gladys, examined the picture again. "It looks like my house."

"It *is* your house."

"Why is my house in the paper?"

"Because it's for sale."

"My house isn't for sale."

Gladys stabbed her finger at the property advertisement again. "Oh yes it is, ducky."

"But who would put my house up for sale?"

Gladys rolled her eyes. "Maybe … Santa Claus, or perhaps the Easter bunny, or the tooth fairy. Or could it possibly be… Dale and Carol-Ann?"

"They wouldn't sell my house without telling me."

Gladys raised her eyebrows.

Cornelia went on, "Anyway, they can't sell my house. It's *my* house."

"They can sell it for you," said Gladys. "Remember signing that silly little power of attorney paper?"

"That was just so they could put the telephone in, and the satellite, and do the improvements."

"It also means they can sell it—on your behalf—if they want to."

"Perhaps it's not my house," Cornelia suggested, peering more closely at the picture. "Perhaps it just looks like my house. How can you be sure?"

"Because I got Tom to pretend to be interested in it, and he called the real estate agent, and asked exactly where it was. I'm telling you—it's your house. And guess what you're asking for it."

"I'm not asking anything for it."

"Guess how much *they're* asking for it, then—on your behalf, of course."

Cornelia shrugged.

"325,000 dollars—U.S.," said Gladys.

Cornelia repeated, "325,000 dollars."

Gladys nodded, and added, "U.S."

Cornelia looked down at the picture once again. "That's a lot of money."

"You bet, old girl."

They were standing in the vestibule of Sunny Haven. Cornelia looked through the glass panel of the door. Beyond the North Head road she could see a fishing boat setting out from the wharf. She looked back at Gladys, then along the east hallway towards her room.

Gladys pressed: "So?"

Cornelia was still holding the newspaper. She opened it out, straightened it, folded it carefully with the front page outwards, and handed it back to Gladys. Her hands fell to her sides. She fluttered them, her fingers moving as if shaking off drops of water.

Gladys said, "Cornelia."

She put her hand gently under Cornelia's chin and forced her to look up from the floor, where her gaze was fixed as her hands and fingers did their dance. Their eyes met, and Gladys said again, quietly, "Cornelia."

As Gladys released her chin, Cornelia looked down again, and said, "It's my yoga class. We do yoga tonight."

Gladys persisted: "The house, Cornelia. Do you want me to do something?"

But Cornelia was already heading back into the common room, looking down, her hands and fingers fluttering again.

*****

Gladys's tires screeched as she accelerated fiercely up the ferry ramp. She swung the car onto the Shore Road and pulled up in front of the store.

Through the display window she could see Carol-Ann behind the counter and Dale stacking cartons in one of the aisles. The door jangled as she pushed it open with her foot, her hands occupied with opening the Boston Citizen. She found the property section and slammed the newspaper down on the counter in front of Carol-Ann.

"What the hell's going on?" she demanded.

Carol-Ann glanced down at the newspaper. "We're looking out for Cornelia."

"So am I."

"You're not paying the fees for Sunny Haven."

Dale, checking to make sure there was no-one in the store to hear the exchange, said, "The fees for the *home*—they add up, Gladys. What we get from the store, and from me doing a few shifts at the plant—that's not making us *rich*."

"But selling the house at an inflated price to some rich American will."

"The money goes into a trust to take care of her."

"Until…" Gladys broke off.

"Until she dies—yes," Carol-Ann supplied. "And that might be in ten years or more. She hasn't got the money to stay at Sunny Haven, and we can't afford the fees for a year, let alone ten years."

"You might at least have told her you were going to sell her house."

"We tried," said Dale. "But you know how *difficult* it can be talking to her lately. I don't think she'd understand. We thought it best she didn't know about it just yet. Then we can *break* it to her gradually."

"She knows already," said Gladys. "I just showed her the ad."

"I don't see what this has got to do with you," Carol-Ann snapped. "You have no right to interfere." She went on, as the door jangled to announce a customer, "I suggest you leave, right now, and let us try and earn a living—a living for us and for Cornelia, that is."

Gladys picked up the paper and left, banging the door behind her.

Chapter Fifteen

Meanwhile, on Deer Isle, Cornelia's yoga class had finished. She sat for a while with the other residents, watching television in the common room. At ten o' clock the activity director clapped her hands and said, "It's getting late, everybody. You've had a busy day and you must be tired." Cornelia, like the other residents, obediently returned to her room. She switched on the television and sat on her bed to watch the news. When she woke it was two o'clock. The television was still on and someone was trying to interest her in buying an exercise bicycle. She switched it off and lay in the dark, wondering why she had her clothes on and why she felt so ill at ease.

What was it Gladys was always saying?

"Get your brain in gear, old girl."

That was it.

Do it, then, Cornelia, she told herself: Get your brain in gear.

She had her clothes on because—that was easy—because she'd fallen asleep watching television. But why the uneasy feeling? She projected her mind further back into the evening until she remembered watching television with the residents. (No wonder she'd fallen asleep. Television always made her dozy.) Before she watched television in the common room, there was the yoga class. Yes—and Gladys had arrived in the middle of the class and said, "Get your arse out here." Just like Gladys to say something like that. They'd talked, in the hallway. Gladys had been worked up about something. What was it? And when they parted—they hadn't hugged.

They hadn't hugged.

They *always* hugged to say goodbye.

But they hadn't, because … because …

Cornelia had walked away!

Her eyes fell on the photograph Dale and Carol-Ann had brought from her house on White Rock Island of herself and Gladys. That would be—

heavens—nearly seventy years ago, when they left high school. Those were the years when her mother's friends said things like, "Cornelia is a … *hand-some* child," and, "Cornelia *could* grow into an attractive woman," the cautious, qualified compliments she supposed referring to her wide nose and full mouth, features which seemed as if they belonged on a larger face, set on a larger body. She was slight, and only medium height, and—peering more closely at the photograph—beside her Gladys seemed perfectly proportioned. Moreover, how ravishing, how twinkling, how *saucy* Gladys looked, in comparison with Cornelia's heavy, brooding gaze. Cornelia's mother told Cornelia, "I wish you'd present yourself like Gladys," meaning pay more attention to your hair and clothes. Gladys's mother told Gladys, "I wish you'd behave like Cornelia," meaning move and talk with her reserve and grace.

Cornelia picked up the photograph. She smiled down at it, then held it close to her chest, hugging her old friend. No wonder she felt so uneasy. How could she have walked away without hugging goodbye, without even saying goodbye?

She needed to talk to Gladys, right now, to apologise, and to explain why she'd walked away like that.

But … why *had* she walked away like that? Why had she been so distraught; too distraught, even, to say a proper goodbye to her oldest, dearest friend?

Yes—there was more, but she couldn't remember.

Get your brain in gear, old girl.

Next time she woke it was four o'clock. At first she thought she was in her old house, with the battered bedside table bearing the photograph of Dale Senior, and the stairs with the bend in them, and the worn and slippery step, and downstairs the front door with the stained glass panel, and the little parlour, and the garden outside with the old wooden chairs among the wild roses. Remembering she was at Sunny Haven, she suddenly, and for the first time, missed her old house badly.

She thought: My house …

My house is being sold.

Gladys told me.

Then I walked away!

Cornelia opened her door onto the dimly lit, silent hallway. She tiptoed to the telephone outside the common room (why hadn't she heeded Gladys's urging to have a telephone installed in her room?) and dialed her old friend's number.

Gladys answered on the second ring. "Cornelia." A statement, not a question.

"How did you know it was me?"

"I've been sitting beside the goddam phone since I got home, waiting for you to call. What took you so long?"

"Sorry."

"For what?"

"For not saying goodbye. For not hugging goodbye."

"My fault, old girl. I shouldn't have sprung the news on you like that. It's really nothing to do with me. And I've got a sorry to say to you."

"What for?"

"I tackled Carol-Ann and Dale about selling the house. I shouldn't have done that."

"You did it for me, for the best, Gladys."

"Well, yes, that—plus me being an old busybody."

"You did it for me," Cornelia asserted, "Just like you told me about the house being for sale. Now I want you to do something else for me, please."

"What's that, ducky?"

"Come and get me. Take me over to White Rock Island. I want to see my house. I don't know how I feel about it being for sale. I think seeing it—being in it—might help me sort out my feelings."

"Well, it's a shock, news like that. It takes a while for it to sink in. Sit tight, ducky. I'll be there as soon as I can. I'll get the early ferry. Look out for me."

At five thirty Cornelia slipped out of the front door of Sunny Haven as Gladys pulled up in the car park.

"Hurry up, old girl," Gladys urged. "They're waiting for us."

"Who's waiting?"

"The guys on the ferry, of course. I told them I was getting you and they said they'd wait. It won't matter if the milk and papers are ten minutes late getting to the island."

Gladys drove fast out of North Head. At Seal Harbour she turned onto the Ingalls Head road, and at Ingalls Point the ferry waited. The crew waved them on and the ferry pulled away. They were the only passengers. Gladstone Ingalls, one of the two members of the crew, plodded across the deck slowly and deliberately, two mugs clasped in one big hand, moving his thick set frame with a slight, gentle roll, as if the ferry had infected him with its own style of passage during the ten years he'd worked on it.

As Gladys wound her window down, Gladstone lowered his big, square head, with its mass of black curly hair springing out around it, and spoke as slowly and deliberately as he moved. "You girls like some coffee?" He passed the two mugs in, then: "Coming home, Cornelia?"

"Don't know ..." She was going to say his name, but found she couldn't remember it, although she'd known him since he was a child, had taught him in school. She looked at Gladys, who mouthed, "Gladstone," and Cornelia finished, "... Gladstone."

"It doesn't seem right, you not being there," Gladstone went on. "We told Dale we'd look out for you if you came back. We always have kept an eye on you—you know that—but I mean a special eye, like, you know?"

"Thank you, Gladstone. That's nice of you."

As they drove from the ferry, they saw Carol-Ann and Dale in the store. Cornelia was silent as they drove the familiar road to her house.

When they arrived and Gladys stopped the car, she sat, still silent, gazing at it. A sign posted at the front of the house declared: *Lomax Realty. For Sale.* It gave a number in Fredericton.

"Are you going in?" Gladys asked.

Cornelia nodded, her eyes still fixed on the house—her house.

"Do you want me to come in with you?"

Cornelia shook her head, still without taking her eyes off her house. Then she patted Gladys's knee. "Thank you—no. But can you come back in an hour and get me? That'll be long enough for me to sort out how I feel."

Gladys said, "I'll be at my place. Call me if you need anything, now you've got the new telephone in your house—and seeing as how you've suddenly got so good at using the phone." Seeing Cornelia's blank look, Gladys added, "You called me from Sunny Haven—remember?"

Cornelia nodded. "Yes. I telephoned you."

Gladys said, "Right. See you soon, old girl."

Cornelia watched her friend drive away, then walked slowly through the front garden to the door. It was locked. She thought: That doesn't seem right. I never lock the door. She walked around to the back of the house and found the key she always kept under the big rock beside the back door.

She let herself in, thinking—Am I trespassing? She dismissed the thought as absurd. It was *her* house, even if it was for sale. But as she ventured further, she felt like an intruder in a strange house: The television in the parlour, the new telephone—red—on a new table in the hallway, the kitchen with new sink and counter tops, the downstairs bathroom with new flush and washbasin, all were foreign to her. She wondered how much Dale and Carol-Ann had spent on what they called the improvements. Were they improvements? She wasn't sure. Had they carried them out for her, anticipating her return (although they'd never spoken of her return when they installed her at Sunny Haven, and she remembered thinking when she arrived—is this my final home?) Or had they carried them out with the idea of making the house a more desirable sale? Was that always the plan? Had they been waiting for her to reach such a state of decrepitude that she would have to move out? Surely not. Dale would never think like that.

She had come back to determine how she felt about her house being for sale, but it didn't even feel 'hers'. She was as uneasy as she had been lying awake in the early morning. She was about to pick up the new telephone to call Gladys to come and get her and take her back to Sunny Haven (she supposed that was her home now—now that she'd somehow lost her house) when she decided to overcome her unease and disillusionment at least enough to look upstairs, to see what changes had been made up there. She climbed the stairs. There was the step she'd slipped on, as worn as ever. At least that was the same. She welcomed its small dereliction.

Cautiously, she pushed open the door of her old bedroom, unsure whether her caution derived from fear of intruding on what seemed no longer her own, or of finding so many changes it would be unfamiliar and lost to her, anyway. She closed her eyes, stepped forward, breathed in deeply.

The familiar memory evoking smells assailed her: lilac toilet water, beeswax, old woolen blanket, dust, where it always collected above the window, rubbery odour of the old life jackets in the closet under the eaves (two adult sizes, for Dale Senior and her, one child size for little Dale).

With her eyes still closed, she moved carefully into the room, felt for the bed, sat on it.

She thought: It doesn't matter if, or how much, the room has changed. For me, it will be the same. It's still my bedroom.

She breathed in deeply again.

Her memory, already triggered by the familiar smells, conjured more smells, old, distant ones. She remembered cod and engine oil and sweat on Dale Senior when he returned from fishing, baby powder and urine on the bedsheets after Dale had crawled in with her and Dale Senior, sex and sweat and semen after loving Dale Senior before he rose to catch the early tide, Dale Senior's shaving cream, wet wool of his sweater.

Yes. Her bedroom. Her house.

She shifted her weight on the side of the bed. It creaked. (If she had shifted the other way, she would have moved silently.) She opened her eyes and looked around. With satisfaction, she discovered her room not only smelled the same, but also looked the same. The coverlet with the rose pattern. The flowered curtains. The photograph on the bedside table, Dale Senior and Dale, Dale Senior in a suit (it must have been Easter or Christmas), looking at the camera, not smiling but not frowning, little Dale clutching his father's hand, looking up at him. The rocking chair, where once she'd sat to nurse and soothe Dale, now where she laid her clothes.

Where she laid her clothes.

Her clothes—there were none on the chair. She always left something on the rocking chair—a cardigan, her sweat pants—ready to throw on in a hurry, but the chair was empty. She looked in the closet and in the chest of drawers. While some of her clothes were at Sunny Haven, enough to make two outfits—one to be worn, one in the wash—most of them should be here. But they'd gone. A first spasm of indignation rose in her.

She went slowly back down the stairs—careful on the worn step—and out of the back door.

Even in her confusion, the garden delighted her, as it always had done. The hedge of wild roses on one side already promised a profusion of blooms, even as the rose hips still clung. The lupines were just beginning to flower, purple and blue and pink. The wild raspberries and blackberries which lined the other side of the garden were a straggle of bare, spindly branches. Really, it was a wild garden, a transition between the domesticity of her house and the wilderness of the woods behind it. At the end of the garden, just before it gave way to the woods, the rose hedge curled in and out again to form a secluded bower where there had always been two old wooden chairs, one for her, one for Dale Senior. She liked to sit there in the afternoon with a cup of tea.

This was where she'd been sitting, with her cup of tea, when they brought her the news, Moses Ingalls—that would be Gladstone's father—and Jeremiah Miller. She knew it was serious by their silent arrival, by the lack of the usual boisterous greetings, by the way they held their caps in front of them, by their grave faces, by the way they stood before her without speaking.

She had to prompt them for their news. "Dale Senior?"

They nodded, and Moses said, "He's gone, m' dear. We're sorry."

Strange how she could be so calm. "A drowning, was it?" Dale Senior had gone out early with the White Rock fishing fleet.

Moses shook his head. "No, m' dear. Heart attack, we think, like his father. We've got him down at the wharf. Doctor's on his way from the big island. Shall we take you down to him?"

"In a few minutes. Let me sit for a few minutes." Her tea cup rattled against the saucer with the shaking of her hands.

"Shall we stay with you?"

"Thank you."

They backed away as if taking leave of royalty, and waited with heads bowed. She hadn't realized she was crying until Moses came forward to offer his handkerchief. It smelled of engine oil and cod, like Dale Senior.

"There, m' dear," Moses said, patting her shoulder.

She put her hand on his, as if comforting him. She thought of Dale, at work at the school, innocent of bereavement among the vitality and joy of the children.

"Dale—has anyone told Dale?"

"No, m' dear, not yet. Would you like us to go down and tell him, or would you like us to take you down to the school and you tell him?"

But island news, especially news of tragedy, travelled fast, and Dale had already heard. Moses and Jeremiah fell back as he hurried around the corner of the house, calling, "Mother. *Mother,*" his voice querulous and uncertain.

"I'm here, dear."

"Mother. *Mother.* What are you *doing* here? How did you *get* here?"

"Your father. A heart attack, they think, on the boat, Moses says."

"Mother, *that* was twenty five years ago."

He was kneeling in front of her, taking her hands in his.

She said, as if it would be a comfort, "He always told me not to worry about him when he was out on the boats. He'd never drown, he said. It would be his heart that would take him, like his dad—like your grandpa."

"Mother ..."

"Were you at the school? Did someone there tell you? I was just coming ..."

"I was on my way to the plant when *people* in the store said they'd seen you at the house. How long have you been here? I can't leave you *here* by yourself. Let me call Carol-Ann and see if she can come up from the *store* and stay with you. Come in the *house* while I call."

He stood and she let him pull her gently to her feet and lead her to the house.

In the kitchen, she said, looking around, "The house is for sale."

He was in the hallway, his hand on the telephone. He paused. "Yes."

"Gladys told me."

"We *were* going to tell you."

"My clothes have gone."

"Carol-Ann took them to get them cleaned for you. They're at the store."

"I wanted to see it, the house, to see how I felt about it being for sale."

"We didn't want to *upset* you with it. Are you ... upset?"

"I felt ... uneasy."

She paused, and Dale prompted, "About the house being for sale?"

Cornelia considered. "Because I didn't say goodbye to Gladys when she told me."

Dale picked up the telephone again. "I'm *late* for the shift. I have to get to *work*. I'll get Carol-Ann to come and stay with you. Then I'll take you back to Sunny *Haven* after work this afternoon. Okay? You can't stay here by yourself. You're much better off, and much *happier*, at Sunny Haven—*aren't* you?"

He spoke hurriedly, then soothingly, to Carol-Ann, on the telephone, hugged Cornelia, and left.

Cornelia called Gladys. "I'm ready. Come and get me. Quick."

As they pulled away, Carol-Ann's car came into sight.

Gladys said, "Shall I stop?"

Cornelia slid low in her seat and said, "Mush, pardner. We can just get the eight thirty."

They drove to, and on, the ferry, which pulled away from the wharf immediately.

As they settled back in their seats, Gladys said, "Well?"

"I'm checking out of Sunny Haven and moving back to White Rock," Cornelia announced. She added, "I won't tell Dale and Carol-Ann, not yet. They want me to stay at Sunny Haven."

"Do you want to live with me?"

"I wouldn't impose on you, Gladys. Anyway, I'd drive you crazy."

"Crazier is what you mean."

"Us gals need our independence. I'll live in my house."

"It won't be a popular move."

"No. But I'll talk to Dale. He'll come around."

"It's not that easy, old thing. I've got news for you. I just heard it, from Fran Miller. Someone's made an offer on your house. It's as good as sold."

Cornelia reflected, seeking a suitable expression of surprise. Finding nothing in her own lexicon, she drew on Gladys's repertoire. "No shit."

"It's true."

Cornelia reflected again. "I'll move back anyway. It's my house."

As Gladys pulled in to Sunny Haven, Cornelia asked, "Will you come and get me tonight?"

"After supper?"

"After bed time. About eleven."

"What are you going to do? Break out?"

"If they know I'm leaving, they'll call Dale and Carol-Ann."

Gladys nodded. "So what am I supposed to do? Climb down the chimney and spirit you away?"

"You just wait outside—at eleven."

"What the hell am I going to do until eleven o' clock?"

"You can visit with me here until ten thirty. Then you leave—pretend to leave—and I'll come out and join you."

"Anything you say, old girl."

They spent the day together, and at ten thirty walked from Cornelia's room to the front door of Sunny Haven and hugged. The night supervisor watched from the office between the east and west wings as Gladys winked at Cornelia and said loudly, "See you on Saturday, old thing."

Cornelia echoed with equal emphasis, "Until Saturday, then."

Back in her room, Cornelia collected the few clothes and other possessions that Dale and Carol-Ann had brought to Sunny Haven with her. She didn't have a suitcase but she found two grocery bags in the garbage in her room and stuffed everything in them. She locked the door and switched off her light. Opening her window wide, she leaned out and looked along the east wing. A few lights were on, but all the curtains were closed, and the front of the building was in darkness as far as the main door, from where light spilled down the drive. She stepped back and assessed the height of the window. The sill was on a level with her waist. She placed her bedside table under the window and tried to climb on it but couldn't lift her foot high enough. She unlocked the door and walked down to the common room, nodding to the night supervisor as she passed. She collected as many *Homes and Gardens* and *Better Livings* as she could find, and set off back to her room. Seeing the night supervisor watching her curiously, she said, "I'm going to read myself to sleep." She locked her door again and piled the magazines on the floor beside the table. Balancing on them, she pulled one knee on to the table, then the other. Kneeling unsteadily, she opened the window wide and threw the bags out. Then, leaning out as far as she could, wriggling and kicking, she manipulated herself over the sill until her fingers touched the ground. She was relieved that the drop didn't seem as far on the outside. She walked herself forwards on her hands until her feet tumbled from the sill. Her knees banged painfully on the ground and her arms gave way and she lay, breathing heavily with her eyes closed.

She froze as a hand gripped her shoulder.

A voice said, "Cornelia?"

She lay still.

The voice said again, more urgently, "Cornelia?"

She opened her eyes and looked sideways and found Gladys's face inches from hers, wet with tears.

Gladys repeated, "Cornelia?"

Cornelia said, "Are you okay?"

"What do you mean—am I okay?"

"You're crying."

"So would you be if you could have seen your arse wriggling out of that window. I've just about wet myself laughing."

"I'm glad I entertained you."

"Sorry. Couldn't help myself. Are you okay?"

"Of course I'm okay."

"Then why are you lying around?"

"I didn't know it was you. I was wondering whether to play stupid or dead."

"Which one did you choose?"

"I thought I could do stupid better."

"Good, because that's what we are."

"Why?"

"Tell you in a minute. Come on. Get your arse moving again."

They grabbed a grocery bag each and crossed the lawn, keeping out of the light from the main door. Gladys's car was parked in the shadows beside the drive. They climbed in and Gladys drove out of Sunny Haven, not putting her headlights on until they were on the road. They looked at one another and grinned.

"Quite the break out," said Cornelia. "But what's the stupid part?"

"The stupid part is—there's no ferry until the five o' clock. What the hell are we going to do for five hours in the middle of the night on Deer Isle?"

They drove to the southern tip of the island and parked as near to the cliff top as Gladys could get.

"Are we the wild things or what?" Gladys murmured.

"Wild things," Cornelia confirmed.

They reminisced about their days as wild things—the day they skipped school and took Gladys's father's boat out without permission and ran it aground on Shoal Island; the day they ran away from home and slept on the beach on the western side of the island, only to find, when they decided to capitulate and return home, disappointed at the lack of search, that Cornelia's father had been watching over them all the time, also sleeping on the beach; the day Gladys said they'd climb the cliff at the Northern Head and they got stuck on a ledge half way up; the day Gladys was allowed to take her father's car for the first time, unsupervised, and, driving too fast to board the ferry, skidded off the ramp.

They dozed fitfully until five o' clock, when they drove back to Ingalls Head and boarded the ferry for White Rock.

Gladstone commented, leaning in the car window to offer coffee, "You ladies are out early again."

"It's a secret, okay, Gladstone, please?" said Gladys. "Don't let on you saw us."

Gladstone nodded, winked and offered a thumbs up.

Gladys added, "Good man, Gladstone."

The road was deserted and the store was in darkness as they drove from the ferry to Cornelia's house.

Cornelia climbed out of the car and told Gladys, "I'd be lost without you, old thing."

"I know. That's why you're going to call me at my place as soon as you're in."

"Why?"

"First—to tell me you're safely in. I'd wait and watch until you're inside but I don't want to sit here and draw attention to us. And second—because you know how you get sometimes."

"You mean a bit vague and forgetful?"

"Just a bit, and just sometimes, ducky."

"I've been doing well, though, haven't I?"

"Yes—that's why I'm worrying. You're overdue for a bout of old age looniness. Now—get your arse inside. Then call me."

Gladys drove away and Cornelia let herself in with the secret key. She called Gladys and said, "I'm in."

"What are you going to do now?"

"Sleep, I think."

"Me too. Call me when you wake up."

Cornelia lay on her bed, adjusted the photo of Dale Senior and Dale so that she could see it in the growing early morning light, and thought: Despite all the excitement, and being up all night, I don't feel one bit tired.

She fell asleep.

Chapter Sixteen

Cornelia wasn't sure whether it was the front door closing or the voices downstairs that awoke her. At first it was just a noise which shouldn't be there, disturbing her sleep.

Oh.

They must be cleaning the hallway. They weren't supposed to start that until the residents went to breakfast.

Oh dear. Then she must have overslept. It was the residents, on their way to breakfast.

No.

She wasn't at Sunny Haven. She was at home. She knew without opening her eyes. She knew by the smell of her own bed and her own bedroom.

Then it must be Dale Senior, trying to leave without disturbing her.

But no—that was long before Sunny Haven, before *now*.

Was it Dale, then, on his way to school?

No. That was before Sunny Haven, too, long before; before Dale and Carol-Ann; before *now*.

Think.

Get your brain in gear, old girl.

She must stop being vague about time.

But—yes—Dale was, somehow, *now*.

Dale was …

Dale was …

Dale was selling the house!

She was home because Dale was selling the house.

She glanced at her watch: Heavens—eleven o' clock. She listened.

"… Built around 1920 by my *father*."

That was Dale. *Now*.

"But it's well built."

Uh-oh. Carol-Ann.

"Of course well *built*. My father knew what he was *doing*."

Dale again, as indignant as he ever became with Carol-Ann.

Now it was a voice she didn't know, a man's.

"It's charming. I admired it—from the outside, of course—that first week I stayed on the island."

A summer visitor?

"… It's as *charming* inside as it is *outside*, and …"

"We've had it modernised, of course." Carol-Ann. Interrupting Dale. "You'll see there are new kitchen appliances and countertops, and we've had the septic system upgraded and the well redrilled."

The footsteps and the voices progressed beyond the front door—"The coloured glass over the door … absolutely charming …"—through the hallway, into the parlour, back into the hallway, into the kitchen, out of the back door, into the garden.

Should she sneak downstairs and out the front door while they were in the back garden? She could walk up to Gladys's house. Or should she hide—in the closet, or in the bathroom (locking the door!), or under the bed? But what if they found her? How embarrassing—to be caught hiding, like a naughty child, in your house—*in your own house*. Perhaps it would be best just to get up, go downstairs, and greet her children and the stranger, as if she had every right to be there.

Which she did, she reminded herself.

The voices and footsteps returned—quickly, too quickly, leaving no time to act. They crossed the kitchen, came down the hallway, started up the stairs.

She froze. Closed her eyes. Feigned sleep.

"… We haven't got around to modernising the upstairs yet."

Carol-Ann's voice.

"Good." A pause, at the top of the stairs, on the landing. "I mean—I like the old style."

The stranger.

The footsteps and voices were at her bedroom door.

"… Oh, quite. We feel the same way."

Carol-Ann, lying through her teeth.

"Dale and I believe it's so important to honour and preserve the past."

The door opening.

"Oh my God."

The door slammed.

Carol-Ann's voice penetrated from the landing outside. "How silly of me. I'd forgotten your mother was staying here, Dale."

"My *mother*? She's in Sunny …"

"No. We agreed she could stay the night—just the one night, last night—remember?"

"But …"

"I'm so sorry. I'd completely forgotten about her. She's sleeping. We won't disturb her. Let's take a look at the spare bedroom."

The voices faded, returned a few minutes later, Carol-Ann still talking. "The house is empty and available immediately, I assure you. Dale's mother is resident elsewhere."

"I quite understand."

The stranger.

The voices began to fade as the footsteps descended the stairs.

"… Just visiting overnight … Do apologise … Marvellous old lady …" Carol-Ann, gushing now. "Eighty-three … So spirited … But forgetful … Obviously forgot we were coming to view the house this morning."

The voices were at the front door. Cornelia crept from her bed and opened the bedroom door a crack, straining to hear.

"… Loved this house since I first saw it … Definitely interested … Would like to confirm my offer …"

"… Discuss terms … Contract … Closing date …"

Carol-Ann again. Dale didn't seem to have much to say. The front door slammed. A car door opened and closed. The engine started, faded.

Silence.

She was shaking. She stumbled back to her bed and sat. Dale Senior, from his photograph, seemed to be watching her. Why should she shake with fear and embarrassment when she was in her own bed, in her own house? Indignation mastering the timorousness and indecision which had gripped her at the unexpected intrusion, she went downstairs and picked up the telephone.

She thought: They'll be back. How long have I got?

"Gladys, I need some food. There's no food here."

"I'll go down to the store and get you some groceries."

"No time. Just bring me anything you can spare."

"What's going on, ducky?"

"I'll tell you later. Quick now."

She replaced the receiver and contemplated the front door, her mind wandering—but with purpose—back to her and Gladys's days as wild things: An argument with their parents … over clothes … "You look like a pair of trollops" … angry and humiliated … running upstairs to the attic, to the Wild Things' club room … sulking … refusing to come down for supper … Gladys's father's footsteps on the attic staircase … "Come down this minute or I'll drag the both of you out of there" … Gladys whispering, "Quick. The chair—under the door handle …"

Yes!

She dragged a chair from the parlour and wedged it under the front door handle.

A car pulled up.

Gladys? Couldn't be. Too soon.

She peeked through the parlour window.

Dale. Getting out of his car. Approaching the front door.

She hurried back into the hallway.

Key in the lock. Turning. Then the handle turning. Dale muttering. The handle turning again.

Would the chair hold?

More muttering.

The door straining against the chair.

Then: "Mother? Are you *there*?" The door straining again. "Mother. Please *answer* me. I can't open the *door.*"

Silence.

Footsteps receding. She glimpsed him passing the parlour window and turning the corner of the house.

The back door!

She'd kept the key from under the rock, and the other key was always left hanging inside, behind the back door. But Dale or Carol-Ann might have taken it. Or they might have left the door unlocked when they came in from the garden with the stranger. From where she stood, she couldn't see if the key had been returned, or if the door was unlocked.

Dale passed the kitchen window. The back door handle turned. The door creaked as he pushed against it. Creaked again—but stayed shut.

Dale appeared at the window, his hand shielding his eyes from the reflections.

"Mother. Are you *there*? Yes—I *see* you."

Yes. She was at the kitchen door and he could see her.

"Open the *door*, please, Mother."

She stepped back into the hallway, out of sight.

"Mother! Are you *all right*? It's just *me*, Dale."

Just Dale. Never Dale Junior. There was Dale Senior and there was ... just Dale. Supposing it was Dale Senior at the door now? He'd have called twice, then kicked the door open, not out of anger, but out of concern, and out of his desire to put things right, always to have everything as it should be.

Twice more, first cajoling, "Mother!" Then pleading, "*Mother.*"

Then—silence again.

Should she look? No—not yet.

Footsteps—around the house. She peered from the parlour window. Dale gave a last look—exasperated, forlorn—back at the house. He drove away. She was shaking again.

Some tea would be nice. She put the kettle on the new stove and looked for tea in the usual place. There was none. The cupboards were empty. Ready for the new owner to fill, she thought. She sat at the kitchen table.

Once, she'd locked Dale Senior out of the house. They'd been married only a few weeks and argued about sex, of all things. It was the first time she'd refused him—a headache, too tired, in a huff over something, she couldn't remember why—and he'd said he might as well have stayed single. He wasn't angry. He was rarely angry, and never with her. It was more like disappointment. He left the house and sat in the garden. She was angry, however (she wasn't sure whether she was angry with him or with herself), and locked the doors. Then waited for him to try and come back in, and grew impatient because he sat outside, apparently content, for more than an hour before he tried. He only had to say, twice, "Cornelia, open the door", and she unlocked it and met him in the doorway, flinging her arms around him.

"Cornelia, open the door."

She took the key from the hook, but waited. She'd make him ask a second time.

The day they were married, when they returned to the house, he'd swept her—yes, *swept* her—off her feet, and carried her through the front door, kicking it wide, as she clung to his neck.

"Cornelia, open the door."

She put the key in the lock.

She'd made him ask twice. That was enough. She didn't want to make him kick the door open. She would open it, and embrace him, and draw him in, and lead him upstairs—like a hussy!

"Cornelia, open the door!"

Three times? Twice would have been enough.

She turned the key part way.

"Cornelia, open the goddam door!"

Wait. Three times. No—four times! And he wouldn't swear like that, not at her.

She glanced through the kitchen window. "Dale?"

No. Carol-Ann, shouting again: "Cornelia, will you open the goddam door?"

Cornelia recoiled. Reached back and reset the key.

Carol-Ann rattled the door. "Open it, Cornelia. What do you think you're doing?" Gentler: "Cornelia, we need to talk about this. I know you're upset, but there's no need to be. This will be for the best, I promise."

"You put my house up for sale."

"We had to. We couldn't afford the fees at Sunny Haven otherwise. This way—selling the house—we'll—you'll—never have to worry about money again."

"How much are you selling it for?"

"We can talk about that later. Just let me in now."

"No." She searched through her mind for an appropriate response. What would Gladys say in a situation like this? Ah—yes. "Piss off."

Through the window, she saw Carol-Ann release the handle, lift her arms in exasperation, and shake her finger at Cornelia, as if admonishing a naughty child.

"I'll be back."

Yet again, Cornelia was shaking. She sat at the kitchen table and closed her eyes. Carol-Ann's peevish voice had turned to a whistling in her head and she wished it would stop.

Again—a knocking at the back door.

Cornelia thought wearily—I can't keep this up. I'll open the door.

She did—and Gladys burst through, dumping a bag of groceries on the table.

"What's going on, ducky?"

Cornelia started to tell her, but Gladys interrupted: "You're burning the kettle dry, old girl. I've told you before not to start doing something else until it's boiled. Can't you hear it?"

"I thought it was a whistling in my head."

"It'll be voices in your head next if you don't get a hold of yourself."

"It was a whistling in my head. It was Carol-Ann's voice. It was whistling in my head."

"Steady on now, old thing."

"They want to sell my house."

"I know that, ducky. I'm the one who told you—remember?"

Cornelia reflected. "Yes. I locked them out. I wouldn't let them in."

"Who?" Gladys grinned. "Dale and Carol-Ann?"

"Yes. And before that there was a man with them. They were showing him around my house. They woke me up. He said he was interested. They left."

"And you won't let them back in. Good for you. This should be a movie: The Siege of the Senile."

"I was going to give in and open the door. I thought you were them, coming back."

"Hang tough, dearie. Do you want me to stay with you?"

"No. I might need you to bring me more food."

"Okay. I'll clear off so you can lock up again before they come back." She grabbed Cornelia to her, hugged her and kissed her on the cheek. She flew out of the door, calling back, "Don't forget to lock up after me. And call me." As Cornelia locked the door, Gladys banged on the window. "Take the friggin' kettle off, old girl."

*****

She must have fallen asleep again. This wasn't mental and physical feeble-
ness, she protested to herself. She'd always enjoyed an afternoon nap, and
it had been an eventful night and morning, enough to tire anyone. She was
in the parlour, in an armchair, and something had woken her. It was late
afternoon. There it was again, a knock at the door. Not the beseeching
knock of Dale, nor the imperious, impatient knock of Carol-Ann. This was
the knock of a real visitor, polite, apologetic, prepared to retreat if unan-
swered. She rose and peered through the parlour window. It was the
stranger, by himself, as far as she could see, come back to claim his
house—*her* house—she thought, indignation returning. He raised his hand
to knock again, hesitated, lowered it. Stepped back, looking at the windows. She retreated out of sight. A moment later she peered out again. He
was walking away. She was sure he was alone. She hurried to move the
chair from the front door.

She called, "Come in."

He'd reached the road. "Are you sure? I don't want to intrude."

She repeated, "Do come in."

As he walked toward the house, he said, "I'm by myself."

She nodded and stepped back to let him enter, thinking: Gladys would
say I'm crazy letting him in like this, not just a stranger, but a stranger who
wants to buy my house—the stranger who wants to buy my house without
even telling me; who comes to view it without even asking me.

Indignation mounting anew, she snapped defiantly, "It's my house. I'm
not selling it."

He nodded. "I understand."

She was still holding the door, and he had paused just over the threshold.

She laughed suddenly. "Whatever would Dale Senior think of me, leaving you standing in the hallway like this? Do come in. Let's sit in the parlour."

He followed her into the parlour and waited until she was sitting in the armchair before settling himself on the settee.

She asked, "Would you like some tea?"

"I'd love some, but I'm not sure you'll find any. The cupboard was bare when I was here this morning."

"Gladys made a relief run."

"Good for Gladys."

"Excuse me for a moment. I'll put the kettle on." At the door she looked back, frowning, thinking: a stranger—in my house.

As if reading her thoughts, he nodded and stood. "I'm so sorry. I should have introduced myself." He held out his hand, approaching her. "I'm Patrick Given."

She laid her hand lightly in his. "Cornelia Morse."

He inclined his head in a little, formal bow. "It's a pleasure to meet you."

Warming to his old fashioned formality, she asked, "And you are from ...?"

"Ottawa, when I'm at home. I travel a lot—business, you know."

She nodded. He sounded like Tom, who always seemed to be anywhere but at his office in Saint John. "Do you have a helicopter like Tom?"

"No. I have a Beechcraft."

"A Beechcraft?"

"It's a small aircraft. I fly to Deer Isle. Who's Tom?"

"Tom—Gladys's son."

She said it as if he should know it. Surely he would know Tom, what with Tom flying around in his helicopter and he in his Beechcraft. Surely the two of them would have flown to the same place, or at least have passed one another in the air.

"Ah. Gladys's son. Of course."

"You must excuse me."

92

She left for the kitchen and he returned to the settee. As she made tea, she heard the telephone ring and thought: Gladys! She picked it up in the hallway and heard only the dial tone. She said, "Gladys?", then, louder, "Gladys!"

Patrick Given came into the hallway, apologetically holding towards her a tiny cellular telephone like the one Tom had given Gladys for emergencies.

"It's mine. I'm sorry. I usually turn it off when I'm visiting ..."

Visiting! She liked him for saying that, and not, *looking at the house I want to buy,* or something like that.

He went on, "... But I was expecting this call. You'll have to excuse me. I have to deal with this." He spoke into the phone, sounding suddenly like a different person. "Tell them no way. It's as per contract or no dice. Yes. No. Okay. Call me tonight." To Cornelia he said, "One more call, then I'll be done. Please excuse me again." He pressed a button on the phone. She started for the kitchen to make the tea, but couldn't help overhearing: "Peggy, I'm turning off. I've heard from Andrew. He's handling it. Now I'll be in conference for a while. Yes, on White Rock for at least another night. Leave a message if anything comes up. I'll check later. Otherwise, I'll call you in the morning. Okay. Thanks."

Forgetting her pretence of not listening, Cornelia said, "In conference?"

Patrick Given nodded. "With you."

Cornelia smiled, flattered. "Oh. Hmmm." She remembered now. That was what Tom said on his cellular telephone when he was visiting Gladys and they were having tea.

When Cornelia returned from the kitchen, Patrick Given was examining photographs on the wall, and commented, "I'll bet this is you and your friend Gladys when you were in school."

Cornelia followed his gaze, studying the two figures, one, Cornelia, slight and scrawny, the other, Gladys, sturdier, both in black shoes, with long white socks, and pleated grey skirts, and white blouses. They were in primary school, before Cornelia became handsome and Gladys glamorous. Cornelia's hair was in a neat ponytail, while Gladys's flew in all directions in glorious disarray.

"We were the wild things," she said.

They sat, and she put the tea things on a small table between them. She looked back at the photograph and touched her hair. Funny how Gladys's hair style now was the neat one, and hers was the confusion. She wondered when the change had occurred.

"I don't know when mine got like this and Gladys got so fussy with hers. She goes to *Holly's Cuts 'n' Styles* every week and has it done. She says mine's a mess."

A beat, then: "Your hair."

"Yes. Gladys says I should take more care of it."

"It looks fine to me."

She touched her hair again, primly.

As she poured the tea, he took a deep breath and said, "Let me tell you how it is."

He sounded like a teacher. She passed him a cup, placed hers on the table beside her, then put her hands on her knees and sat straight in what she and Gladys always thought of, when they were schoolgirls, as the attentive position.

"We were at school together. They called us the wild things."

He nodded. "When I enquired about buying your house, I didn't know the whole situation. I still don't know it. All I knew was that this house, which I'd admired when I stayed on the island, was for sale."

"Are you a summer visitor?"

"Not really. I spent a week here recently. And I was here once before, when I was small. My parents brought me."

"How old are you?"

"I'm fifty. The house…"

94

"Married?"

He paused; shook his head. "No."

He sounded uncertain. And sad. His eyes—they were brown, she'd noticed—seemed to cloud.

He looked away.

*****

The cliché of their affair—childhood friends become lovers, although that took a few more years—jarred with the eccentricities of both their subsequent careers. After college he joined a newspaper in Ottawa, where he accidentally unearthed a national political scandal involving the underhand and illegal transfer of government funds to the party in power in the guise of bestowing grants to promote multiculturalism. He became a media celebrity and invested the money he received for interviews and articles in educational software in what he intended as a flippant gesture of altruism, only to discover to his surprise that what started as a respectable amount quickly became a significant amount. He formed his own investment company, and found himself, at the age of thirty, with leisure time to spare while he monitored the continued growth of his interests.

At the same time as he relinquished his temporary celebrity and soared to private success, Penelope soared to equally unexpected but spectacular public success, from commercial art student after high school, to photographer's assistant, to photographer's model (the girl booked for a shoot failed to arrive, and the photographer, in desperation, asked Penelope to stand in), to international model.

Meanwhile they argued. Just as once it had never occurred to them that they would ever be apart, they had also assumed that they would be together when Penelope finished school. Patrick had assumed that Penelope would join him in Ottawa; Penelope that Patrick would return to Toronto. But Patrick had set up his company in Ottawa, and Penelope needed to be in Toronto to advance her career. She begged Patrick to return to Toronto. He said she didn't understand that his new business contacts were in the capital. He implored her to come to Ottawa. She accused him of trying to limit her career. The first time they argued—Patrick was home for the weekend—he left without saying goodbye. Penelope followed him to Ottawa a few days later. In the tumult of a passionate reunion, they promised never to argue again; never to spoil their love and friendship. She looked forward, she said, to seeing Patrick in Toronto next weekend. But he had meetings in Ottawa; perhaps Penelope could come back to Ottawa again. But why should she be the one to travel again, as if she was chasing him? Very well: He would come to Toronto the following weekend. That wouldn't work; she was away the following weekend doing a shoot. They argued again; parted bitterly. Patrick cancelled his meetings and went to Toronto the next weekend, to surprise Penelope. He found she had a sudden engagement in Montreal and wouldn't be back until Monday.

So the pattern of their relationship was set—passionate reunion and distraught parting; parallel paths that suddenly and briefly met, flared and splintered anew. Their meetings became increasingly unpredictable as their respective careers made them more difficult to arrange. Patrick grew accustomed to seeing Penelope more often on the covers of magazines glimpsed in Munich, London, Paris, than in real life. She grew accustomed to telephoning him when she was briefly between engagements, then flying to wherever his business had taken him, so that their reunions took place around the world. But as her fame grew, so did the demands of her career, and often their meetings were cut short by sudden calls from her agent: she was needed for a shoot in Milan; she had the opportunity for an appearance in Berlin and couldn't afford to miss it. The first time their reunion was interrupted before it could be consummated—a cover shoot for *Lustre* had to be completed the following day in order to accommodate the famous photographer's changed schedule—they declared it would not happen again; Penelope would simply stay incommunicado. But the next time they met—in Paris—even as they sat in the sidewalk café on rue de Rivoli where they'd arranged to meet, it was Patrick whose cell phone rang and whose executive assistant told him he should fly immediately to Boston to take over negotiations of a deal in danger of collapse. When he told Penelope he had to go, she accused him of putting business ahead of her. He retorted was that different from her putting her career before him. She said she couldn't afford to miss opportunities at this stage of her career; he said he couldn't afford to let a deal fall through at this stage of his business. She left him sitting at the sidewalk table, his cell phone still in his hand. They saw one another at the airport, he on his way to Logan, she to Heathrow. They didn't speak.

*****

Patrick's tone and stance had stayed Cornelia's enquiry.

She apologised, "I'm being nosy. Sorry."

"Not at all. I want you to know these things before I tell you my plan."

"What plan?"

"About the house … your house. I plan to spend more time on the island, and I want to buy a house so that I have somewhere to stay, instead of renting, or staying at the bed and breakfast. Now—I have bought your house …"

Cornelia protested, "It's not for sale. It's my house."

Patrick Given held up his hand. "… And my lawyer tells me everything is in order, and that means—everything is in order."

He sounded so confident, so authoritative—like he had been on the telephone—that she was silenced, cowed. She hung her head and her shoulders drooped. He put down his cup and knelt in front of her so that he could see her face.

"I'm sorry. I didn't mean to sound brusque."

"It's always been my house. I live here."

"I was told you'd moved to the seniors' complex on Deer Isle."

"I moved back."

"Tell me."

So, while he still knelt before her, Cornelia told him about her fall down the stairs; about her move to Sunny Haven; about Gladys telling her the house was for sale; about her clandestine return. "Then you found me in bed."

"I'm so sorry."

"Dale and Carol-Ann have no right to sell my house."

"Actually they do have the right, legally if not morally. That's what power of attorney is for."

"That was just for the improvements, not so they could sell the house. I didn't know power of attorney meant they'd sell it."

"I can have my lawyer take a look at the power of attorney, if you like. But in the meantime, they do have the right, and I have bought the house."

Cornelia muttered, weakly but defiantly, "It's still my house."

He nodded. "I understand."

After a few seconds of silence, he said suddenly, "Here's my idea: Could we share your house? It might be the simplest thing, and the most economical—for you."

She looked at him. Although they'd now been introduced, he was still a stranger. "What do you mean—share?"

"When I visit White Rock, which isn't very often, I'd stay here. The rest of the time, it would be your house, just as it's always been."

The front door opened. Dale and Carol-Ann hurried in, stopping abruptly when they saw Patrick Given on his knees in front of Cornelia.

Dale said, "Mother, there you *are*. Are you all *right?*"

Carol-Ann said to Patrick Given, "I'm sorry. She'll be leaving immediately."

Rising quickly from his knees, Patrick Given said, "No need to apologise."

Carol-Ann admonished Cornelia, "Cornelia, dear, you have to leave so that …"

Patrick Given interrupted her. "Mrs. Morse, Dale, you must excuse us. Mrs. Morse Senior and I are in conference ..."

Seeing Carol-Ann's eyebrows shoot up, Cornelia echoed, "We're in conference."

"… And we have a few more things to discuss, if you'll allow us."

He was that different person again, the one who'd spoken earlier on the telephone. Cornelia watched him usher her children easily into the hallway and out of the front door, speaking all the time. "… No need to apologise … must excuse us … will explain later …"

And they were gone.

In the doorway of the parlour, he smiled and said, "Well? What do you say?"

"Still my house?"

"Still your house. I'd be an occasional guest."

She repeated softly, "My house."

"Probably you should talk to someone about this. I'd suggest discuss it with your children, but that may not be the best thing. How about your friend, Gladys?"

"Yes. Gladys. We were the wild things, you know."

"I know."

Cornelia called Gladys, who questioned her closely about her visitor, then said, "Don't trust him. Don't agree to anything. I'll be over in a minute or two."

It was nearly an hour before Gladys arrived. Cornelia and Patrick Given were in the back garden.

Gladys shouted, from inside the house, "Cornelia, where the hell are you?"

"That'll be Gladys," Cornelia confided to her guest.

When Gladys found them, Cornelia announced, "Gladys, this is Mr. Patrick Given. Mr. Given, this is my friend, Ms. Gladys Cronk."

They shook hands.

Gladys said, looking the stranger up and down, "I know you."

He nodded. "I visited the island a few weeks ago. We met at the store—briefly."

Gladys took Cornelia's arm and drew her aside. Patrick Given withdrew discreetly.

"This guy's okay," Gladys asserted. "I called Tom and he checked him out."

"Does Tom know him?"

"No, but I guessed he was some big shot businessman from Ontario from what you told me, so I had Tom make a few calls to his business pals up there. He says he's straight up honest and you can trust him. All Tom's pals say he's famous for it. Big money, too. Tom says you can't go wrong, what with Carol-Ann screwing you with the power of attorney and all, not to mention the improvements to the house to be paid for somehow. He says it's a good deal, and do it."

They turned in unison towards Patrick Given and Cornelia said, "You're on."

Chapter Seventeen

Two months later, in the late afternoon, Cornelia was sitting in one of the old wooden chairs in the wild rose bower. Lulled by the distant shouts of children at play, she'd been daydreaming of her teaching days. From there her mind had wandered on to the end of her time at the school, to the birth and early childhood of little Dale, to the time when Dale Senior was so busy with the fishing that he was always down at the wharf.

A man came around the side of the house. It was probably someone looking for Dale Senior, she thought, something to do with supplies for the fishing. It was always a problem getting the supplies in.

"Dale Senior's down at the wharf," she called.

"It's me. Patrick. Patrick Given."

She echoed, "Patrick. Patrick Given." Then: "Are you looking for Dale Senior?"

He shook his head, smiling, and repeated, "Patrick Given. How have you been?"

Not looking for Dale Senior. Perhaps something to do with the store, then. Looking for Dale. A delivery for the store.

"Dale's not at the store—he's at the plant—but Carol-Ann's there. She can deal with it."

"I've come to stay."

"To stay." A guest. A friend of Dale's, come to stay. "I'll get the spare room ready."

"I'll take care of that."

He held out a bouquet of flowers, daisies and baby's breath and rosebuds. It was always nice when guests brought flowers. Old fashioned, but none the worse for that.

"So kind."

Where had he bought them? Certainly not on White Rock Island, or on the big island. He must have come from the city, bearing flowers, like Tom did for Gladys.

"Did you see Tom?"

"Ah—no. Where is he?"

"In the city, of course. In Saint John."

"I came from Ottawa."

"Ottawa! Tom goes there, I think, sometimes."

"He does. He told me."

"Told you! Did you see him?"

"Not today."

She held the flowers to her face, breathed them in, and repeated, "So kind." She looked up at him. He'd come to stay. A guest. "I'll get your room ready."

"There's no need."

"Just make yourself at home."

He looked as if he was about to protest, then smiled. "That's kind of you."

She went inside and in the spare room upstairs turned down the bed, which she left always made up. She opened the window a crack. (She must remember to tell him to close it later, with the nights getting colder already.) Looking out of the window, she saw him standing beside the chair, talking on a cellular telephone, gesticulating forcefully as if his listener was with him.

Talking on his cellular telephone.

Like Tom.

The telephone rang in the hallway and she hurried downstairs to answer it. That would be Gladys. She was staying in Saint John with Tom and called every day, on Tom's cellular telephone, to check on her.

Gladys said, "I thought you were out."

"I was upstairs getting the spare bedroom ready."

"Is Patrick there?"

"Patrick?"

"Patrick Given."

Yes! Of course. Her guest was Patrick Given. She shared the house with him—*her* house, as he kept insisting they call it.

She said, nodding into the phone, "Patrick Given. Patrick Given's here."

"Are you managing all right?"

"Oh yes."

"See you in a day or two, then. Say hi to Patrick. And Tom says hi to both of you. 'Bye, ducky."

Yes. Patrick Given. The cellular telephone. The aeroplane—the Beechcraft! Like Tom and his helicopter. Patrick Given had stayed once before, a few weeks after they'd agreed to share the house. Tom had been on the island, too, staying with Gladys, and the two of them, Gladys and Tom, came to visit.

Cornelia remembered now, remembered Gladys announcing on the phone, "We're coming to supper, old girl, the precious boy and me."

"Lovely. I'll make a chowder."

She remembered Patrick returning from the factory as she was gathering ingredients. They'd prepared supper together. When Gladys and Tom arrived, they were in the kitchen, and Patrick was wearing one of Cornelia's aprons.

As Patrick and Tom shook hands, Tom said, "I've heard lots about you."

"Oh dear."

"Nothing but good. You've saved the island, I'd say."

"That's putting it a bit strongly. It's a sound investment, I think."

"I hope it is—for your sake."

Patrick's phone rang, and excusing himself he went into the hallway to talk on it, his hands gesturing. A moment later Tom's phone rang, too, and he retired to the parlour to talk. When the men returned, almost simultaneously, Gladys had her hands on her hips.

Seeing her, Tom said, "Uh-oh. Better look out, Patrick. I think we're in trouble."

"It's time for the two of you to be in conference," Gladys announced.

Tom said, "Yes, ma'am." He pressed a button on his phone. "Katy, I'm in conference for a couple of hours."

Patrick said, "Oh. I understand," and also pressed a button on his phone. "Peggy, I'm off. In conference."

He and Tom returned their phones to their pockets. They stood before Cornelia and Gladys, and Tom pronounced, "We're all yours, ladies."

As they dined, Tom questioned Patrick about investments, high yield stocks, and foreign ownership. Patrick interrogated Tom on the economic forecast for the province, cross border trade, provincial tariffs, and federal trade regulations.

Finally Gladys said, "Boys—enough."

Patrick said, "Sorry. We're being boring."

Tom protested, "What's the matter, Ma?"

"Business talk—nothing but—is the matter, precious boy."

"I wish you wouldn't call me precious boy."

"That's what you are—even when all you talk about is boring business."

"Well … What would you like to talk about?" Tom asked.

Gladys suggested, "Tell us about yourself, Patrick."

"There's not much to tell. I have a company, Given and Associates, which is doing quite well …"

"Impressively well," Tom put in. "I looked it up."

"… And I live in Ottawa—and on White Rock Island, of course."

Gladys started, "And are you ..?"

Cornelia interrupted: "No, he's not married—he told me—and he's too young for you."

"Rats," said Gladys. "You've got a girlfriend, I bet. One of those smart Ottawa cookies, a corporate lawyer, or a magazine publisher, or an advertising executive."

Cornelia remembered how Patrick had reacted—his eyes clouding, looking away, shoulders slumping, lips tightening—when she'd asked him if he was married, and now she saw the same response gathering in him.

*****

A week before his first excursion to White Rock Island, they had met, the first time in three months, in London. Patrick was there to attend a conference he didn't really care about but which gave him the opportunity of charging to his company a visit to a city he liked. Penelope was called there unexpectedly because the weather and the light were predicted to be exactly right early the next morning to do a fashion shoot for *Beau Monde*. The famous photographer had arranged for part of Wardour Street to be closed for the shoot. Knowing Patrick was in London, she telephoned him breathlessly at the Dorchester. It was late afternoon. Patrick said come straight up to my room; we haven't been together for three months. Penelope said let's have tea first. They met in the lobby, Penelope glittering in a short white dress, her fine, pale blonde hair streaming around her shoulders like the feathered tendrils of ornamental grasses, an irresistible and apparently unaware magnet for the eyes of everyone in the busy lobby. Standing to greet her, Patrick marvelled anew at her attractiveness. He agreed with the fashion journalists who wrote that Penelope's fame as a model derived from her unassuming looks, which embodied and survived the cliché of being the attainable, pretty girl next door. (Although now in her early thirties, she still looked—effortlessly—barely twenty.) She was called the Not Model—not haughtily beautiful, but pretty; not thin, but certainly not overweight; not intimidatingly tall, but not short; her famous complexion neither pale, nor burnished, but warm, with a hint of rose, as if she was always about to blush. Her face in repose was sad, with her slightly downcast mouth, her eyes so luminous they appeared tear filled. Her slow smile, her mouth at last turning up, her eyes crinkling, was famous.

As they embraced, Patrick murmured, "Let's make tea short."

They sat in the restaurant, ordered, and her cell phone rang.

She answered and protested, "But, Don, you said he didn't need to do a set up this evening ... I know he's famous but ... I *know* it's a great chance for me, but ... Oh very well. I'll be at the door." As the waiter delivered tea, she explained to Patrick, "The famous photographer—he is famous, really, and it is a great chance for me—wants to do a set up now, ready for the morning. He hasn't got time then because he has an afternoon shoot in Rome. Don's sending the car round. Why don't you come and watch?"

"Peggy's calling me here at five. I've got to speak to her, and I don't want to use the cell."

"Peggy?"

"My executive assistant—remember?"

"Oh yes. Of course."

"Will I see you after the set up?"

"I'll come right back. We'll have supper if it's not too late."

He saw her to the door, aware of the eyes following her, envying him, knowing who she was, wondering who he was, then took tea by himself. At five o' clock exactly Peggy telephoned and he completed business with her. The company was buying a pulp mill with a reputation for environmental irresponsibility and Patrick wanted to be sure there were no outstanding claims against it and to know the cost of upgrading the operation so that it exceeded environmental regulations and was beyond reproach. Peggy had been speaking to government and private environmental agencies. The pulp mill company was pressing for a decision, suggesting someone else was interested in taking over the operation. The environmental agencies were checking records and data. Patrick knew Peggy could handle

the preparations for the deal, but he didn't want her, or one of his associates, to be under pressure from either side, and was ready to take over the
negotiations if necessary.

At ten o' clock he was in his room studying some of the environmental
data provided by the government and faxed to him by Peggy. A soft knock
at the door announced Penelope's return.

Patrick said, "Let's eat in the room. I'm starving."

"I mustn't eat now, not until after the shoot." She gestured downwards
from her stomach to her thighs and shrugged. "You know. Sorry."

"I'd been picturing a romantic late night supper." He said it lightly, but
had been anticipating it keenly.

"Sorry, Patrick."

"Oh well. Drink?"

She shook her head. "Mustn't."

He ordered a hamburger and ate it sitting on the bed, Penelope beside
him, her arm draped over his shoulders. In between bites, he rested his
hand on her knee.

When he finished, Penelope said, "Tell me what's happening in Ottawa."

The telephone rang.

"Ignore it, Patrick."

"Can't. It might be Peggy."

"Oh. Peggy."

He spoke into the phone. "Good … Well done … Great … Tell them
they'll just have to wait … Good work, Peggy. Thank you. Call me as soon
as you hear anything."

Penelope had moved to the window while he spoke and was gazing at
the street below. He stood behind her and put his arms around her and
nestled into her.

She murmured, "I can't."

He was stunned, as if she'd slapped him on the face.

She bit her lip, looking down. She rushed on, "Don says I mustn't do it—have sex—the night before a shoot. He says it shows in my face. The makeup can't hide a sort of glow."

He said bitterly, "What's wrong with a sort of glow?"

She answered seriously. "Don says it conflicts with my girl next door image."

"So now Don dictates not only when we can be together, but when we can make love."

She retorted, "And Peggy decides when we'll have time to talk."

The telephone rang. Patrick ignored it. They faced one other.

Patrick said, "This is hopeless."

Penelope started to cry. The telephone, which had stopped ringing, started again.

Patrick said, "Penny," and moved to hug her.

She said, moving into him, "Don says I mustn't cry. It shows in my eyes the next day."

He moved back from her. "Will Don allow us to hug?"

She giggled through her tears, uncertain whether or not he was serious.

The telephone stopped ringing; started again immediately. She moved away from him as he seized it and snapped, "Yes?" Then: "Sorry, Peggy. Go on ... Wonderful ... Well done ... Get all the papers ready and arrange a meeting for—I wonder how soon I can get back—oh, you've booked me already. What time? What flight number? Okay, arrange a meeting for late tomorrow and we'll sign everything then. Sorry you've had such a late night. That's great work, Peggy. Thank you."

He made a note of the flight number and time, and looked up.

Penelope was gone.

He telephoned her at her hotel but was told she was taking no calls. When he insisted they put him through, his call was directed to Don, who said she was in her room but he didn't want her disturbed before the shoot. Patrick slammed the phone down. He thought about going round to the hotel but was afraid the inevitable confrontation with Don would make things worse between Penelope and himself, and would trouble her seriously enough for her not to be at her best for the early shoot. At two in the morning he gave up trying to sleep and went for a walk. For two hours he wandered the streets of central London. He had breakfast at Oxford Street station and caught the underground to Wardour Street, the end of which he found cordoned off and patrolled by a security guard. He watched from behind the barricade. The street was empty but for a few carefully chosen and placed vehicles, and a motorhome. The famous photographer fussed behind his equipment in the middle of the street, while two assistants adjusted reflectors and lights. Then Penelope, flanked by two stylists, swept from the motorhome. Patrick gasped. The security guard uttered a long, low whistle, and even the famous photographer, inured to beauty, was momentarily frozen in admiration as he glanced up from his Bronica. Penelope wore a long red gown of such light, flimsy material that it wafted around her as she walked. She scintillated in the early morning light filling the street.

Patrick murmured unthinkingly, "Penelope."

The security guard, overhearing him, said, "Don't tell me you know her."

Patrick nodded. "We grew up together."

The security guard contemplated Patrick, assessing his credibility. "Are you serious?"

Patrick nodded again.

"Do you want to get closer? I can let you in. Just keep clear of her agent—that bloke by the van. He won't want her disturbed."

"Thanks. I'll watch from here."

Penelope, her head down, arranged her body in the pose dictated by the photographer and manipulated by the assistants. The stylists made last minute adjustments to her face and dress and hair. One, stooping, peered closely at her eyes, shook her head slightly, applied something to the skin around them, stepped back, nodded. The photographer said, "Let's go." He bowed behind his camera. Penelope's body, without moving, seemed to radiate a new sensuality. She raised her head, and saw Patrick at the end of the street. Her body slumped. The photographer said, "Penelope. Let's *go*." Don threw his arms up in a dramatic gesture of exasperation. The stylists rushed forward for new adjustments and the assistants minutely manipulated her pose. This time she didn't look at Patrick, and with a nod to the security guard, he left.

Since then he'd telephoned twice and although he'd called her cell, both calls had been diverted to Don, and he'd hung up. He'd seen her on the cover of *Chic* and *Toronto Weekend*, and in the pages of *Elegance*. (The passenger beside him on a flight from Calgary to Ottawa was looking at the magazine, noticed his glance, and said, "She's something, isn't she?") He'd also seen her—imagined he'd seen her—in Vancouver, Seattle, Boston, Marseilles, Hamburg and Rome. He carried her image so constantly that it was easy for him to imprint it onto any woman bearing the slightest resemblance seen from a distance, even as he told himself it was impossible that it was her.

But it was not impossible. He went to Salzburg, for pleasure, and was sipping coffee at a sidewalk café near the Mozarteum when he saw her. He looked away, telling himself he was imprinting her image again. He looked back. It was Penelope, walking ostensibly alone, but with the stylists and Don at a discreet distance alongside and behind her, and a photographer bobbing and weaving in front, shooting pictures from low angles. When Penelope saw Patrick, she faltered. He held his coffee cup still below his mouth. Their eyes met and locked. He saw her teeth bite at her lower lip and was pleased at the secret agitation it revealed. His hand was shaking, spilling coffee. Who would look away first? He bowed his head to his coffee. She swept past him, and the photograph that appeared in *Allure*—it became well known and established the photographer's reputation—showed the beautiful, famous face and body ignored by the sullen café occupant too intent on his coffee even to notice, let alone appreciate, such sublime loveliness.

*****

Catching Gladys's eye, Cornelia shook her head briefly, warningly.

Covering, Gladys said brightly and quickly, "Tom's turned from an island boy into a city boy. He lives in downtown Saint John."

Patrick asked, "Apartment?"

"Townhouse. Restored nineteenth century."

"Nice." Tentatively, "Plenty of space …"

Gladys put in, "He shares. With Adrian."

That had been a month ago, Cornelia remembered now. They'd had a nice evening, the four of them.

Returning to the garden, she said, "You're Patrick Given. We share the house."

"I hope I'm not disturbing you, arriving suddenly like this."

"No. It's nice to have you." She nodded, thinking of the supper with Patrick Given and Gladys and Tom. "You helped me make the chowder.

Chapter Eighteen

It was the evening of the Christmas concert at White Rock Island School. The teacher, Mrs. Wilhemina Griffin, who wore a new blue suit decorated with a light up reindeer brooch, had transformed one of the classrooms into an auditorium by placing the school's twenty desks (twelve of them in use, the remaining eight evidence of the school's declining enrolment) together at one end of the room and covering them with sheets of plywood. Invitations to the concert had gone to parents and family and friends, which in effect had invited the whole population of the island. The audience was arriving with seats in hand, knowing the paucity of chairs in the school, and in any case unwilling to be seated for an hour or more on the small school chairs even if they were available. Already the classroom boasted a variety of seating—elegant antiques from the older homes (not regarded as antiques by their owners), plastic beach chairs, a rocker, a couple of deck chairs, and the old pew which had once stood in the Baptist Church porch and which now usually stood at the side of the playground. Meanwhile, in the other classroom, members of the audience were depositing breads, sweets, desserts and cakes in preparation for the post-concert lunch.

Cornelia, as a former teacher at the school, always received a special invitation, and a reserved front row seat. She sat at the end of the row, beside Gladys, who was at the piano ready to accompany the children. Tom sat behind Gladys, prepared to jump up and turn the pages at her command. Cornelia kept looking around for Patrick, who had called earlier in the week.

"It's Patrick," he'd announced, cautiously gauging the level of Cornelia's awareness that day.

"Patrick," she'd repeated, placing him. Patrick Given. They shared the house, *her* house. She was in the garden last time he arrived. They had supper with Gladys and Tom. He had a cellular telephone, like Tom, and a Beechcraft.

"Are you in the Beechcraft?"

"No. I'm in Ottawa, at the office. I'm coming to White Rock on Friday, for Christmas."

"We share the house."

"Yes. I'm coming to stay. May I bring someone, a friend?"

"You don't have to ask, Patrick."

"I know. But I don't want to suddenly spring a stranger on you, especially at Christmas."

"It will be a pleasure to have her … him …"

"It's a her. Her name's Penelope Diamant."

"Is she your …" Careful. His shoulders sagging, lips tightening, eyes clouding, looking away. She thought of it as *Patrick's girlfriend look*. Don't say *girlfriend*. "Is she a business colleague?"

"An old friend. She's a model."

"Oh. Lovely. How exciting."

"She's in Buenos Aires this week, doing a show, but she'll be back in time to come to White Rock with me."

Cornelia called Gladys and told her Patrick was bringing someone for Christmas. "Her name's Penelope."

"Is she his girlfriend?"

"He said she's an old friend. She's a model."

"I bet she's a loose woman. Models always are."

Now Cornelia craned her neck to see through the audience crowding into the classroom. Patrick had said they would arrive on Deer Isle in the Beechcraft around noon, and would catch the first ferry they could to White Rock. She'd told him if she wasn't at their home she would be at the school concert, and he should come, too, and bring Penelope Diamant.

"But I'm not part of the community. I'd feel like an intruder."

"Oh yes you are part of the community. Everyone knows you."

Mrs. Griffin stood at the front of the room, making pushing motions with her hands to quieten the audience. She welcomed everyone, wished them Merry Christmas, and concluded, "Sit back, relax, and enjoy … Christmas Around the World."

The children, wearing cardboard headpieces denoting various countries, climbed onto the makeshift stage. The audience aah-ed and clapped. As Gladys raised her hands over the piano keys to play the introduction, the audience's attention suddenly swept from the front of the room to the back, where a woman, a stranger, hesitated just inside the door. She'd entered silently, but the audience seemed to sense her discreet arrival, and their eyes were drawn to her.

She was dressed entirely in white, boot cut jeans flaring over ankle length leather boots, knee length fitted wool coat open revealing a cashmere sweater, patterned scarf wound twice around her neck, wool toque pulled low from which nevertheless a few wisps of blonde hair escaped to hang in fine tendrils on each side of her face. She carried a tiny white bag with a ruff around the zippered top. She pulled off her hat and her hair cascaded around her shoulders and nearly to her waist in a blonde waterfall. Seeing the audience looking around, she bit her lip and one hand flew to her mouth, two fingers twitching at her lips. She looked behind her as if for reassurance.

Gladys's hands were frozen in midair by the audience's sudden shifting of attention from the stage to the back of the room. She looked around, opened her eyes wide, leaned close to Cornelia, and muttered, "It's a fucking snowman."

"It must be Penelope," Cornelia whispered.

"Scrawny bint, isn't she?"

"She's pretty."

Patrick appeared, squeezing through the door behind Penelope, whispering apologies to everyone around him. They sat at the back of the classroom, Gladys resumed her piano introduction, and the concert began. Afterwards, the audience crowded into the adjoining classroom. Midway through the lunch, a telephone rang, as Penelope fielded questions from the curious islanders, while Patrick stood beside, and slightly behind, her. (Yes, she lived in Toronto, in an apartment; no, she hadn't been to White Rock before, but she had been to Deer Isle; yes, that was her on the cover of *La Vie* last month; no, she hadn't been in *People* magazine and—laughing—would rather not, thank you very much.)

Cornelia and Gladys looked accusingly at Patrick and Tom, who held up their hands, protesting innocence.

Patrick said, "Not mine. I'm in conference."

Meanwhile Penelope was searching in her white bag and produced a tiny, purple cell phone. She smiled apologetically around and spoke into it, sounding at first disappointed, finally resigned: "No ... oh no ... well, yes ... yes ... yes, all right."

Biting her lip, she turned luminous blue eyes on Patrick, who said, "Now what?"

"I have to go." A murmur of disappointment rose from the crowd around her, and she addressed them. "That was Don, my agent." They nodded, as if understanding all about agents. "He says he's booked me for a Christmas Eve charity gala in Washington, which he says I absolutely have to attend, and for a new year's day photo shoot in Switzerland." She added, looking around, "It's for skiing outfits, you know."

Her audience nodded understandingly again.

Penelope continued, "Don's sending a plane up to Deer Isle tonight. I'm so sorry. I was really looking forward to spending Christmas here, with you, on White Rock." Turning to Patrick, she said, with her audience still listening, "Sorry, Patrick, but Don says I have to do this, if my career means anything to me."

On Patrick's face and in the movement of his body, Cornelia noticed *Patrick's girlfriend look*, a combination, she thought, of disappointment and resignation and sadness. Not anger.

Like Dale Senior—not angry.

Patrick said, "You'll have to wait until tomorrow. There's no ferry to-night."

Gladstone spoke up, gallantly, "I think we can do something about that, Mr. Given. We'll get your young lady over to the air field."

Patrick said to Penelope, suddenly and abruptly, "Let's go then," and headed for the door.

Penelope looked around at her audience, biting her lip again.

"He's just disappointed," Gladstone assured her. "He'll get over it."

Gladys grinned at Cornelia and whispered, "Our Gladstone's quite the man of the world, isn't he?"

Cornelia said, "Let's go and talk to Patrick."

As Penelope said goodbye to the children and adults around her, and signed a last few concert programmes thrust at her by the older girls, Cornelia and Gladys hurried after Patrick. They found him outside, pacing, hands in his pockets.

"Never mind, Patrick," said Cornelia, putting her hand on his arm to still him. "It was nice to meet Penelope even if it was for just a short while."

"We haven't seen one another for months—not since we decided it was a waste of time to go on ... to go on ..." Patrick paused, searching for words.

"Courting," Gladys supplied.

"Thank you. Not since we decided it was a waste of time to go on courting when all we were doing was upsetting and hurting one another because we could never manage to be together for long without one of us getting called away. Then she called me last week, after all this time, and said she missed me, and could we be together again. Of course I said yes,

116

but I had to come to White Rock Island, and she said she'd come too; she'd love to come—if I'd let her. And now she's leaving."

Cornelia said gently, "She has to work. That doesn't mean she wants to go."

Gladys added, digging him in the ribs, "You've still got us, you know." She winked lewdly. "We'll give you a good time."

"I'll see her to the plane and then I'll be back, if I can persuade Gladstone to wait for me."

When Penelope came outside she hung on Patrick's arm. "I'm so sorry. I really want to stay, but Don says I have to accept these engagements if I'm serious about my career."

As they left with Gladstone, Penelope was whispering in Patrick's ear, and he was smiling and nodding.

Chapter Nineteen

Cornelia called Gladys. "I'm on the telephone."

"I know you're on the goddam telephone, ducky. You called me on it, right?"

"I mean I'm on my cellular telephone. Patrick bought it for me so we can stay in touch."

"What colour is it?"

"Green."

"Well aren't you the cool chick, with your green cell. That's what you call it, by the way. You don't say—I'm on my cellular telephone. You say— I'm on my cell."

"I'm on my cell," Cornelia repeated, nodding. "Patrick bought it for me so we can stay in touch."

"You told me that already, old girl, about five seconds ago. Are you two in love or something, that you have to stay in touch all the time?"

Cornelia found herself blushing, ridiculously. "Don't be silly, Gladys. It's so he can tell me when he's coming, so I don't get ... so I don't get ..."

"Confused is the word you're looking for, old thing, like you are now. He'll call you so when he arrives you'll know it's him and not a mad rapist, right?"

"So I know it's him—yes."

"What's wrong with the phone at home?"

"He says this way he can let me know he's coming, even if I'm not at the house, because often he suddenly decides to come. This way he won't worry me when he arrives. And he says when this phone rings, I'll know it's him. Sometimes, with the other phone, I'm not sure who's there, even when they tell me, but when this phone rings, I'll know it's him."

*****

It was spring of the new year, and he seemed to call her from all over the world.

"Hi, it's me. Patrick."

"Where are you?"

"I'm in Rome."

"What are you doing there?"

"We have an interest in a couple of businesses here and they're thinking of expanding. Where are you?"

"I'm on the old chair in the garden."

"I can picture you. I'll join you there on Friday. I'm flying to Ottawa tonight, then I'm coming straight on to Deer Isle."

A few weeks later, he called to say he wasn't going to be on the island for a couple of weeks, but he wanted to be sure she was all right.

When she expected him, she always aired his room and turned down the bed sheets. He told her she didn't have to do that; she said she knew she didn't but she liked to do it. He left a few clothes at the house and she took to washing them. Again, he said he didn't want her to do that, and she said *she* wanted to do it.

She always asked him, whenever he called, where Penelope was, and what she was doing, and whether he'd seen her. The answer was usually somewhere exotic—Milan, Paris, Berlin—and, no, he hadn't seen her for a few weeks, but expected to spend a day with her next week, before she went to Vienna, or London, or Athens. The next time they spoke, he'd relate how they'd had only a couple of hours together before she had to fly out on a new assignment Don had found for her. Twice Cornelia saw her picture on the front of magazines in the island store. Carol-Ann always brought in extra copies when that happened.

One Sunday afternoon when he was there she said, "I want to go to the western beach."

"Across the island?"

"Where Gladys and me used to go."

"That's quite a hike. It takes me nearly an hour to walk there."

"I'm a good walker."

"I know, but…"

"Not as good as I used to be, but I still get along quite well."

She looked at him, nodding firmly. She was determined to go. She'd had the dream again, the dream about Dale Senior showing her Morse Cove, and saying it was the key to the island. She thought being close to the secret cove might reveal the meaning of the dream.

Patrick said cautiously, "We'll drive as far as we can, then we'll see."

They decided the trail through the woods across the island was too rough, so they drove to where the houses and the paved road ended at Southern Point, and onto a dirt road that rounded the tip of the island and climbed steeply before petering out among the slabs of rock marking the beginning of the white Southern Point cliffs. Leaving the car, they followed the trail along the cliff top. It wound through scrubby fir and tamarack, through which they could hear, and occasionally see, the waves pounding far below, then descended through thinning woods until it emerged onto a lowering mass of rock that descended in tiers to the sea like huge steps. Patrick held Cornelia by the hand as they walked carefully along the uppermost tier until a last wide, smooth rock gave way to bracken, through which the trail wound on. At the same time the wall of rock became a tumble of smaller stones shelving to the sea. Patrick took both Cornelia's hands to help her climb down from the slabby rock on to the trail, then walked closely behind her as she picked her way through gnarled roots and between the snagging raspberry and gooseberry bushes plucking at her coat. When the trail degenerated into a muddy spring fed morass, he said,

"Wait", and forced his way off the trail and through the brambles, and disappeared among the shelving rocks.

Cornelia remembered this muddy place from the time she and Gladys had run away from home. Gladys, flying along the trail ahead of her, had jumped in it, spraying mud up her legs and on her dress. Cornelia had followed suit.

"Fine thing if Dale could see you now," Gladys taunted. "I don't think he'd want a filthy scrap like you for his girl with mud up your arse."

"I'm not his girl," she retorted. "We don't even speak."

That was a lie. They'd walked home from school together one day the previous week, when she didn't walk home with Gladys the way she usually did, because Gladys had to stay behind for not doing her homework. That was in the days before the older kids went to the high school on Deer Isle. They were fourteen. She and Dale had cut across the barrens behind the school. Dale said, "Look—blackberries," and picked her some. That was all he said, apart from, "See you later," when they reached her house. But that was enough to make her his girl.

"And I'm sure Walter Jordan would like to see what sort of a lady you are, with mud up your fanny," Cornelia said.

"I'll show him that and more," Gladys retorted.

"The things you say," Cornelia gasped, clambering out of the mud.

Patrick returned, struggling through the bracken with a large, flat rock in his arms.

"Stand back," he warned.

Cornelia stepped back a few paces. Patrick tried to place the rock in the middle of the puddle, but dropped it the last few inches. Muddy water sprayed widely. Cornelia looked down at it dripping from her coat. She wiped it from her face.

"Sorry," said Patrick.

She looked at him and laughed. "You're covered."

"Give me your hand. Use the rock as a stepping stone. At least your feet won't get wet, even if the rest of you is covered in mud."

They set off again on the trail. The mud underfoot became sand as the bracken thinned and gave way to dunes—and, suddenly, rounding Cronk's Point (named after Gladys's great grandfather), the white sands of the western shore appeared, stretching before them in a concave arc, their purity interrupted only by a few outcrops of rock and scraps of bladderwrack. Despite the effort of her walk, Cornelia felt like running and skipping down to where the incoming tide pulsed gently, as she and Gladys had done the day they ran away.

They had stood, mesmerized, at the end of the trail as the beach unfolded in front of them, deserted and apparently untouched, as if unknown to people.

"Holy-ee shit," Gladys breathed.

Cornelia echoed, "Yes, really, holy." She was going to echo Gladys's mild blasphemy, but, like her friend, was overwhelmed. She breathed again, sincerely and truthfully, "Holy."

"I should have brought my camera and taken a photo to show Penelope," Patrick said. "She likes beaches."

"I saw her on a beach, on the cover of a magazine."

"That was in Cannes."

"Do you and Penelope go to the beach?" Cornelia asked cautiously, remembering Patrick's drooping shoulders, his girlfriend look.

"We never seem to have time."

"Where do you go when you're together?"

"We usually just go out to eat. Then her cell phone rings—sometimes mine, but usually hers—and she has to rush away."

Cornelia peered at him from the corner of her eye. The girlfriend look was there, certainly, but he was the one who'd brought up the topic of Penelope. Perhaps he wanted to talk about her.

She ventured, "Couldn't the two of you change your schedules to give yourselves more time together?"

"We've tried, but it doesn't seem to work." He sighed and added, "Last time I saw her, Don called her for an engagement two hours after we met, and I told her—again—there was no point in our carrying on the way we have been." He looked away, eyes clouding, shoulders drooping.

"What did she say?"

"She said if that was how I felt, she was sorry—but she'd go along with it."

"So are you still … friends?"

"We've been friends since we were kids."

"I mean are you still … courting?"

"I don't know. That was the end of the conversation. I haven't heard from her since, and I haven't tried to call."

"Poor Patrick."

"Pathetic Patrick."

Cornelia patted his arm. They stood still where the trail dipped to the beach.

Cornelia gazed at the unblemished length of sand.

"Let's go, ducky," Gladys had shouted suddenly, breaking the reverent silence and grabbing Cornelia's hand. They launched themselves on the sands.

Patrick held her two hands again as she stepped from the trail to the beach. She stopped and breathed deeply.

"Out of breath?" Patrick asked.

"No. Oh no. I'm just enjoying the smell of the beach. It reminds me of picnics when we were little kids, and of long walks with Dale Senior, and of the time Gladys and I ran away and slept on the beach—just over there."

She pointed to the dunes that lay between the beach and the forest, to a place marked by two smooth, white rocks spaced a few feet apart.

They'd woken between the white rocks to the sound of the gulls and the incoming tide. They looked at each other, shocked anew at their defiance.

"Do you suppose they're looking for us?" Cornelia wondered.

"Who cares?"

"There'll be hell to pay when we go back."

"We're not going back. We're going to be beach nomads. They can visit us if they like, but we won't go home."

The sun was gaining warmth, dispelling the chill they felt from their night in the open.

"Let's go for a paddle," Cornelia suggested.

"Don't you want to sit and rest?" Patrick asked.

"No. I don't need to rest. I want to go for a paddle," Cornelia insisted. She said softly, "Gladys and I tucked our skirts in our knickers that morning when we went paddling."

They'd pranced to the water's edge, where they strutted in the surf.

"Steady on," said Patrick, pretending shock.

"Gladys said our legs were like alabaster. I said no—like ivory."

As they sat on the sand to remove their shoes and socks, Cornelia surveyed her veined, mottled legs. Patrick helped her to her feet. They ventured down the beach and into the sea, Patrick holding her hand to steady her against the incoming waves.

"On hot days when we were walking here, Dale Senior used to carry me out into the surf and drop me," Cornelia reminisced.

Patrick grinned. "Don't get any ideas."

She looked at the forbidding cliffs bordering the beach, with their sentry line of rocks extending far into the surf. Could Dale Senior really have led her around those rocks and past the cliff? Morse Cove seemed as elusive in reality as it had when she tried to recall her dream, as elusive as Dale Senior's enigmatic message that Morse Cove was the key to the island. She watched a portentous wave spend itself along the line of rocks until it reached her feet in a gentle lapping. She shivered.

"That's enough. My feet are getting cold."

Patrick led her back up the beach, where they sat again.

"Now I'm cold," Gladys had grumbled. "Let's run, to warm up." They jogged for half a mile at the edge of the surf. Then, turning, Gladys said, "Race you back."

They raced along the beach, jumping rocks and splashing through tide pools, disturbing the gulls, which rose and wheeled, keening, before settling again on the beach behind them. Back at their starting place Cornelia was ready to collapse on the sand, but Gladys said, "Keep going as far as the rocks. We'll swim." At the end of the beach they climbed along the rocky outcrop that jutted into the water, presaging the wall of rock, the start of the Southern Point cliffs, that rose just beyond it. They stood on a flat rock at the base of the outcrop, surveying the deep, clear water before them. The line of rocks extended further into swirling water, but here the waves washed gently over the ledge and over their feet. They held hands, still breathing hard and sweating from their running and climbing.

Gladys said, "Ready?"

Cornelia nodded.

They threw off their dresses, joined hands again, looked once more at each other, grinning, and jumped. Gladys's hand slipped from Cornelia's as they went under. Cornelia spun underwater, kicked, and shot to the surface, gasping. She looked around for Gladys. Saw her still under the water. Her body rose slowly and bobbed just below the surface. Cornelia scrambled onto the rock and, kneeling, reached for Gladys. She hauled her onto the rock beside her, where she lay unmoving. Cornelia seized her hand, gasping, "Gladys … Gladys … Can you hear me, Gladys?" Was she breathing? Cornelia leaned over her friend, her cheek close to her mouth. "Breathe, dammit, Gladys." She seized her by the shoulders and shook her.

Gladys lay lifeless. Murmuring, "Gladys … Gladys …," and crying, Cornelia bent close over her friend's face. She whispered, "Oh, Gladys," and kissed her. Gladys stirred. Cornelia rolled her onto her side.

Gladys coughed. "Blecchh. You kissed me."

"I thought you were dead."

"You don't get rid of me that easily."

Cornelia said again, still crying, "I thought you were dead."

Gladys sat up, shook her head, and grinned. "Kiss me again, then."

They embraced and kissed. Trembling, they sat with their arms locked around each other, gazing at the sea.

Cornelia's cell phone was ringing somewhere. "That must be Gladys. Only Gladys knows my number, apart from you."

As she searched in her bag for it, Patrick said, "Was Gladys all right?"

She hadn't realized she had been giving voice to her memories. "Oh yes. The shock of the cold water knocked her out. She came round as soon as I dragged her back on the rock. And my father was there all the time, although we didn't know that until later. He said he was about to come to the rescue when he realized Gladys was all right."

The voice on the phone said, "Cornelia?" A man's voice. Only Gladys and Patrick knew her cell number. She looked at Patrick.

He said, "Who is it?"

"Only you and Gladys know my number."

"Is it Gladys?"

"A man."

The voice on the phone was saying, urgently, "Cornelia, are you there?"

She said into the phone, "Only Patrick knows my number. Patrick and Gladys."

"It's Tom here."

"Tom! How do you know my number?"

"Gladys gave it to me when you got your phone." His voice disappeared and was replaced by a crackling, hissing sound. There was silence, then, "Can you hear me? I'm in the helicopter, on my way to White Rock. Listen. Something's happened to Gladys. Her number rang on my phone but there was no-one there when I answered. That means she needs help. It's our emergency signal."

"I thought you were Patrick. But he's here with me."

"Can I speak to him?"

She passed the phone to Patrick. "It's Tom. Gladys is in trouble."

Patrick said into the phone, "Tom? … Western beach … Gladys … Most likely at her house … There in about an hour …"

They climbed from the beach to the trail, Cornelia in front, picking her way along the root strewn trail as fast as she could, Patrick close behind her. Twice, in her haste, she stumbled and would have fallen had Patrick not grabbed her arm and steadied her.

The second time he said, "This isn't going to work. You're going to injure yourself."

"But we have to hurry."

"I'll carry you. Here."

With amazing ease—was he very strong, or was she really so light?—he swooped and picked her up, cradling her, saying, "Put your arms round my neck and hang on."

He set off, striding back along the trail. When he stopped to rest, he carefully set her down and walked in slow circles, breathing deeply and swinging his arms, before taking a deep breath and saying, "Let's go."

"Are you sure you're all right?"

"I'm fine. You?"

"I feel I'm a burden."

He swung her easily into his arms again and said, smiling, his face close to hers, "You couldn't be a burden if you tried."

She lowered her eyes from his. "Thank you."

He said, gallantly, "It's a pleasure."

She thrilled, to be held so easily, to surrender so helplessly. Dale Senior had carried her like this over the threshold when they were married, as if they were in a romantic movie. He said, "Hold tight, little lady," and before she realized what was happening he seized her and his arms were under her and she was happily and helplessly trapped against his chest, his face close to hers. She flung her arms around his neck and leaned her head on his shoulder, at the same time protesting, "You'll hurt yourself."

He grinned. "You're just an armful of air."

"He said I was an armful of air."

"He?"

"Dale Senior" —as if Patrick should know her thoughts.

He kicked open the front door and she said, "Put me down now." But he carried her straight upstairs, as she protested, "You'll give yourself a heart attack."

"You won't give yourself a heart attack, carrying me, will you?"

Patrick smiled and shook his head. "Dale Senior was right. You're just an armful of air."

"Silly."

Cornelia's mind was cluttered with images of what might have happened to Gladys. She thought of all the times they'd joked together about Tom's dear, fussy insistence on her friend always carrying her cell phone and being ready to press the button which rang straight through to his phone if she was in trouble. What kind of emergency was this, where Gladys had telephoned but was unable to speak? An accident, like when Cornelia had fallen downstairs? But she'd still been able to speak, in between those bouts of sleeping. Surely Gladys would have been able to say *something*, if she'd fallen and was lying hurt?

"If I'd had a cell phone I would have been able to call."

Patrick nodded and grunted, breathing heavily.

If not a falling kind of accident, perhaps a car accident? She pictured Gladys aware that a disaster was about to happen—her car, out of control, going too fast as usual, heading for a ditch, or—heavens—the cliff, and Gladys having time just to press the button that rang straight to Tom's phone before she went off the road, or over the cliff.

Cornelia glimpsed Patrick's car through the trees.

Her father had been waiting in his truck where the trail emerged onto the road, having seen them set off from the beach, and having hurried back along the woods trail in order to drive around and meet them.

"How did you know we were here?" Cornelia challenged sullenly.

"I'll tell you later."

"I expect you're mad."

"I expect I am. So's your mother—yours, too, Gladys. Get in, the two of you."

They climbed in the cab beside him. They held hands. He sat with arms folded. Cornelia saw him looking in the mirror at her and Gladys, and caught the twitch of his mouth as he regarded their unkempt hair and bedraggled clothes.

"You're a couple of wild things," he said, shaking his head.

They giggled, looked at one another, their hands still clasped tightly.

They were back at the car. He set her down gently.

"Tom always said she drove too fast."

He looked up blankly from where he was resting, leaning against the car, said, "Ah," as if suddenly understanding, and, "I don't think it's a car accident."

He opened the car door for her.

As she eased herself in, she said, her eyes filling with tears, "Then what?"

Quietly, gently: "Let's go and find out."

They were silent as Patrick drove fast around the southern head, to the road, and to Gladys's house.

He said, "I'll go in and see if she's there. You wait here." She began to protest but he said, "Just for a moment—wait," and set off toward the house. She opened the car door and rocked twice to give herself momentum to rise from the seat and climb out. As she did so, a beating in the air announced Tom's arrival. The helicopter circled over the meadow behind the house before setting down there. Tom and another man, carrying a bag, jumped out and ran, stooping low, across the meadow and around the house. At the same time Patrick emerged.

Cornelia heard him say, "Stroke, I think."

Chapter Twenty

After her stroke, the first sound Gladys articulated was, "Sh …" Her lips were trembling and her face was contorted as her head lolled to one side and she rolled her eyes toward Cornelia.

Cornelia put down her knitting and said, trying to calm her excitement, "Yes, Gladys?" She added, encouragingly, "Sh …"

Patrick was working at the table in the parlour. He looked up from his notepad.

Gladys repeated, "Sh …"

She'd been six weeks in hospital in Saint John, and another six weeks in rehabilitation, where Tom spent every day with her, taking time off work. Then he flew her back to White Rock Island in the helicopter, with the doctor in attendance, and left her with Cornelia and Patrick, promising to be back at least once a week with the doctor.

Patrick had sold a large part of his company, keeping only what he called his pet projects, one of which was the Defiant Island fish plant. He still travelled for his other business interests, and kept his apartment in Ottawa, but was spending more and more time on White Rock Island.

"So—are you retired now?" Cornelia asked when he explained.

"I'm half retired. I'm fifty, after all—nearly old enough to retire properly, if I wanted to."

"What does Penelope think?"

He'd shrugged, downcast, looking away, then asked whether she would mind if he made White Rock his home.

She said, "Of course I don't mind," then added, "That would be lovely."

So Patrick had begun to call the island, and not Ottawa, his home, and with Cornelia had spent six weeks nursing Gladys, who tried again: "Ssshh …"

"Shall?" Cornelia prompted.

"Sssshhhh …" Gladys persisted.

"Shoes. Are your shoes hurting your feet? Do you want a different pair?" Patrick ventured.

Gladys's head, still lolling to one side, shook in fierce spasms, her mouth working. "Ssshhhh …"

"The sun's too bright!" said Cornelia. "Is it shining in your eyes? Sh-sh-sh-shining …?"

Gladys's mouth and lips searched furiously. "Sssshhhh …"

The dining room was now Gladys's bedroom. Patrick helped her walk from there to the kitchen for breakfast, and from the kitchen table to the armchair in the parlour, where she spent her recuperative days. Every day she moved her right arm a little more, but she struggled to keep her head from falling to one side, and speech eluded her. The doctor said she would recover physically except for the loss of some movement on one side, and eventually she would regain her speech.

"Ssshh …" Gladys started again.

Leaning forwards, Patrick and Cornelia encouraged together, "Yes? Ssshhh …?"

"SSHHHHH … SHIT," Gladys roared.

Patrick and Cornelia applauded.

Cornelia added, suddenly, "Do you mean you want to ..?"

Gladys shook her head and shoulders, making flapping motions of denial with one claw like hand.

"Shit because of what's happened—because of the stroke?" Patrick suggested.

Gladys raised a trembling hand with thumb erect, nodding and bobbing her head.

"But you're getting over it, like we keep telling you that you will," Cornelia said. "You'll be the old Gladys in no time."

Patrick called Tom to tell him of Gladys's progress.

Tom said, "Let me speak to Ma."

As Gladys listened on the telephone, Patrick and Cornelia saw her lips moving, trying to form the words that eluded her. Her lips made little popping sounds.

Tom said, "I hear you, Ma."

Gladys was shaking and tears were rolling down her cheeks.

Patrick leaned close to Gladys and spoke into the telephone for her. "Tom—she says, precious boy."

*****

Another six weeks passed, and Cornelia, Gladys and Patrick were sitting around the kitchen table for supper, a bottle of wine between them. They raised glasses, Gladys's triumphant but trembling hand slopping most of her drink on the table.

"Welcome back, Gladys," Patrick toasted. "You're just in time for Christmas."

She was walking with the aid of only a stick. Although she struggled all the time for words, often unsuccessfully, her speech was returning, and her head stayed almost constantly erect. Only one side of her body resisted recovery.

They drank, Gladys dribbling joyously and carelessly, wine dripping down her chin and into her lap.

"I'm going to get you a bib," Cornelia warned.

Gladys started, "F ... f ... f ..."

Cornelia said, "I know. You don't have to say it."

They heard the front door open and a voice called, "Anyone home?"

Gladys's head jerked up from her glass and her eyes opened wide. "T ... T ... Tom!" It was one of the first words she'd regained.

Tom appeared at the kitchen door. Dark circles under his eyes betrayed lack of sleep. Instead of his customary work dress of cords and sweater and field jacket, he was wearing a sweater and jeans. But while he was usually immaculate even in these—"executive scruffy chic for casual Fridays," Gladys liked to tease him before her stroke—now the sweater was dirty and the jeans creased. His hair was tangled and greasy.

"You look as if you slept in your clothes—tried to, anyway," Patrick laughed.

"I did."

Tom stood behind Gladys and with his arms around her neck lowered his head towards her. She half turned and raised her head so that his forehead rested in her hair.

"P ... P ..." Her eyes filled with tears. "Shit."

"Precious boy," Tom said for her.

"Where's the ..?" Gladys stopped; started again. "Where's the ..?" Her mouth moved, groping. Then: "Shit."

"Helicopter?" Patrick supplied.

"He ... Hel ... Helicopter," Gladys finished.

"I came on the ferry for a change, Tom said lightly, adding, "The company's cutting back on flying time."

Patrick was looking evenly at Tom. Catching his eye, he nodded and said quietly, "Brunswick Oil is downsizing—right? I heard."

Tom released Gladys, slid into the empty chair beside her; rested his elbows on the table and lowered his head into his hands. His voice emerged, muffled. "I'm not with the company any more. They claim it's downsizing. I say it's prejudice."

Tom was on Gladys's unresponsive side and she was reaching a trembling arm across herself, trying to touch him.

Patrick said, quietly again, "Tom," and when Tom raised his head, indicated Gladys's straining hand. Tom took it, and their hands rested, clasped, on the table. Cornelia reached across and stroked Tom's hair.

Patrick poured another glass of wine and said, "Here, Tom." When Tom lifted his head, Patrick added, "Am I in the way? Do you want me to leave?"

Tom shook his head.

Cornelia cradled the side of Tom's face with her hand and murmured, "Poor Tom."

They sat in silence, unmoving. Gladys and Cornelia gazed at Tom's troubled face, while Patrick looked down, rolling his wine glass between his hands.

At length he asked, "Do you want to tell us?"

Tom nodded slowly, sniffing and wiping his eyes with his sleeve, the women still holding and stroking his hand and face. "Sorry about this. There's not much to tell. Adrian's gone. He took off last week. I had no idea it was coming. He's not just gone. He's disappeared and there's no trace of him. And I'm not going to look for him."

Cornelia said, "Oh, Tom, after all these years."

"That's not the end of it. He took all the money from the joint accounts."

"I can get someone on to that," Patrick offered quickly. "You'll get it back—guaranteed."

Tom shook his head. "No. Thanks. I just want to be rid of him now and … and … I don't want him in trouble with the police. He had some trouble before, years ago. They'll bring all that up again and I don't want to put him through it. I don't want to … to …"

"You don't want to hurt him," Patrick finished.

Tom nodded, and Patrick added, "Of course you don't."

"It's funny to be alone after fifteen years."

"You're hardly alone."

"You know what I mean."

Patrick nodded.

They sat in silence again until Tom continued, "Word got out and everybody was talking about it, of course. Then, two days ago, the personnel manager—that's the personnel manager that I hired, dammit—called me in—called me in; didn't come to my office even—and said he regretted that because Brunswick Oil was downsizing they had to let me go. When I pressed him for more information he said the company was aware I was having some family problems, and thought an extended leave of absence would help me cope with my present difficulties. What he meant was they didn't want people like … like me—especially when they cause gossip."

"I can have my lawyers take them to court. They'll get you your job back, with compensation, if you want it."

"Thanks—but to hell with Brunswick Oil. I couldn't go back."

"I understand."

"All I've got is a couple of hundred dollars I had in a separate account, and six months severance pay, so I cancelled the lease on the house. And came here."

Gladys said, "Welcome home, p … p … precious boy."

Chapter Twenty-One

In late April, Patrick and Tom were preparing to go fishing in Patrick's boat. It was the first time they'd left Gladys and Cornelia alone for more than a few minutes since Gladys's return from hospital. Even with her stick she still stumbled and either Patrick or Tom would be close behind to catch her or steady her. Often she still searched for words, using an exasperated "Shit" as the signal for the others to complete her speech.

Cornelia, meanwhile, still had what she called her vague days. One day the previous week she'd dozed in the parlour and, on waking, had gone to the kitchen, where she found Gladys making tea.

"Gladys!" Cornelia greeted her. "When did you arrive?"

"I live here, you silly old fool," Gladys answered.

She lived there, with Cornelia and Patrick, because she'd sold her own house, secretly and in a hurry, while she was in hospital recuperating from the stroke. Fearing she would never recover sufficiently to live alone, she anticipated moving into some sort of home, and wanted enough money in her account to secure entry to an establishment of her choice. She'd checked up on these things, she told Tom and Cornelia and Patrick later. Tom, upset and hurt, remonstrated with her. He would have paid for a home. Or she could have lived with him in Saint John. She raised her eyebrows. Well, he would have found a way. She retorted that even if he had found a way, she still didn't want to be dependent on him, or on anybody. She'd simply buy a new house now. Cornelia, after consulting with Patrick, suggested she live with them. Gladys demurred, but Cornelia insisted until she accepted. Patrick offered to move out to leave room for the two of them, but Cornelia said absolutely not. There was plenty of room. The dining room would become Gladys's bedroom. It was downstairs, and they didn't need a dining room because they always ate in the kitchen anyway.

"We'll be a ménage a trois," she concluded.

Six weeks later the ménage a trois became a ménage a quatre with the arrival of Tom, who, with Patrick's help, turned the attic into another bedroom, insisting it would be a temporary arrangement.

As the men prepared to leave for their fishing trip, Patrick said to Cornelia and Gladys, for the third time, "Are you sure you'll be all right?"

"Of course we'll be all right, you silly boys," Cornelia insisted. "We always got on fine before you were here and we'll get on fine without you under our feet for a couple of hours."

Patrick said to Tom, "Of course they'll get on fine—as long as they don't fall downstairs, or forget who they are…"

Tom picked up, "… Or forget who we are, or get themselves put in a home …"

"You know what I mean," said Cornelia, adding, as she made shooing motions with her hands, "Off with you now."

"Call on the cell if you need us," Patrick said.

"Do you remember which key to press?" Tom put in.

"Of course we remember which key. Now—go," said Cornelia, pointing at the door.

"You're like a couple of old women, with your worrying," Gladys called from her armchair in the parlour.

At the wharf, Patrick and Tom surveyed the old fishing boat Patrick had bought. It was a small inshore lobster craft and looked like a toy moored at the wharf alongside the island fishing fleet. Its original owner, one of the White Rock fishermen, had named it, ironically, *The Millionaire*, and Patrick had kept the name.

Looking at it, Tom said, "Are you?"

Patrick shrugged. "A few times over."

Tom grunted.

"What's up?" Patrick asked.

"I guess it's just as well you are a millionaire, with me living off you."

"You're living with me—with us—not off us, and certainly not off me. We all share living expenses."

"I happen to know you're putting in more than your share. Cornelia and Gladys might not realize it, but I do."

Patrick shrugged again. "I owe Cornelia and Gladys plenty for making me a home here."

"It's your house."

"It may be in my name, but it wouldn't feel like a home without them—and without you—there. It's your home, too."

"But I'm not contributing my share of expenses."

"Who cares? And you will contribute, in time. It's not your fault you got cleaned out by Adrian and screwed by Brunswick Oil, and it's not your fault there are so few jobs on White Rock."

"I should leave the island and find something."

Patrick punched him lightly on the shoulder. "Something will come up, sooner or later."

He headed the little boat past the barricade of white rocks that shielded the harbour entrance and out into the open sea. They stood side by side in the cabin, rocking in unison as they reached the ocean swell beyond the shelter of the island. A mile from shore, Patrick cut the engine.

They fished in silence, unsuccessfully, until Patrick suggested, "Let's try further out."

As he restarted the motor, his phone rang and he handed Tom the wheel while he searched in his pockets for it, apologizing for the call, not because it was an interruption, but because he knew it was a reminder to Tom of how much he missed his cell phone, with the satisfaction and the excitement it denoted of being constantly in demand, constantly sought after.

"That's got to be Peggy or the plant or the women at home," Patrick muttered.

"My money's on Peggy or the plant. I don't think pride would allow Ma or Cornelia to call us even if something did happen."

Patrick laughed as he took the call. "Patrick Given here." Then: "Damn," and again, "Damn." Tom looked at him and raised his eyebrows as Patrick repeated, "Damn." He went on, "Well it can't be helped. If you can see this shift out I'll be in for the next one, and I'll sort something out then. Thanks, Mac. Oh—and put yourself down for double time this shift, for taking care of things."

He put the phone away and said, again, "Damn."

Tom said, "The plant, I take it."

"Fred McLennan, the shift foreman."

"What's up?"

"I'll tell you later. I need to think for a bit." He looked at the sea in front of them. They were beyond the Northern Head cliffs. White Rock Island lay behind them and Deer Isle to the east. "This'll do. Let's get our lines out."

For half an hour they fished in silence, until Patrick said suddenly, "Would you do something for me?"

"What?"

"Manage the plant."

"What about Jimmy Guptill?"

"He's gone."

"When?"

"Half an hour ago. That's what Mac called about. Jimmy's the new manager of the Aquaculture International plant on Deer Isle. They offered twice what I've been paying him. He took it—and walked out."

"Couldn't you match them?"

Patrick grinned. "I could—but I won't. Will you do it?"

"I might have grown up on White Rock Island, but I don't know much about fishing and fish processing, certainly not enough to run a fish plant."

"You know about company finance, and strategic planning, and managing people, and you're good at all of those. Anything else you need to know you'll learn fast."

"I don't want charity."

"I don't do charity when I'm doing business. You know that. I need someone to manage the fish plant. I can't do it because I've still got too many other things on the go. So—do you want it? I'll match what you were getting with Brunswick Oil."

Tom reached out a hand. Patrick took it, and they stayed with hands clasped.

Chapter Twenty-Two

A month after Tom took over as manager at the Defiant Island plant, Gladstone radioed Dale from the ferry.

"I've got a bunch of guys in suits on board. Two car loads of them. I think one of them's the premier—small, dark, beaky guy. I overheard them saying they were going to tour the island and visit the plant. D'you suppose Patrick knows they're coming?"

"Patrick's in *Ottawa*. I'll run over and *warn* Tom."

Cornelia and Gladys arrived at the store as Dale left for the plant. Carol-Ann was behind the counter.

"You two behave yourselves now," Carol-Ann warned. "There's suits on the way."

"Suits?" said Cornelia.

"She means big-wigs," explained Gladys.

"*Think* they're big-wigs," Carol-Ann corrected. She bustled from behind the counter with blood pressure apparatus. "Give me your arm, Cornelia."

"I'm all right."

"I know. Just like to be sure. Do you want me to check you, Gladys?"

"Not bloody likely."

Cornelia turned the pages of an *Island Gazette* on the counter with her spare hand as Carol-Ann wound the rubber around her arm.

"How's your memory?" Carol-Ann asked.

"My memory?"

"Wait." Carol-Ann concentrated on timing and reading the gauge, then continued, "Good. Well?"

"Well what?"

"I asked you a question."

"Did you? What did you ask?"

"I asked how's your…" She broke off as Cornelia and Gladys giggled. "I give up. I guess you're okay."

"It comes and goes, doesn't it, Cornelia?" said Gladys.

Cornelia looked up from her reading. "What comes and goes?"

Carol-Ann muttered, "Oh my God."

"Your memory, ducky. You're okay today, so far, but your memory wasn't good yesterday, was it?"

Cornelia frowned, thinking. "I don't remember."

Gladys and Carol-Ann groaned.

Cornelia said, "Thank you for checking me, Carol-Ann."

Two long, black cars drove up from the ferry and stopped outside the store. Seven men and one woman emerged from them. At the same time Dale appeared, crossing the road on his way back from the plant.

"Suits," said Gladys, watching the newcomers through the window. "Bleccch."

"Behave," Carol-Ann warned again.

Gladys produced a shopping list and set off into the aisles. Cornelia continued to peruse the *Gazette*.

The visitors swept into the store, the man at the head of the procession announcing, "The Premier of New Brunswick—Keeping in Touch with the Ordinary People of the Province."

Bernard Appleby, the small, dark, beaky man correctly identified by Gladstone, paused in the doorway, beaming. With no-one looking in his direction, his smile disappeared quickly.

One of his aides, the lone woman in the entourage, was consulting papers on a clipboard as she confided to him, "… Only store on the island. No subsidy or grants that we know of …"

The premier interrupted, "But the ferry—half a million a year, did you say?"

The aide consulted her notes. "Yes."

"And it's considered part of the road system of the province, so the islanders pay no toll, no fare?"

"No. Nor the tourists."

"Nor the store, of course. Amazing. They get subsidized shipping and delivery. Make a note of that."

One of the men murmured, "Old lady. Photo op, sir." He beckoned to another man, who came forward raising a camera.

The premier, with a brief nod to Carol-Ann as he walked in front of her, stood beside Cornelia, saying, "It's always a pleasure to meet the senior citizens of this province."

His head slanted courteously towards Cornelia, he turned to smile at the camera. Dale entered the store and walked between the photographer and his subject as the flash fired.

"Excuse me, sir," the photographer said.

"Gee. *Sorry,*" said Dale, adding, "You did of course *ask* the *lady* whether she wanted her photo taken, didn't you?"

An article in the *Gazette* had caught Cornelia's eye. It reported that the annual White Rock Island Craft Fair would be held in the community hall next Saturday. She remembered baking things for it, banana bread and carrot cake and molasses cookies, to raise money for the school. Then she'd spend the day behind the stall, serving, parceling up, and gossiping. Dale Senior arrived unexpectedly at the fair one year, back early from the fishing. That was the year, the only year, the fancy silversmith from the mainland took a stall. He came only that one time because no-one, except Dale Senior, bought his creations, beautiful though they were. The islanders couldn't afford them.

Cornelia smiled at Dale Senior. "You're back early."

He reached over the heads of Myra Wormell and Leola Moses, who were bending over the stall while they debated the rival merits of banana bread and carrot cake. His fist was closed around something.

He said, "For you."

She held her hand under his closed fist and he released a brooch into it, a small, silver dolphin.

He said, "It's a dolphin."

"Yes."

"The silversmith said when he finished the piece and examined it, he thought it was exuberant and graceful and beautiful. I said that's like my wife. Like you."

Myra and Leola looked, smiling, from Cornelia to Dale Senior. Cornelia's eyes filled with tears. She'd worn it every day since then. She was wearing it now. She fingered it, snug against the wool of her fall jacket. They'd been married less than a year.

A tear spilled onto the *Gazette*.

Bernard Appleby frowned, looked at his aides, and said, "Ma'am…"

"Dale Senior gave it to me. We'd been married less than a year."

Carol-Ann said, "Cornelia."

Gladys, arriving back from her sortie into the aisles, said, "She's gone again. She'll be back."

"My brooch. My dolphin brooch. Dale Senior said it was like me."

"I know, old girl."

Carol-Ann, who'd been answering questions from one of the premier's companions—How long had the store been in operation? How many people did it employ? —took Cornelia's hand. "Cornelia, dear. You're crying."

The premier, catching the photographer's eye, stood beside Gladys and said, "It's always a pleasure to meet the senior citizens of this province."

"Frig off," said Gladys, and made rabbit's ears with her fingers behind the premier's head as the flash fired.

The photographer said, "Oh, Jesus."

The aide who had been questioning Carol-Ann turned his attention to Dale, who had taken his wife's place behind the counter.

"Do you make a good living from the store?"

"Do *you* have webbed *feet*?"

"Do you have to work hard to make a go of the store?"

"Does a dog *shit?*"

The premier, overhearing, said, "I think it's time for us to be moving on."

Gladys said, "Good idea, ducky." As the islanders watched Bernard Appleby and his entourage set off across the road toward the plant, she added, "Who the hell was that?"

Over at the plant, Tom was helping out in the cleaning and packing room. They were short staffed—two of the women had stayed home to nurse sick children—and he was anxious to get the catch frozen and shipped. He saw the plant's visitors pass the door as they followed signs pointing the way upstairs to the office. He waited for them to return, knowing there was no-one up there.

One of the aides looked into the cleaning and packing room and said, jovially, "Don't you people have a boss somewhere?" The aide saw some of the workers glance in Tom's direction. He took in Tom's stained apron, his dirty *Defiant Island* cap, the paring knife he was deftly wielding, his hands dripping with fish guts and grease, and said uncertainly, "You, sir, are the … er …?"

Tom nodded. "The Defiant Island plant doesn't have a boss in the sense you're implying, but you can talk to me."

The aide turned and beckoned to the premier and his companions. He announced loudly, "Allow me to introduce …" —he paused as if waiting for a drum roll— "…The Premier of New Brunswick—Keeping in Touch with the Ordinary People of the Province."

The workers continued gutting, not taking their eyes from their flashing knives.

Tom said, "We're busy, you know."

The aide said quietly, "But … the *premier.*"

"I don't care if it's Jesus Christ. We're still busy."

The premier came forward, saying, "Mr. Thomas Cronk, formerly of Brunswick Oil."

Tom nodded.

The premier extended his hand, looked at Tom's gut smeared hands and knife, and withdrew it. He said, "It's always a pleasure to meet the workers of this province." He stood alongside Tom, looking up and smiling.

The photographer raised his camera.

Tom pointed his knife at the photographer. "No."

The photographer lowered the camera.

Tom told the premier, "You and your people are always welcome to visit—but now is not a good time, with this catch to get cleaned and packed. If you want to make an appointment to visit at a better time, I'd be glad to show you around and talk."

The photographer had backed away. He raised his camera again, aiming it to include the premier and some of the packers.

Tom warned, "You ask my permission before taking any photographs in the plant."

"Do you mind if I take a picture of the premier among your workers?"

"Yes."

Bernard Appleby, watching Tom resume work, commented, "The plant has an interesting history."

Tom grunted.

"Defiant Island has been doing well."

"Yup."

"But fish stocks are uncertain ..."

"Maybe."

"And with the economy of the province the way it is, you can't rely forever on the government to keep small scale rural operations like this viable."

"We don't look to the government for help."

Ignoring Tom's response, the premier went on, "With these things in mind, I was surprised Mr. Given undermined the offer from International Consolidated."

Tom stopped work and looked up. "Meaning?"

"I'm just saying that with the future so uncertain, and with Mr. Given's lack of experience in the fishing industry, and with the relative insecurity of his company compared with the stability and breadth of I.C.E., your workers might have been better advised to entertain more seriously such a generous offer. I might add that I'm sure if approached in the right manner Mr. Wise would consider reopening negotiations."

"I take it Mr. Wise is a friend of yours."

"An acquaintance."

"A supporter."

Dale arrived to help with the shift.

Tom called, "Dale, Mr. Appleby and his friends are leaving. Could you show them out, please?

"It would be my *pleasure*," said Dale.

The premier turned to go, turned back to Tom, and said quietly, "Don't misunderstand me. I'm not threatening you or Mr. Given or the plant. I'm simply advising you that in the context of changing societal attitudes, it's my job, as fiscal manager of the province, to ask awkward questions about how government money is spent, money, after all, that rightfully belongs to the ordinary people of the province. For example, I have to ask how long isolated communities like White Rock Island can survive in the twenty first century—and how long do they *deserve* to survive."

"You've been saying that for the three years you've been in power, and I don't see much happening yet."

"It's still early days for us. People need time to adjust to the prospect of change, but I believe the majority of my constituents are coming to the realization that the unproductive way of life enjoyed by some of the people of this province, because of the isolated areas in which they choose to live, may be unsustainable in a social climate dominated by a global economy that necessitates objective economic rationalization. In other words, this government, on behalf of the ordinary people, has to question how long the majority of the population can afford to subsidize the outdated way of life of a minority. And I believe that most of the people in the province are now ready to accept a rationalization of the way we live, and of where we choose to live."

"That's because most of the people in the province live in urban areas—as you well know, of course—and won't be too concerned at services to rural areas being cut back."

Bernard Appleby shrugged. "As premier, I have an obligation to respond to the will of the majority of the ordinary people of the province. I expect to receive a renewed mandate in the election I intend to call next year, and then we'll see."

With Dale at their head, the premier and his aides swept out.

Chapter Twenty-Three

In mid-summer, Penelope arrived on White Rock Island, unexpectedly. Tom and Patrick were at the plant. Cornelia and Gladys had given up reading after their afternoon tea, and were dozing in the parlour. They jerked awake at the knock on the door.

"I was asleep," said Cornelia.

"Me too," said Gladys.

"Did I wake you?"

"No. It was the knock at the door."

"Was there a knock at the door?"

"That's what woke you."

"I wonder who it is."

"You might go and see. That'd be quicker than me struggling out there."

Cornelia nodded. "Yes ... yes ... But you're walking quite well now, aren't you, Gladys?" As she rocked in her chair to gain momentum to rise, she went on, "You don't depend on your stick as much as you did just a few weeks ago, do you?" She stood, leaning on the arm of the chair. "Your mother always walked with a stick, even when we were young, didn't she? My mother had one, too, although she didn't always use it. I think they were a sort of fashion accessory."

The knock sounded again, twice and louder.

"Someone's knocking at the door," said Cornelia. "I'll see who it is."

"Good idea, old girl."

As Cornelia set off, there was a single, quieter knock at the door. She stopped. "Whoever it is, is knocking at the front door. 'Magine—the *front* door. We never used the front door when we were children, did we? No-one did. Everyone used the back door. There really wasn't any need to have a front door at all, except I suppose if you didn't have a front door then you wouldn't have a back door, because you wouldn't call it that, you'd call it just … the door. And then people couldn't decide to go to the back door when they felt they knew you well, instead of to the front door, when they were strangers, which would be a shame, don't you think, because when they went to the back door it showed they weren't strangers any more, although of course everyone knew everyone on the island in those days, so there weren't any strangers around, which meant everyone went to the back door, anyway. And no-one ever knocked, did they? They just walked straight in the kitchen, through the back door."

She nodded, savouring the memory of visitors who dispensed with the formality of the front door, arriving unheralded and confident through the back door. She set off toward the kitchen, heading for the back door.

Gladys, watching her, shook her head.

There was a moment's silence when Cornelia reached the kitchen. Then, "Gladys, I'm in the kitchen. Why?"

"You were going to answer the front door but you headed for the back door instead."

Cornelia reappeared in the parlour. She sighed. "This seems to be one of my vague days, but I have been doing well, haven't I? I don't think I can remember when my last vague day was, can you? But then I don't suppose I'd remember a vague day because I'd be … vague about it, anyway. It would be a vague memory. You don't seem to have vague days, do you, Gladys?"

Gladys prompted, "The front door, ducky."

Cornelia was looking back into the kitchen. "Do you think we should get a bigger table in the kitchen? Tom says we could do with one now that we eat in there all the time. We always used to eat in the kitchen when we were children, didn't we? We never ate in the dining room. It seems silly calling a room the dining room when you never dine in it, doesn't it?"

Four loud knocks sounded again.

Cornelia started. "There's someone at the front door. The *front* door."

Penelope had her hand raised to knock again as Cornelia opened the door. She lowered it, saying, "I didn't hear you coming. I hope I'm not disturbing you."

"We were asleep," said Cornelia, by way of explanation for her tardiness in answering the door.

Penelope took it as a reprimand. "I'm so sorry."

"Who is it?" Gladys called from the parlour.

"A lady. She says she's sorry we were asleep." Cornelia turned back to Penelope. "Why are you sorry we were asleep?"

"I mean I'm sorry I'm disturbing you."

"Who is it?" Gladys called again.

"A lady. She's sorry she's disturbing us."

Penelope, in slim indigo jeans that hugged her legs and a cashmere tee shirt of light mocha, her hair hanging in fine crinkles, reached for Cornelia's hand and shook it. "You're Cornelia, aren't you?"

Gladys's voice sounded again from the parlour, louder. "Cornelia, who is it, for krissake?"

"A lady. She says I'm Cornelia."

Penelope leaned forward so that she could see into the parlour and called, "And you're Gladys. How are you, Gladys?"

Cornelia, searching for a reason for a well dressed visitor to come to the house, said, "Are you doing a survey?"

"No. I came to see ..."

"Are you a Jehovah's Witness?"

"No. I ..."

Gladys interrupted. "You're ... you're ... you're ... Shit."

Penelope took a step backwards.

Cornelia said, "Do you have to go?"

Gladys's voice sounded from the parlour, starting again. "Patrick's friend. Cornelia, it's Patrick's friend. P ... P ... P ... Shit."

Cornelia said, "When she forgets words she says 'shit.'"

"I'm Penelope."

Cornelia smiled slowly. "Yes." She remembered. "Yes. Penelope. Gladys, it's Patrick's friend, Penelope."

She ushered Penelope into the parlour and said carefully, remembering Patrick's girlfriend look, "Does Patrick know you're coming? He's not here. He's ..."

Where was Patrick? He and Tom were at the house. They all had breakfast together. Yes—and Patrick and Tom left together to go ... fishing? No. That was another day. They went to the hardware store on Deer Isle to get wood to make shelves in Tom's room. But that was another day, too. Then they went to Deer Isle and Patrick took Tom for a ride in the Beechcraft. But, no, that was also another day.

She remembered Patrick and Tom saying, as they left that morning, "Call if you need us, girls." They always said that. They always had their cellular telephones—no, their *cells*—with them so they could come quickly if she or Gladys needed help, if anything happened. She and Gladys still had their cell phones—it was cool to say cell phones, or just cells, not cellular telephones, Gladys kept reminding her—although Patrick or Tom, or both of them, were almost always close by these days. Patrick and Tom said keep your cellular telephones—your *cells*—with you all the time in case of an emergency, in case you can't get to the telephone in the hallway. They said just press this button and it will ring straight through to us.

"We just have to press a button and it rings straight through to them," Cornelia said.

"Excuse me?" said Penelope.

"She means on the cell phone," Gladys explained, then added, "She can't remember where Patrick is. Give her a moment."

"Patrick's at the plant, with Tom," Cornelia announced, triumphant.

"Bingo," said Gladys. "Penelope, get your arse over here and help me up. Cornelia, put the kettle on."

"The kettle ..."

"For tea, for our visitor."

"Tea—for Penelope," said Cornelia, leading the way into the kitchen while Penelope helped Gladys.

They took their tea in the garden. Cornelia and Gladys sat on the old chairs among the roses, while Penelope sprawled on the grass at their feet.

"Your ... Your ... Mind your ... j ... j ... Shit," Gladys said. She leaned forward, waving her hand at Penelope's legs.

"My jeans," Penelope supplied.

"Mind your j ... j ... jeans, on the grass," Gladys warned.

Cornelia was enjoying the smell of the wild roses. Dale Senior had loved it, too, when they sat together in the bower, hidden from view among the roses. When she knew he was on the way home from the fishing, and it was a fine evening, she used to wait for him there. He always guessed where she was and came straight around the house without entering it. Sometimes he tried to creep along the border of the rose hedge so that he could surprise her.

"I always heard him coming," she said.

Penelope looked at Cornelia, then at Gladys.

"Dale Senior," Gladys explained. "Right, Cornelia?"

"Yes. Dale Senior. He loved the smell of the roses. He used to bring me wild roses when we were courting. He bought me this brooch." She fingered the tiny silver dolphin. "He used to ... Are you still Patrick's girl-friend?"

"There you go—beating about the bush again," said Gladys.

"Yes. No. I don't know," said Penelope. "We've been together and apart so many times, I just don't know any longer. Patrick told you about how he said there was no point in our carrying on the way we had been, didn't he?"

Cornelia nodded, remembering their conversation on the beach, the day Gladys had her stroke. "I asked him were you still courting. He said he didn't know."

"I didn't know either. He didn't call me, and I wouldn't call him, for ages—until last November, when I thought I could stay in Ottawa for a few days, and I wanted so badly to see him, so I called, and he said it would be wonderful to see me, and we had our reunion ..."

"Lovely," said Cornelia.

"This is better than the soaps," said Gladys.

"Then Don called—my agent, you remember—and said he'd had a call from the Premier of British Columbia—the *Premier*—asking whether I could do a charity show for people living on the street in Vancouver. There was that big snowstorm, and the weather was staying so cold, and they were trying to find shelter for the homeless. The show was arranged on the spur of the moment, and I can't—Don says I can't—turn down those things. He says I can't afford the bad publicity it would make if we turned it down, and I wanted to do the show for them, for the homeless, anyway. So I had to leave Patrick after only a few hours, before we had ..." —she glanced quickly at Cornelia and Gladys, blushing— "... just one night together. Patrick said he understood—he always says that—but he was very upset, and we haven't been together since then."

"How long are you staying this time?" Gladys asked.

"I have to be in New York for a show at the weekend, so I'll have to leave tomorrow or early the next day. Is there somewhere I can stay on the island, a bed and breakfast, or a guest house?"

"You'll stay here, of course," said Cornelia.

"Will that be all right with Patrick, do you think?"

Cornelia and Gladys exchanged a quick glance.

"You mean—he doesn't know you're here?" asked Gladys.

Penelope nodded. "I didn't dare tell him I was coming. He was so upset last time we met and I was called away. I was afraid he wouldn't want to see me."

She started to cry. Gladys patted her on the shoulder, and Cornelia said, "There, there, dear."

They heard a car pull up.

"The boys are home," said Gladys.

Patrick stopped so suddenly as he came out of the kitchen door that Tom, following, walked into him. He looked at Penelope, who stood uncertainly.

"Surprise," she said.

"I thought you were in Spain."

"I was. Then I was in Montreal, and I asked Don if there was time for me to come to White Rock before I went to New York."

"Why didn't you tell me you were coming?"

"I was afraid."

"Afraid—of me?"

"Afraid you wouldn't want to see me."

Patrick said, "Oh, Penelope."

He strode forward and embraced her.

"Lovely," said Cornelia, clasping her hands under her chin.

"I told you—this is better than the soaps," said Gladys.

Half way through dinner, Penelope's phone rang. She looked around the table, biting her lip. "Sorry. I have to answer it. Please excuse me." She rose from the table and they heard her voice in the hallway. "Don, you said ... No, Don, I won't ... I don't have to be there until the weekend ... But you said ... I thought the flight was arranged ... All right ... I know it's not your fault ... All right ..."

They heard Penelope snap her phone shut, then the sound of stifled sobbing.

Patrick threw his napkin on the table. "I'd better see what's going on."

He returned from the hallway with his arm around Penelope, who was still crying. He steered her back to her chair. She sniffed and looked around. "That was Don. He says the Passamaquoddy Sound forecast for the next few days is for mist, and it's likely the plane won't be able to get off Deer Isle. I have to go now—the plane's waiting—or I won't get to

New York in time for the show, and it's an important one, a big one—a really big one. I was going to stay for a day or two, if you'd let me. I'm letting you down again, Patrick, and I'm being rude to all your friends. I'm sorry. I'm so sorry. I'll call Gladstone to give me a ride."

Patrick said, "I'll take you to the airfield."

"You don't have to."

"I know."

*****

The airfield was dark except for the lights of Penelope's plane, waiting with engines throbbing. Patrick stopped the car beside the hut that served as airfield office, weather station, maintenance depot and customs clearance house. Two deer walked through the lights of the plane. Patrick's Beechcraft stood in the darkness on the other side of the hut.

They hadn't spoken since leaving the house, except to wish Gladstone good night on the ferry. When Gladstone offered, "It's always a pleasure to see you, Miss Diamant. I wish we could see you more often," Penelope started to cry, and Patrick left the car to console Gladstone in his distress at upsetting Penelope.

They sat in the darkness, still silent, until Penelope said, "I wanted to stay, Patrick. Really—I planned to stay."

"I know."

"I'm sorry."

"You don't have to say sorry. It can't be helped."

The wind, gusting intermittently across the field, buffeted the car.

Penelope said, "Will you at least hug me before I go?"

"Of course."

They hugged, leaning awkwardly across the front seats of the car. Penelope nestled her head into Patrick's shoulder.

He said, stroking her hair, "How long have we been friends?"

157

Penelope sniffed. "For ever. Since we were kids in Toronto."

"I want us to be friends, not lovers. We're not lovers, anyway. We're never together."

Penelope withdrew her head from Patrick's shoulder. "How can we not be lovers, Patrick, when we love one another?"

"But our loving one another is causing us more grief than joy, isn't it? You were crying at the house tonight, and you're crying again now. I can't bear seeing you like this, and I don't want to feel so … so … dependent on a few moments of happiness with you to sustain me through weeks—months—of being without you."

"I have my career. I'm proud of being successful, and earning well, and being able to give money to my parents."

"I'm proud of you, too. But do you know something? I avoid magazine racks because I know there's a good chance I'll see your picture there. And I avoid certain television stations because I'm afraid you'll be on them."

"That's silly, Patrick. Why?"

"Because it's like being slapped in the face with how much I miss you. I want to see your picture on magazine covers and on television and be proud of seeing my old, special friend so famous, without feeling such a pang of missing her that I have to look away."

"You know you could travel with me, don't you? Then we could marry. You said they don't need you all the time at the office in Ottawa, or at the plant here, and you could do most of your business from anywhere in the world."

"You mean follow you around, and stand around with Don and the others, while you work?"

"What would be wrong with that?"

"I'd feel like a dependent."

"You could work for me … Look after the contracts, do the books …"

"No."

Penelope pushed herself away from Patrick, her limpid eyes glistening with tears. "So?"

He took her head in his hands, brushing gently and ineffectually at her tears. "So there's no point, is there? We're ... we're ... *lacerating* one another."

Outside the car, they embraced. Penelope clung to Patrick, released him, pressed herself fiercely against him once more. As she pulled away, the wind caught her hair, whipping it across Patrick's face. He put his hands up to keep it from his eyes and its fine, blonde tendrils twined themselves through his fingers. Penelope inclined her head toward him while he untangled her hair and gently smoothed it with both hands against her head. His hands rested there, then slipped across her shoulders, and down to his sides.

She walked quickly to the plane, her hair streaming behind her.

*****

Patrick and Tom went fishing a few days later.

Tom said tentatively, "I don't mean to interfere or pry, but—why don't you ask Penelope to marry you?"

"I have, often."

"Oh. Sorry. What does she say?"

"She says she doesn't want to give up work."

"She wouldn't have to, would she? I mean, she may be trotting all over the globe, but you'd at least have some time together."

"Like we do now, you mean?" Patrick said bleakly.

"Sorry—again."

"It wouldn't be a marriage, never being together. She says I could travel with her—she said it again the other night—be her accountant, and then we could marry and be together all the time."

"Doesn't sound a bad proposition to me," Tom said, laughing.

"I thought about it. But I have my work, too, and my … my …"

Tom prompted, no longer laughing, "Pride?"

"Independence."

They fished in silence for a while.

Then Tom asked cautiously, "So—where are you now, you and Penel-ope?"

"Nowhere. Finished."

"Sorry. How did she take it?"

"She was crying."

"How about you?"

Patrick turned away and stared at the horizon.

Chapter Twenty-Four

Two years later Tom was in Samuel's fishing boat three miles off shore, confirming at first hand the bad news he had been growing aware of during the previous six months.

The first year of the Defiant Island fishery had gone well. In the second year, although the catch was down, increased storage capacity at the plant kept the supply of fish to the new markets consistent, and business remained good. Now reserves were dwindling rapidly as the catch stayed markedly down, and the fishermen were making gloomy forecasts about the fish stocks around the island.

Samuel, who was in his seventies and had been fishing from White Rock since he was twelve, said, "The fish simply aren't there. Two years ago we thought it was just a bad year. Last year we thought they were bound to recover for next season. But they're not breeding like they used to. The scientists they sent down from Fisheries can't understand it. It's the same from here to Newfoundland. There's no reason for it we can see. There's just less and less fish."

"Any suggestions?" Tom asked.

"We have to stop fishing now—right now. Government's going to order it soon, anyway, but they'll put it off as long as they can and by then there'll be no fish left in these waters. We're the only ones fishing them, and I say—we say, the fishers—we should stop now otherwise there'll be none left for the future—not ever."

Samuel's young partner, Jeffrey, added, "We don't intend to be—we *won't* be—the ones they'll be talking about in the future, the ones that fished the White Rock Island waters dry."

Samuel pointed towards shore, to a cluster of aquaculture sites. "See them?"

Tom nodded. "What about the aquaculture? The news isn't any better there, is it?"

"No better. We're producing plenty of fish, as you know, but they're no good. The disease is making them not fit to sell. They taste all right, and they're safe to eat, but with their scales flaking off, they look diseased because—well, because they *are* diseased."

Jeffrey elaborated, "They're getting smaller and weaker, too. Another six months and they really won't be fit to eat, because there won't be any meat on them."

"So ..?"

The fishermen nodded grimly, confirming what Tom already knew.

"So we have to cull them—all of them," said Samuel. "It's the only way to stop the disease. Then we have to leave the sites empty for a year at least, probably two or three years, until the water's clear."

"What do we do in the meantime?" said Tom.

Samuel and Jeffrey grunted and resumed their work.

*****

When Tom called Patrick in Ottawa to confirm the news about the precarious state of the White Rock fish stocks, Patrick said he was prepared for it.

"You mean you've got a plan?" Tom asked.

"Not yet, but I've got some ideas. First, we need a new Defiant Island product."

"We'll need a new market, too, then."

"Not necessarily. People are buying our fish not just because they like the fish but because of the romance they associate with it."

Tom scoffed, "What romance?"

162

"The romance of it coming from a little island in a body of water they didn't even know existed. They love the *idea* of it—of their consuming a product from what they perceive to be such an exotic locale."

"You can be the one to tell the crowd at the plant they're working in an exotic locale."

Patrick laughed, even as he insisted, "Our customers aren't just buying fish. They're buying a bit of Defiant Island, a bit of White Rock. They love reading that little potted history of the island we put on the back of the package. They feel they know the island. They care about it. The market analysis people find it in every survey they do. So, like I said, what we've got to come up with is a new product. A new Defiant Island product. I've got a market research firm working on it now."

*****

Two weeks later Patrick arrived at the plant. He'd crossed from Deer Isle on the first ferry of the day, and had brought two sets of papers, one the new marketing plan, complete with a suggested new product, the other, an offer to buyout the Defiant Island plant.

It had come, not unexpectedly, from International Consolidated, who Patrick knew had been watching Defiant Island's difficulties with interest. As soon as he received it, he asked Peggy to find out what she could about the background to the offer. After a day on the phone, she reported that all she could discover—from an old boy friend working for I.C.E., she confessed, sheepishly—was that there was a highly secret business plan being produced in conjunction with, but separate from, the buyout offer. Pressed to reveal its contents, the old flame said he would love to, for the sake of their former relationship and in the hope of rekindling it (she wasn't sure how sincere he was), but—he was speaking seriously now—only Conrad Wise, for whom he had no liking, and his closest associates, knew its contents.

After thanking Peggy for her efforts, and gazing thoughtfully out of his window for a few minutes, Patrick had picked up his phone to call Mike at Soames's Investigation and Security.

Now Tom asked, glancing through the offer, "What do we do?"

"We're obliged—not legally, but morally—to present it to the staff, and to the fishers. It's a generous offer, after all. Conrad Wise is coming down tomorrow and he'll go over the details with them."

Tom scowled. "Do we have to listen to his bullshit?"

Patrick shrugged. "I feel we should. Wise asked for the meeting. I don't trust him any more than you do, but, who knows, maybe the staff and the fishers will want to accept it. And I'm not one for secret dealings."

"Is there anything we have to do before the meeting, like prepare a rebuff?"

"There's no need. I'll leave it to the staff to oppose it, if they want to. But—if Mike Soames calls, I need to speak to him as soon as possible. I told him to try every number he's got for us until he gets an answer, day or night."

*****

Conrad Wise was scheduled to come on the noon ferry, but didn't arrive until six o' clock. From his office window looking out on the harbour, Tom watched the car drive up the ferry ramp and park beside the plant. He quickly gathered the last of a pile of documents churning from the fax machine and stapled them together. The top paper was headed, 'Soames's Investigation and Security. Urgent. Confidential.'

Tom punched numbers into the telephone. "Mike? I've got 'em. Thanks. We owe you."

The chairman of I.C.E. marched into the office.

Tom greeted him. "Welcome back to the island."

They shook hands, and Conrad Wise said, "Mr. Tom Cronk—a pleasure."

Tom led him to the cafeteria, where Patrick was explaining to the plant workers and to the fishers why he had asked them to meet. With a brief nod to Patrick, Tom handed him the documents.

Patrick shook Conrad Wise's offered hand and commented, looking behind him for the two executive assistants, "You're alone today."

The chairman smiled. "Sometimes I can persuade my assistants to let me go solo."

Patrick introduced him to the staff. There were a few mutters of recognition and suspicion, which turned to murmurs of surprise as the chairman outlined his plan to buyout Defiant Island, the amount he was prepared to pay, and the immediate bonuses to be awarded to all workers signing on to work for, and to supply, International Consolidated.

"You take a chance with me, of course," Conrad Wise admitted, "Just as you took a chance with Mr. Given and his company two years ago. Mr. Given tried hard, but—I say this not to be critical, but realistic—he has failed you. I can only promise what he promised you, namely, that I will do my best—my company will do its best—to make the Defiant Island fish plant a viable business. The offer I am making today, to buy the plant, and to pay signing bonuses to you, the workers and suppliers, is proof of my good faith and my sincere wish for the plant to succeed."

Conrad Wise paused before adding, "You might consider the political climate in which the offer is made as further proof of my good faith. As you know, Mr. Bernard Appleby and his Progressive Democratic Alliance have recently been reelected on a platform promising further restructuring and rationalization of the finances of the province, in order to reflect more accurately the changing lifestyles of the present century. Mr. Appleby raises the legitimate question of whether an isolated, rural way of life, like yours, is sustainable with the limited financial resources available to the province. I make the offer to buy Defiant Island despite knowing the hardships such a policy would bring to any business operating in a remote, rural area like White Rock Island. Let me put it another way: Your community needs a friend with political and financial connections if it is to survive, and I am suggesting that friend might be International Consolidated—and me."

When Conrad Wise asked if any of the workers had questions or comments, no-one responded until Samuel offered, "Patrick—Mr. Given—he speaks for us."

Conrad Wise turned to Patrick, who had taken a place among the plant workers and fishers after introducing the speaker. "Well, Mr. Given. It seems you are to be the spokesperson for the islanders again, except that this time you do not have the luxury of speaking incognito."

Patrick was perusing the documents sent by Mike Soames.

Conrad Wise prompted, "Mr. Given, do you have any comments?"

Patrick looked up from the documents, wondering at Mike Soames's ingenuity, and hoping that his methods had been within the law. "I have no comments, Mr. Wise, but I do have a question or two."

"I'll be happy to respond."

"The questions are in regard to these documents, prepared by your strategic management department and entitled, Commercial Benefits of the Defiant Island Product Name."

Conrad Wise said sharply, "Those documents are confidential."

"No doubt that would be your wish at the present, but as I have a copy here you may consider them in the public domain."

"This is unethical."

Patrick shot back, "No more unethical than lying to people you hope to employ."

"I have no comment to make on those documents."

Patrick ignored the chairman and continued, "My first question is—could you be more specific about the date of your proposed closure of the White Rock Island plant? Your strategic management department suggests it be closed between one month and six months after acquisition."

"That's what you call doing your best for the plant, is it?" one of the women packers called out to Conrad Wise.

He repeated, "I said I have no comment to make on those documents."

Patrick went on, "With regard to the name, Defiant Island, you say—your strategic management department says, that is—that although the plant will be closed within six months at the outside, nevertheless the Defiant Island name will continue. How will that be achieved?"

"I have said twice already that I have no comment to make on those documents."

"Perhaps I can answer for you, using these documents prepared on your behalf. It says here, on page six, I quote, 'We consider it impossible for the White Rock Island plant to operate efficiently and profitably, because of its size, the limited resources available, and the limited skills and intellect of the available workforce. Moreover, the shortcomings of the workforce are compounded by the accepted culture of government subsidies being relied upon to maintain the operation of the fish plant and, indeed, the very existence of the island community itself. Despite this, we are surprised to note that products bearing the Defiant Island name are not only popular among consumers—inexplicably, they outsell our own similar products—but are also highly respected by others in the industry. With all this in mind, it is our proposal that the Defiant Island name be retained, although its association with White Rock Island will obviously be severed, for use on as many product lines manufactured by the various International Consolidated companies as can accommodate it, which we postulate will enhance their credibility and their marketability. In short, we ditch the plant but use the name.'"

The workers and fishers sat in silence, looking from Patrick to Conrad Wise, until Samuel snarled, "You bastard. Do you have anything to say about what Mr. Given just read?"

"Only to repeat that these are confidential documents ..."

"I'm not *surprised*," Dale interjected.

"… And, furthermore, give no more than a hypothetical treatment of the possible buying of your fish plant, prepared—yes—at my request by one of my departments, which was given the brief to explore all possible scenarios following the purchase. This does not mean that any of it will happen. It's a hypothesis, a scenario—not a plan of action."

"Which brings me to my final question, then," Patrick put in. "If it's not a plan of action, what does this note at the end of the documents, in your handwriting and accompanied by your signature, mean?" Patrick held up the documents, pointing to a scribbled addendum at the foot of the last page, as he read, "This sounds good. Let's do it."

Conrad Wise snarled, "Not only have you illegally acquired confidential documents, but you have also stolen my personal desk copy."

"It's not your desk copy," said Patrick. "It's a photocopy of your desk copy."

Above the laughter at Patrick's comment, and the growing mutters of anger and scorn directed at Conrad Wise, Tom, still at the front of the room, announced, "Does anyone else have any questions or comments for Mr. Wise?"

"Just one comment," shouted Samuel. "Mr. Wise, you know what you can do with your offer to buy our plant—and our name."

He rose to leave, the other fishers and the plant workers following.

"I guess that's the end of the meeting," Tom said to Conrad Wise. "Thanks for coming down."

Conrad Wise spat, "You'll regret this. You'll be finished within six months." He turned to Patrick. "And you—you'll be sorry, too."

"I apologize for bringing forward the documents in that way, but I felt our staff had to know the whole picture before making a decision."

"Last time I was here you questioned my integrity …"

"No—I questioned your business plan."

"To me, that means you question my integrity. Moreover, you did so in the guise of a casual visitor to the island, without revealing your own business interest ..."

"I had none at the time."

"... Thereby breaching the code of ethics of the International Manufacturing and Marketing Council ..."

"Your complaint to that effect didn't go far with the Council."

"... Which forbids anonymous dealings and demands full disclosure of all business interests at all times in all dealings with fellow members. And not content with that, now you use underhand, scurrilous and illegal methods to undermine a business offer—an offer which amounts to a gesture of philanthropy—made by me in good faith towards these poor islanders whom you have let down by the shortsightedness of your operation and by your own business inefficiency and naïveté."

As he spoke, Conrad Wise walked towards the still seated Patrick, until he was leaning over him, his finger, pointing and menacing, only inches from Patrick's face.

Tom, seeing some of the fishers and plant workers pause at the door to watch, and fearing they would move in to defend Patrick, came forward to intervene. "Mr. Wise ..."

"Let me finish." Conrad Wise flashed his arm backwards in Tom's direction. He turned on Patrick again.

Patrick rose, his hands in his pockets.

Conrad Wise tapped his index finger on Patrick's chest as he spoke. "I don't take kindly to my integrity being questioned, nor to the undermining of my business offers, which I have said are made in good faith. I promise—you will regret this."

He stared at Patrick, then stalked through the group of islanders out of the room.

Dale said quietly to Patrick, "You *really* know how to make yourself *popular*, don't you?"

*****

Patrick and Tom worked late at the plant. At nine o' clock Tom called Cornelia and Gladys to say they'd be home in a few minutes.

"How was the meeting?" Cornelia asked.

"It was … interesting. We'll tell you all about it when we get home. Do you need anything?"

"Get some cheese from the store," Cornelia suggested. "We'll have a bedtime snack. But hurry. They'll be closing soon."

Patrick said he had a few papers to fax to Peggy, and would meet Tom in the car park.

As Tom left the plant, he noticed Conrad Wise's car among the vehicles in the lineup for the last ferry of the day. He walked on to the store, where Dale and Carol-Ann were preparing to close. While Dale marked the cheese on the tab shared by Cornelia, Gladys, Tom and Patrick, they talked about the meeting, and about the uncertain future of the plant.

"We'll hang in—somehow," Tom promised.

"I guess we chose the right *name—Defiant* Island," Dale said.

Tom strolled back towards the plant. The horn on the ferry sounded for the waiting vehicles to load and he veered towards the wharf. He wandered along it and stopped, leaning on the parapet. His gaze swept over the lights of the ferry below him, over the fishing boats moored beyond it, over the white rocks dimly visible at the mouth of the harbour, to the open sea beyond. He reflected on the optimism he'd expressed to Dale about the future of the plant. Was it misplaced? How could it survive, with so few fish coming in? But without it, how long would the island community survive, with its economic mainstay gone? The younger generation would find something else, somewhere else, but his own generation, in their fifties, would be hard put to change careers. He'd already found that out for himself. And the older generation—Cornelia and Gladys—would be distraught, witnessing the loss of the community they'd lived in all their lives. What would they do? Stay on in a doomed, dwindling community? Or be forced to settle somewhere new for the last years of their life? If the plant was going to fail, it had better fail quickly, he decided gloomily. The longer they hung on, the harder their eventual failure would be on them all. Conrad Wise had accused Patrick of being naïve. Perhaps Wise was right. Perhaps it was time to give up. Where did defiance end, and naïveté start?

At the same time as the last few vehicles boarded the ferry and the horn sounded again, announcing its departure, two figures appeared from the direction of the plant. They ran down the slip to Conrad Wise's car. Tom heard Gladstone say, "Just made it, boys," as he secured the chain across the loading ramp behind the last of the vehicles.

Then, above the grumble of the ferry as it pulled away from the slip, more voices.

"We got him."

Tom, leaning over the parapet, strained to hear.

"No scars? Nothing broken?"

"A bit of blood. Nothing serious."

"Enough to make him think twice before getting in your way again."

Tom shouted, "Gladstone," waving at him to stop the ferry.

Gladstone, uncomprehending, busy coiling ropes, waved back as the ferry, gathering noise and speed, made for the harbour entrance.

Tom ran towards the plant.

*****

Cornelia said, "The boys are on the way home. They'll be tired after all this fuss and bother with the plant. Tom's going to bring some cheese. We'll have a grilled cheese snack."

"I'll supervise," Gladys offered. "Help me up, ducky."

Cornelia stood before Gladys, holding out her hands.

Gladys gripped them tightly. She laughed, looking at their joined hands. "What a mess. Bones and veins and mottled skin."

"That sounds like a song," said Cornelia. She began to sing, improvising a melody, "Bones and veins and mottled skin ..."

Gladys stumbled as Cornelia hauled her to her feet, and Cornelia said, "It's just as well you've got me to take you around the house."

"At least I can remember where I'm going," Gladys retorted. "With your legs and my memory, I guess we'll make it."

Cornelia, with one hand on Gladys's shoulder and the other around her waist, asked, "Okay?"

"Give me my stick and let's boogie," said Gladys. "Where are we going?"

"To the kitchen, of course."

"Just checking."

They set off for the kitchen, Gladys grasping her walking stick with one hand and Cornelia with the other.

While Gladys sat at the table and Cornelia laid out cutlery for the snack, Cornelia said, "I keep dreaming about Dale Senior."

"That's nice. I wish I had a hunk to dream about."

"Oh, Gladys. I'm sorry. I'm being thoughtless."

"Forget it, ducky. One man was enough for me, and since he turned out to be rotten, I've never wanted another one. What do you dream about?"

"About Dale Senior, I said."

"But what happens? Is it a screwing dream?"

"Gladys!"

"Just asking."

"We're at Morse Cove. Dale Senior used to take me there ..."

"I knew it was a screwing dream."

Cornelia said coyly, "Well, sometimes … But that's not the dream. In the dream, Dale Senior says, 'Morse Cove is the key to the island.' His grandfather always told him that. It's where I wanted to go when you had your silly stroke. I got Patrick to take me to the western beach, but I couldn't imagine getting around the rocks and into Morse Cove so I didn't even suggest it."

"I knew you were at the beach. That's why I had to lie around so long, waiting for you to come and help me. Anyway, no-one's been to Morse Cove for years. What made you think you could get there?"

"It was just an idea, because of the dream. What do you think it means, me dreaming about Morse Cove? And why do I keep dreaming about it now?"

"Haven't a clue, old girl. It's nice to dream about Dale Senior, though, isn't it?"

"Oh yes."

"It's cute you still miss him, after all these years."

Cornelia sat with Gladys at the kitchen table and rested her chin in her hands. She smiled. "Oh yes."

*****

Patrick had faxed a dozen pages to Peggy, with advice on how to deal with the documents, imagining her rolling her eyes at his fussy instructions, which she almost certainly did not need. He stuffed a few papers into his briefcase to go over later with Tom, at the house, and put the lights out in the office he and Tom shared. On the way out he looked in the cleaning room and talked to some of the plant workers. He called, "'Night, all," lifted his hand in response to waves from the staff, and left the plant. He heard the ferry sound its horn down at the wharf as he closed the door behind him. Tom was not at the car so he looked towards the store to see if he was coming. He saw him leaning against the parapet above the ferry and thought—Tom's worrying about the plant. I won't shout to him and disturb his thoughts. I'll stroll over and join him.

Picking his way through the patch of darkness between the plant and the harbour lights, he paused to watch the ferry prepare for departure, Gladstone on the scow, looking up at the cabin.

He heard a hurrying scuff of feet behind him. His jacket was wrenched from his shoulders and jammed tight around his chest, pinioning his arms. He felt himself spun around. He doubled up, retching, his stomach driven in on itself. His hair was seized, his head jerked up and then wrenched down, hard. His nose smashed into something. His knees buckled. He fell face downwards in the gravel. As he lay, his head was raised again by the hair and smashed back against the ground. A boot drove into his ribs. He pushed himself up onto all fours to retaliate. Another boot, from the other side, this one under him and into his stomach. He sprawled. A boot in the side of his head. He threw an arm up to protect himself.

The ferry sounded its horn again.

Running feet—away, not towards.

*****

Gladys said, "The boys are taking their time."

"They'll be along," said Cornelia. "Be patient with them. They're worried about the plant. Well, we all are." She added, "That dream—about Morse Cove, and about Dale Senior saying—his grandfather saying—Morse Cove was the key to the island. Do you suppose I'm dreaming about it now because I'm worrying about what's happening at the plant?"

*****

As Tom ran across the road toward the plant he glanced at the window of his and Patrick's office. No light. So Patrick was on his way out, or had stopped in to see the evening shift cleaning the catch that had come in earlier, or was talking to the staff, or was at the car already, or … He ran to the car first. No Patrick. He swerved back toward the door of the plant. Ran inside. Put his head around the door of the cleaning room.

"Seen Patrick?"

"Looked in a few minutes ago. Chatted a bit. Said goodnight," one of the women said, not pausing in her work.

Tom ran back outside. He paused at the door, looking towards the car. There was something near it. He could just make it out—a heap of something in the patch of darkness between the light thrown from the harbour and the light spilling from the door of the plant. Discarded sacks? Flattened cardboard boxes? He heard a groan as he ran to it. He knelt beside it.

"Patrick!"

He felt Patrick's head, which lay at an awkward angle, one arm thrown over it. Tom moved his hands cautiously to Patrick's face. Sweat? No—too thick. Blood.

"Jesus, Patrick. Can you hear me? What happened?" He guessed the answer even as he asked, recalling the two figures running to the ferry just before it pulled away. He cradled Patrick's head.

"Bastards … Waiting for me …"

"I know. Lie still. Is anything broken?"

"Don't think so."

"Keep still, just in case." He saw Dale leaving the store and shouted his name.

Dale looked around.

"Over here. Quick."

Dale arrived at a run, peered down at the two men, saw Patrick's face, and said, "Jesus. What *happened*? I'll get Carol-Ann."

He called Carol-Ann on Tom's cell phone. She flew from the store seconds later, a small case in her hand. Patrick was struggling to raise himself.

Carol-Ann ordered, "Lie still. Tom, keep him still. Dale, I need a light."

"Flashlight—in the trunk," said Tom.

Carol-Ann knelt beside Tom. She placed her hands on each side of Patrick's face, assessing his injuries as Dale shone the flashlight. She took latex gloves from the case and pulled them on, and with a wad of cotton wool wiped blood from his forehead and cheek.

As she worked she said, "Do you know what happened?"

"Got jumped. Two of them. Smashed my face in the ground. Kicked me."

"What's your name?"

"Patrick Given. You know that."

"What's my name?"

"Don't you know?"

"Don't be a smart arse. Tell me."

"It's Carol-Ann Morse, nee Banks. You know what you're doing, don't you?"

"I should do. I used to be a nurse." She sat back, saying, "Not too bad. I don't think you'll even need a stitch. What day is it?"

"Friday, I think, isn't it?"

"What's your phone number?"

"Are you looking for a date?"

"I said don't be a smart arse."

"603-755-9053. My office. Private line. I haven't got concussion."

"Hmmm. Where do you hurt?"

"Ribs. They kicked me."

Carol-Ann ran her hands down Patrick's sides.

He gasped. "There."

"Anything else?"

176

"Stomach's sore. They kicked me there, too. Just winded, though. I'm all right—really. Let me up."

"You may have broken ribs. You should have an x-ray."

"They can't do anything if I do have broken ribs. They'll just tell me I'll be sore for a week or two."

"You will be."

"I'll be okay. Come on—let me up."

Dale and Tom looked at Carol-Ann for approval, then helped Patrick to his feet.

She said, "You'd better come over to the apartment and I'll clean and bandage you properly."

In the apartment over the store, as Carol-Ann cleaned and bandaged the cuts on Patrick's face, Tom telephoned Cornelia and Gladys and told them Patrick had had a little accident; was all right; there was nothing to worry about; they'd be along soon.

Then he questioned Patrick. "Did you say there were two of them? Did you see them?"

"Yes, there were definitely two of them, but no, I didn't see them."

"It was those cronies of Wise. I saw them running to the ferry. I'm going to call the police."

"No. I couldn't identify them …"

"But I saw them running from the direction of the plant, and I over-heard them saying they'd got you."

"Did you hear them say my name?"

"Well, no …"

Carol-Ann put in, "Keep still. Don't get yourself excited. You may be in shock."

Patrick went on, "Also it was dark and you're only guessing it was those two."

"I know it was those two."

"So do I—but we'd be shaky identifying them."

"But ..."

"And there's something else. Those documents I quoted from at the meeting, the ones Mike sent us. Don't ask me how he got them, but they came from Wise's desk—from his *desk* in his personal office. I can't imagine how he got them short of breaking in and stealing them, and I don't want that coming out in court, for Mike's sake as well as our own. Wise knows that, and he'd make sure it *did* come out."

"So we let them get away with it?"

Patrick shrugged.

Carol-Ann stepped back and inspected her work. "You'll do. But I'm serious—you may be in shock, and you should get an x-ray for your ribs, and get yourself checked out in case the kicking did any internal damage."

"Thank you. I'm glad you were around to help."

Carol-Ann said to Tom, "Take him home and keep him quiet. Don't let him sleep for a while."

"I hate to see them get away with this," Tom muttered.

Dale said quietly, "I've got an *idea*. We'll take them off the *ferry*—I'll radio Gladstone and *warn* him—and, ah, let them know we don't appreciate their *business* methods. All right, Patrick?"

Carol-Ann and Tom were helping Patrick to his feet. As he straightened he winced and sagged between them.

Carol-Ann said, "Let him down again."

"I think I'm going to throw up."

Dale grabbed a bowl and Patrick vomited into it.

"I said you should get yourself checked for internal injuries," Carol-Ann said, wiping his mouth, her arm round him.

"It's just shock. I'm okay. Really—thank you." He looked up at Dale and Tom. "Those bastards—get them. Just the two—not Wise."

"He's the one who set it up," Tom protested.

"I know. But he's not the one who carried it out. We get those two and no questions will be asked. It'll be tit for tat and that'll be the end of it. If we rough Wise up we could end up in trouble with the law ourselves. It's not worth the risk. What's the plan, Dale?"

"The only plan right now is for you to go home and rest," Carol-Ann ordered. "Tom, get the car while Dale and I take him downstairs." When Patrick started to protest and Tom hesitated, she snapped, "Let's go—now!"

Dale said, "We better *do* it, guys."

*****

The ferry was ten minutes from putting in to Deer Isle when it slowed and turned, executing a wide circle. Gladstone had left the cabin to speak to the drivers of all but one of the dozen vehicles aboard. As the ferry turned away from Deer Isle and started on a second wide circle, Conrad Wise, the driver of the vehicle he'd ignored, wound down his window and shouted at Gladstone, "You—what the hell's going on?"

Gladstone ambled to the car. "Low tide. We have to wait for it to rise before we can put in to Deer Isle."

The executive assistant sitting beside Conrad Wise in the front seat said, "It's high tide. I noticed coming out of the harbour."

"It drops very suddenly," Gladstone explained solemnly, with one eye on the lights of an approaching fishing boat. He added, "Excuse me, gents."

He picked up a rope thrown from the fishing boat, pulled the vessel alongside the ferry, and lashed the crafts together. Samuel, Jeffrey, and two other island fishermen jumped aboard and joined Gladstone and the drivers of the other vehicles on the ferry, who had surrounded Conrad Wise's car.

"'Evening, Gladstone, boy," said Samuel. "I guess you got the call on the radio from Dale, too."

They heard the doors of Wise's car lock. Gladstone unhooked an emergency hatchet from the side of the ferry and drove it through the passenger side window.

"If you'll excuse us, Mr. Wise, we'll be taking these young fellers for a ride with us," Samuel announced. "If you'd like to wait at the ferry landing on Deer Isle, we'll be delivering them back to you in an hour or two."

As he spoke, Gladstone and the fishermen pulled the executive assistants from the car and dragged them across the scow. One of them wrenched his arm free and threw a punch at Samuel. Gladstone intercepted the blow and twisted the executive assistant's arm behind his back, doubling him up and pushing his head against the side of the scow. Wise opened his door and climbed half way from his car.

Samuel, looking back, warned, "You'll stay there, if you please, Mr. Wise."

Conrad Wise sat back in the car and closed the door. The fishermen threw Wise's companions into the fishing boat. Gladstone untied the rope and as the fishing boat pulled away into the darkness the ferry resumed its course towards Deer Isle.

*****

On the insistence of Cornelia and Gladys, Patrick went reluctantly to bed when Tom delivered him home.

Before he went to his room, Gladys hugged him painfully, promising, "We'll get those … those … b …, b …"

"Blackguards," Patrick suggested.

"Buggers," Tom surmised.

"Bastards," Cornelia supplied. "She means those bastards."

"Those b … b … bastards," Gladys confirmed.

Tom assured the women that Patrick's assailants were being dealt with. Cornelia took the toasted cheese supper up to Patrick.

180

While he ate, painfully working his jaw, she sat on his bed and stroked his hair, murmuring, "Poor boy. Poor boy."

Tom poured a glass of scotch for them all. Gladys had gone to bed, so he delivered her drink to her room and then took Tom's up to him.

"You okay?"

"I'm okay. Thanks."

"Thanks for nothing. I shouldn't have left you alone."

"You weren't to know those two were hanging around."

"I should have been suspicious when Wise appeared at the plant saying he was alone. Should have known his goons were hanging around somewhere. Sorry."

"Please, Tom, don't apologise. No-one's to blame."

"I just wish I'd been there to help you."

"I know—but it can't be helped. Thanks for what you did. I'm glad you were there." Patrick held out his hand. "Careful—it's sore."

Tom clasped Patrick's hand gently in both of his, shook it carefully, and held it.

When Cornelia called, "Herbal tea, Patrick?" Tom said, "Time for your next visitor."

Cornelia resumed her place at the bedside.

Two hours later Tom was sprawled in the living room. His cell phone rang. "Dale?"

"*Mission* accomplished. Samuel and the *guys* took them off the ferry and *delivered* them to the wharf on Deer Isle a couple of hours later."

"*Two hours?* What did they do to them all that time?" Tom imagined Samuel and his partners bludgeoning Wise's colleagues for two hours.

"Nothing *much*. Just took them for a *ride*—up through the eastern passage between Deer Isle and Horse Island, and *twice* round Gannet Rock."

"And the tide was turning, and the wind was westerly—right?"

"Yup."

"I almost feel sorry for them. Were they ill?"

"Started *puking* before they even reached the *passage*. Then hardly stopped to breathe. They weren't in good *shape* when they got back to the wharf. One of them couldn't even *stand*, just kept throwing up over himself. Then when they took them off at the wharf, the guys opened the door of the *car*—Wise was waiting, like they told him to—and threw them in, and one *puked* over Wise. I think you can tell Patrick that *retribution* has been exacted."

"Thanks, Dale." Tom shut off the phone and muttered, "Not quite."

Chapter Twenty-Five

A week later Patrick and Tom asked the plant workers and the fishers to meet in the cafeteria.

Patrick, his face still bruised but healing, started, "I'm trying not to feel like Conrad Wise, getting you together again like this."

There was some uneasy laughter, and a few calls of, "No way."

Patrick continued, "But things are serious, as you know. The catch is down—way down—and is still going down. We don't know why the fish stocks are so low. The scientists are working on it but they won't have an answer for months, and even then the answer, whatever it is, may not help us. On top of all this, the government has renewed its threats about cutting back on services to rural and isolated areas—and that means us. No-one knows exactly what that means—the premier is very tight-lipped about it—but it's something else we may have to contend with."

Samuel interrupted. "But the new minister, the one who'd be dealing with cutbacks and such, that Gorman Grant, he's from Cape Sable Island, so he's from an isolated area himself. Maybe that means the government is having second thoughts about the cuts."

"We can hope so. But whatever happens, if we're going to keep the plant going, we have to be ready for some tough times, and we have to think differently. For a start, with fish stocks so uncertain, we need a new product, which will mean a whole new way of working, here in the plant and out on the boats. As you know, I've had some friends working on some ideas, researching possible products, and they've come up with a project. That's why we're here today, so that Tom and I can share the plan with you, and you can tell us what you think of it, and whether you think it'll work."

Patrick looked around at the twenty plant workers and the dozen fishers. Their eyes were fixed on him. He glanced at Tom, beside him.

Tom urged, "Go on."

Patrick announced, "We're going to knit."

A beat of silence followed before Samuel said, "Patrick, boy, I can't knit. I've never knitted in my life."

"I don't mean you—unless you want to. I mean here in the plant, we knit."

"Knit what?" one of the women asked.

"Sweaters. Toques. Scarves. Anything. The market research shows two things. One—people in central Canada and the eastern States—I mean city folk, mostly—want to buy woolen goods from here in the east. Two—if the goods have our name on it, *Defiant Island*, they'll sell, because we've built up a following with the fish products. You heard that from Conrad Wise's secret documents. His research found the same thing."

"Where do us fishers come in?" Samuel asked.

"The fishing boats would have two roles. They'd bring the wool from the mainland to be worked here, and then deliver the goods back to the mainland. Also—you could sell from your boats."

"Like we sometimes sell fish at the wharf when the tourists are in?" a fisherman asked.

"Just like that—except that we'll be more organized doing it. We'll go into ports, especially when the cruise ships are in, maybe even arrange to meet them out at sea."

A plant worker broke the thoughtful silence. "I'll be happy to give up fish gutting and packing, but someone's going to have to teach me to knit. I started a pair of socks for the husband, for Christmas, two years ago, and he's still waiting."

"There's enough people on White Rock who can knit, and they'll teach us," Patrick promised. "If we're successful, we may have people knitting in their homes. In fact, you could all knit at home, doing your own hours—we'll pay hourly or piece work, whatever you want—and we could use the plant just for packing and shipping."

"I could sell the *stuff* right in the store, have a *special* section with a display," said Dale. "It'd be better than the *tourist* stuff we sell now."

"We could do tours of the plant," one of the plant workers suggested.

"Yes—and finish the tour with a trip on one of the boats," a fisherman put in.

"You'll have to let us know what you think of the plan," Patrick concluded.

Tom said, "I think you know already."

Chapter Twenty-Six

Cornelia and Gladys were on the old seats in the garden, knitting scarves. They were being paid for piece work rather than hourly because, as Gladys told Tom, "We're so damn slow you'll have to pay us more than you sell them for. Anyway, we're not doing it to get rich. We're doing it for Defiant Island."

"For White Rock Island," Cornelia added.

Gladys had decided knitting would be good therapy for her still not fully recovered right side, which inhibited movement of her right arm, hand and foot. Apart from that, and apart from her failure to discover some words, for which she still substituted 'shit', she was now, a year later, fully recovered.

Cornelia was unchanged except that her vague days had grown still vaguer and more frequent. Gladys watched her carefully when she was knitting on a vague day. She'd learned to do this after Cornelia, experiencing three vague days in a row, had knitted a scarf eight feet long.

Patrick and Tom, home early from the plant, emerged from the kitchen, carrying glasses and a bottle of champagne.

"Take a break, ladies," said Tom. "We're celebrating."

"Is it my birthday?" Cornelia asked.

Gladys said, "Ha, ha."

"Just kidding."

"What are we celebrating, precious boy?" Gladys asked.

"We're celebrating the fact that we're not just breaking even this quarter. We're making a profit!"

At the end of the first quarter they were operating at a loss, as they'd expected. They'd hoped to break even by the end of the second quarter, but had to wait for the third quarter before this happened. Now, with the tourist season at its height, they were meeting their goal of making the plant self-sufficient.

As Tom poured the champagne, Patrick said, "It's the cost of the raw material that's holding us back. If we could cut down what we pay for the wool, and for bringing it from the mainland—I don't mean the fishers bringing it across, but getting it from the farms to the wharf—the plant would be something like ten per cent more profitable. If only we could raise sheep here on the island."

"Why not?" said Gladys. "They could graze on the beach. They eat rocks, don't they?"

Cornelia murmured, "That dream …" Her voice tailed away.

"Are you going vague again, ducky?" Gladys prompted.

"That dream—about Morse Cove, and Dale Senior—I told you about it …" Cornelia went on.

"The screwing dream?" said Gladys.

"… About Dale Senior's grandfather saying Morse Cove was the key to the island." Cornelia was staring at the half finished scarf in her hand. "Wool … sheep …"

"We're losing her," said Gladys. "Earth to Cornelia. Come in, Cornelia."

"The meadows … Tom, when's low tide?"

"In about two hours. Why?"

"No—not just low tide today. The real low tide. The lowest tide."

"Not for another three months. Why?"

"I think we should go to Morse Cove."

*****

They rounded the outcrop of rock and Samuel turned the fishing boat toward land. They were coming by sea because they didn't want to wait for the low tide that might permit access from the western beach to Morse

Cove, and, in any case, said Patrick, if the cove was not accessible from the sea the plan wouldn't work.

Surveying the choppy waters ahead of the boat, Tom said, "Are you sure it wouldn't be better going in through the cliffs?"

"This is the easy way," Samuel promised. "Unless you want to break your neck—then through the cliffs is a good way."

"So the choice is break your neck—or shipwreck yourself."

"That's about it. Look. It's round that shoal—see the jagged rocks sticking up when the swell goes down—and then there's a narrow channel between that outcrop and the wall of rock that separates Morse Cove from the western shore beach. It looks like it's all solid rock over there, but there's a way through, although it's not flagged. They never bothered to mark the channel in the old days. They just knew the way through."

He brought the boat closer to shore, then turned it to run parallel to the shoal.

Jeffrey, leaning over the side of the boat watching the rocks, shouted, "Samuel, hold it still. I can't see where the ridge ends. We may be on top of the shoal now."

Samuel reversed the motor and held the boat steady. He called, "Take the wheel."

Jeffrey came into the cabin. He was trembling. "I don't like this, Samuel."

Samuel repeated, "Take the wheel. Do exactly as I say." He looked at Cornelia and Gladys, who sat close in the stern, holding hands. "Girls, got your life jackets buckled and snug?"

They nodded.

He turned back to his crew. "Tom, watch the starboard. Patrick, the leeward. Shout if we get too close to the rocks. I'll watch the front." As he squeezed past Patrick, who was already leaning over the side, he muttered, "I'm not sure I can do this. My grandfather could do it, and my father knew it and told me the way through, although he never did it himself. The days when they used the cove were long gone by then."

"We'll make it," Patrick said.

Samuel lay on the prow, his eyes fixed on the water below. Without looking up, he signaled to Jeffrey to take the boat forward. Tom and Patrick strained to see into the water on each side. The boat inched forwards.

Patrick shouted, "Rocks. Right beside us."

"Put her in reverse and hold her," Samuel called.

The engine roared as Jeffrey slammed it into reverse. Samuel lay beside Patrick watching the jagged points of rock.

"My fault," Samuel muttered. "I remember now—father said the shoal curled out to sea just before you reach the channel through it. We have to turn towards open sea, then straighten up and aim at the cliff. Just when we think we're going to run into it, we throw her sideways, and sideways again straight after, else we hit another bunch of rocks that juts out from the cliff."

Samuel looked back to the cabin, pointed towards the open sea, and called, "Easy." The boat eased forwards, turning away from shore.

"Now—aim for the cliff," Samuel shouted. As Jeffrey turned the boat back, Samuel pointed to a place where the water swirled ferociously. Beyond, it seemed to pour towards land in a narrow chute, and further beyond slammed into another outcrop of rocks. "Tom, look there. Is it the end of the shoal?"

Tom leaned further over the side, peering at the swirling water. "Can't see. Wait. Yes—it's clear."

"Hard towards the cliff," Samuel roared over his shoulder to the wheelhouse, pointing to the wall of rocks.

His young partner wrenched the wheel hard over.

"Open her up or the current will carry us back onto the shoal," Samuel shouted.

Jeffrey, his eyes fixed on the rocks, reached down and eased the throttle open.

"Harder!" Samuel ordered.

With the throttle fully open, the fishing boat lurched and rolled as it fought against the current roiling landwards between the cliff and the shoal. Just as the boat seemed doomed to smash against the rocky outcrop it now faced, Samuel roared, "Hard to landward. Full throttle. Hard!"

As Jeffrey spun the wheel, Patrick, who had been hanging over the side watching for rocks, pulled himself backwards to avoid his head smashing against the rocks as the boat was thrown from side to side.

Samuel shouted, "Starboard hard—*hard*—and cut the engine."

The boat gave a final lurch as it rounded the rock outcrop and freed itself from the onrushing current in the channel. It rocked briefly before lying still and silent as it reached calm water and Jeffrey cut the engine.

Samuel sat on the prow like a figurehead, smiling in satisfaction.

Tom, leaning against the cabin, shook his head and murmured, "Is it real?"

Patrick, joining him, breathed, "It's perfect."

"Something, isn't it?" Samuel agreed.

Cornelia and Gladys, their hands still joined, gazed at the white sandy beach and narrow strip of dunes, and the meadows stretching away behind them.

Gladys said, "Is it a m … m … Shit."

"Mirage?" suggested Cornelia.

Gladys nodded. "Is it a mirage?"

"It's real. It's just like my dream."

"It's a great place for screwing."

"Gladys!"

"Well done, Samuel," said Tom.

"You can thank my dad. He remembered the channel."

"You got us through, you and Jeffrey," Patrick said. "I've never seen navigation—and nerve—like it."

"But is it realistic to expect other boats to come through there?" Tom asked.

"Oh yes—with the channel marked and after a few runs, they'd come through easy. Right, Jeffrey?"

Jeffrey, leaning from the door of the cabin, wiped his face with his sleeve. "If you say so, Samuel."

"Take us in. We'll moor over there and take the dinghy ashore."

As the boat moved slowly through the calm waters of the natural harbour, Patrick repeated, "It's perfect. A protected, accessible harbour ..."

"Accessible?" Tom queried.

"With channel markers and practice—yes. Samuel says so. Right, Samuel?"

Samuel nodded.

"And ice free?"

Samuel nodded again. "You get ice along the shore further up the coast, but not this end, and never in this bay. Water's warm here for some reason, my grandfather always said."

Patrick went on, "We have meadows, and we have boats for transport, and we have a harbour from where we can move the raw material around to the plant, so ..."

"So we raise our own sheep!" Tom finished for him. "So much for the cost of buying the wool, not to mention bringing it over from the mainland ..."

"We can cut costs by something like twenty per cent—thirty per cent! —and on top of that we'll have woolens that are produced exclusively on the island."

Gladys interrupted. "Aren't you boys jumping the gun? Shouldn't you be consulting the owner of the land about your plans?"

Patrick and Tom looked guiltily back at Cornelia and together said, "Sorry, Cornelia."

"We got excited," said Tom.

They glanced at one another and stood with heads down.

"You look sheepish," Gladys said.

She and Cornelia held on to one other as they spluttered with laughter.

"Wild things," muttered Tom, shaking his head.

When she'd recovered, Cornelia said, "Dale Senior's grandfather always said Morse Cove was the key to the island. Dale Senior never knew what he meant, although he loved this place. Perhaps his grandfather imagined something like your plan. Of course I don't mind if it's used for raising sheep."

With the boat moored, Tom and Patrick brought the dinghy alongside. Samuel and Jeffrey passed first Cornelia, then Gladys, over the side, and Tom and Patrick eased them into the dinghy.

"Why don't you drop me and I'll swim ashore if it's easier," Gladys suggested, as she dangled between the fishing boat and the dinghy while Patrick and Tom got a grip on her arms. They gently lowered her. Tom tucked her reluctant right foot under the seat, stepped back, and flipped over the side of the dinghy. Cornelia and Gladys shrieked with laughter again.

Tom's head emerged from the water. "It's warm. It's *so warm*."

"I told you," said Samuel.

Patrick rowed the dinghy ashore while Tom swam and waded in. Samuel and Jeffrey motored the fishing boat around the natural harbour, stopping every few minutes to peer into the water. Cornelia and Gladys strolled slowly up the beach toward the meadows, Cornelia relating her dream again.

Patrick had his hands in the water. "It's amazing."

Tom, wringing water from his shirt, said, "I suppose it stays warm because it's so protected. Even with the tides, much of the water in here must stay the same, so it gets—and stays—warm."

Patrick, his hand still in the water, was thoughtful. "You know, there are certain fish you can raise in warm salt water. Do you suppose we could try some new aquaculture, as well as raise sheep?"

Chapter Twenty-Seven

Tom was in Ottawa, researching experimental aquaculture, visiting scientists, and lobbying the fisheries department for approval for an experimental fish farm on White Rock Island. He'd spent three days in laboratories and offices, and was satisfied that he had the information and the support Defiant Island needed. He'd booked a flight home for the next morning. Meanwhile, as the work day ended and the sidewalks grew crowded with office workers joining the tourists, he had one more item of business to attend to. He was on Slater Street, beside the rotating doors of one of the functional, characterless tower blocks that dominated that area, inspecting the brass plates which announced the company head offices inside. He found what he was looking for: International Consolidated Enterprises. He crossed the street and sat at a sidewalk café. He punched a number on his cell phone and a woman answered. "International Consolidated."

"Mr. Conrad Wise, please."

"Mr. Wise is in conference."

At least he's here, Tom thought. "Can I call back?"

"He won't be through until six, but he'll be here in the morning. You could try him then."

"I'll do that. Thank you."

Tom thought—that means he won't be going far tonight. I'll look around while he's occupied.

He entered the building and went to the fifth floor. He stepped from the elevator, not into a hallway, as he'd expected, but into a spacious reception area. A woman sat at right angles to the elevator, a sign on her desk stating *International Consolidated Enterprises. A. Mitchell. Receptionist.* Across the room, Conrad Wise was standing with his back to Tom, talking to two men.

The receptionist said, "Can I help you?"

"Is this Cross Canada Imports?"

"One floor down."

"Sorry."

He returned to the waiting elevator, keeping his head down and his back turned as Conrad Wise looked across the room at the visitor. Tom pressed the ground floor button. Conrad Wise stepped to one side so that he could peer into the elevator. He took a few steps towards it. Tom pressed himself against the side, as far out of sight as possible.

As the doors started to close, a man carrying a briefcase hurried from an office across the room, calling, "Hold it, please."

Tom pretended not to hear or notice him. The doors were almost together when the man jammed his foot between them. Conrad Wise was behind the receptionist's desk, peering at the elevator. The doors were clamped around the man's foot.

They parted slowly and he entered, with, "Didn't you hear me?"

Tom ignored him and pressed the ground floor button again. Conrad Wise, his head craning to see behind the door, approached the elevator.

The man, seeing him, said, "Can I help you, Mr. Wise?" and moved to hold the door open.

Tom pushed him aside. The doors closed and the elevator began its descent.

"Do you mind?" the man complained.

"I'm in a hurry," Tom said.

When the elevator reached the main lobby, Tom stood back to let the man with the briefcase exit first. Then he followed him. The man walked fifty yards down Slater Street before turning into a side street, where he crossed the road and entered a parking garage that rose several levels.

Tom waited for him to disappear inside, then sauntered to the attendant's kiosk. "My girl friend told me to meet her at her car but I don't know where she's parked. Are there assigned spaces?"

"Not by name, unless she's real important, just by company. Who's she work for?"

"International Consolidated."

"Level Four. All of it. Stairs are over there. Elevator there." The kiosk attendant called after Tom. "Hey—most of them are gone."

"I'll take a look."

Tom took the stairs to level four. He peered from the stairwell. The office closing rush seemed to have abated and there was no-one around. Only a few cars remained. The elevator was at the other end of the level. He guessed that the International Consolidated executives would park near it. He walked quickly across, looking back at the stairwell and ahead at the elevator, ready to hide behind a pillar or one of the few cars if people or vehicles appeared. A dozen parking spaces near the elevator were marked with titles. Tom looked along them. He saw Executive Assistant on two and muttered, "Bastards." He walked on until he came to the space marked Chairman. The car with the tinted windows was there. Tom wondered how much the cleaning bill had been for the vomit left by the executive assistants after their forced boat ride with the White Rock fishermen. He looked around again. He was alone. He glanced at his watch: four-thirty. The receptionist on the telephone had said Conrad Wise was in conference until six o' clock. Was she telling the truth, or was she just screening an unwanted caller? The elevator rattled. It stopped at level four. Tom ran to the nearest vehicle, half way back towards the stairwell, and crouched behind it. A security guard walked from the elevator and began a circuit of the parking area. At the same time a man and woman emerged from the stairwell. They exchanged a few words with the security guard before the woman approached the car behind which Tom was hiding. The man and the security guard walked to a car on the other side of the floor, where they continued to talk. Tom, squeezed between the front of the car and the wall, crouched as low as he could. The woman climbed into the car and reversed, leaving Tom exposed. He froze, his eyes fixed on the security guard and the man, still talking, and the woman at the wheel. She looked behind her as she reversed, and then quickly across at the men as the car moved forward. She waved, looking in their direction. They saluted her in return as she drove past, without looking in Tom's direction. He wondered whether to run or to freeze. He chose the latter, sinking even lower to the ground. The man opened his car door and climbed in. The security guard shouted something. Tom tensed, ready to flee, gauging the distance to the stairwell. He could outrun them, he was sure. The security guard laughed and slapped his hand on the roof in farewell. The man drove away. The security guard sauntered after the car and turned into the stairwell. Tom rose shakily and returned to the elevator, which was still at level four. He'd intended to wait in the International Consolidated parking area, but decided it was too risky, with so few hiding places, and people still leaving, and the security guard doing his rounds. He took his fish gutting knife from his pocket and stuck the rear tire of Conrad Wise's car before getting into the elevator. At ground level he emerged casually and looked around. The woman's car was at the kiosk and the attendant was dealing with her. The man's car arrived behind her. Tom strolled from the parking garage and returned to Slater Street. At the sidewalk café he ordered a coffee and unfolded the *Ottawa Star*. He fixed his eyes on the door of the office building across the street. Half an hour later he ordered a second coffee and a sandwich. Another half hour passed and he drank a third cup. It was getting dark.

And it was six o' clock.

He waited another half hour, drank another cup of coffee, and was about to temporarily abandon his quest, surmising that there was another exit from the office tower, or another route to the parking garage, when Conrad Wise emerged. He was flanked by the two men with whom he'd been in conversation in the office. They stood talking for a few minutes before parting company, one man heading away down Slater Street, the chairman and the other man walking together towards the side street. Tom thought: One down. He crossed the road and followed them. At the car parking garage they entered the elevator. Tom vaulted the low wall of level one and made it to the stairwell without the kiosk attendant seeing him. He ran to level four and peered from the stairwell. He was faster than the elevator. The level was deserted. He ran to a pillar in the centre of the floor and pinned himself against it. The elevator light signaled arrival at level four. Conrad Wise and his companion emerged, spoke briefly, and went to their cars. They bent to unlock their doors. Tom held his breath, frozen. The man drove away. Conrad Wise reversed, stopped, reversed again, pulled forwards. The door opened. He stood with his hands on his hips looking in disgust at the slashed rear tire.

Tom left his hiding place and approached Conrad Wise silently from behind.

Chapter Twenty-Eight

Tom idled the engine outside the channel, waiting while one of the fishing boats motored through, taking a load of wool around the coast to the plant. Patrick sat with him in the stern of the sixteen foot dory, Cornelia and Gladys, bulky in life jackets and Defiant Island sweaters, in the middle. They'd brought a picnic. The fishing boat passed by and Tom steered the dory through, confident in the difficult waters through practice and with the help of the channel markers Samuel had installed. As they entered the cove, the scene that opened before them, although they knew what to expect, was still a surprise.

It was a year since their first visit to Morse Cove, and Patrick and Tom wondered with pleasure at the success of their enterprise. The Defiant Island plant had its own flock of two dozen sheep, cared for by the plant workers, who took turns being shepherds, living for a week at a time in the small, comfortable cabin they'd built in the shelter of the cliff. Tom had asked for volunteers to act as shepherds, and had offered to pay time and a half for the week, thinking it would be an unpopular chore. However, the plant workers turned down the offer of extra pay for the work, and swamped him with requests for what they called the shepherd stint. He now had a waiting list of six months. The former fishing boats took the wool from the cove to the plant, and from there left for the mainland and the eastern States, delivering Defiant Island woolen goods, and mooring for several days at a time in the harbours at Boston, Portland, Halifax and Saint John, meeting cruise ships whenever they could. Twice in the past year cruise ships, which were not stopping at any of these ports, nevertheless moored off White Rock Island, while the Defiant Island fishing boats, dwarfed by the huge visiting vessels, moored alongside so that visitors could come aboard and choose sweaters and scarves and hats. Tom already had twelve visits lined up for the following season, four of them new shipping lines. Tourists had come in increasing numbers to White Rock Island to visit the plant, and to stay on the island. Gladstone had made extra ferry runs to avoid lengthy line ups at the wharf on White Rock Island and on Deer Isle. Two new bed and breakfasts had opened near the plant. Dale and Carol-Ann organised walking tours to the western beach, from which visitors returned in rapture and wonder.

Meanwhile, on one side of Morse Cove, yellow striped flounder were being raised in two small aquaculture sites. Tom had secured federal government approval to experiment with raising the fish after government scientists had confirmed that the extraordinarily warm water made it suitable for that species. There was limited demand for such a specialised fish, but consumers and restaurants were willing to pay high prices for the comparatively rare food, giving the Defiant Island plant a good return for its investment. Moreover, it kept the aquaculture operation small and manageable, which was necessary while they established and expanded the woolen business. Samuel and Jeffrey took the first thousand packets of frozen Defiant Island flounder to the mainland, delivering eight hundred of them to previously established markets, and the remainder to restaurant owners who contacted them on board as soon as they heard that the Defiant Island boat was in port.

Cornelia saw with satisfaction what she imagined Dale Senior's grandfather had foreseen, despite the tragedy that had driven his family from the cove: a self-sufficient community thriving in a locale as peaceful and picturesque as anything she could imagine. She liked to think that Dale Senior himself, like his grandfather, had envisaged something like this, and she held conversations with him whenever she visited Morse Cove.

While Cornelia and Gladys strolled to the top of the beach and settled themselves for their picnic, Tom went to check on the aquaculture site and Patrick the sheep operation. He found the shepherd in the back meadow, near the cliffs that bounded Morse Cove, rebuilding a stone wall which had partly collapsed. As Patrick expected, everything was going well, and he soon began a leisurely stroll back through the meadows towards the beach. He stopped on the way and sat on one of the old stone walls. He pulled a crumpled paper from his pocket, opened it and smoothed it. He read it for the tenth time. It was a letter from Penelope. They hadn't met for three years. Now she wanted to visit, to see him again. He reflected on the irony of her contacting him now, when he had found the emotional peace and independence—on White Rock Island, and especially in Morse Cove—that he had sought for so long. He wondered whether seeing her would destroy his peace—or complete it.

He began a reply: *Dear Penelope: It would be lovely to see you. Can you come to White Rock Island? It's impossible for me to be away at the moment, with the Defiant Island business expanding fast—faster than we anticipated—and the aquaculture experiment just bearing fruit (fish, I should say). May I lay down a condition—a pleasant one, I think—for your visit? Will you agree to spend a week here, where I'm writing this, in Morse Cove? I'll be the shepherd for the week, and you will be my companion. Our only other companions will be the aquaculture workers, who come in by boat every morning, and the sheep, the flounder, the eagles and the gulls. (There may be a seal or two around, as well. They're anxious to sample the flounder, but have been unsuccessful so far.) The way in, by sea, is exciting but safe, now that we've marked the channel and practiced maneuvering the boats in and out. I have to warn you, also, that it's isolated— your cell phone will not work because of the high cliffs surrounding the cove—but it is breathtakingly beautiful and peaceful. Call me on my cell phone—it'll have to be when I'm not in the cove—and let me know if you still want to come. I'm hoping you do. Your—Patrick.*

Chapter Twenty-Nine

Patrick was in Ottawa to talk with his financial manager about the performance of one of Given and Associates' business interests.

When he arrived in his office, Peggy said, "Mike Soames called in yesterday. He said you'd asked him to continue monitoring the activities of International Consolidated."

"Right."

"He left this for you, and he said had you heard about Conrad Wise."

She handed him a copy of an e-mail from Conrad Wise to Bernard Appleby. It was marked Confidential.

"How does he get this stuff?" Patrick murmured.

"Don't ask," said Peggy.

Patrick read: "This memo, and the donation to follow, will confirm the continued support of International Consolidated for your Progressive Democratic Alliance, and for your own political ambitions in the province, as well as beyond it, at the federal level.

"The support, as you will understand from our earlier conversations, is not quite unqualified, coming, as it does, with the understanding that your government will continue and intensify its sensible and overdue drive to rationalize spending so that the province in your stewardship may become debt free, subsidy free, and financially self-sustaining, with corporate taxation at acceptable levels, thereby establishing itself as an area worthy of our future investment.

"We at International Consolidated are particularly interested, as you know, in your efforts to rationalize the population landscape of the province. Rural and isolated settlements, we feel, must come to understand that they cannot continue to be subsidized by the rest of the province and, indeed, through transfer payments, by the rest of the country, albeit indirectly. Therefore we endorse your policy statements—not yet fully acted upon, I should point out—that commit the Progressive Democratic Alliance to forsake the worthy and well intentioned, but also misguided and doomed, attempts of former governments to sustain an illogical and outdated rural way of life in the province, and to press ahead with the actions—drastic, perhaps, but necessary—as outlined in your Policy and Action Paper 15463.

"Give my warm regards to your father. I look forward to seeing you at the Empire Club in the near future."

Patrick shook his head as he read.

"Bad?" Peggy asked.

"Could be. What did Mike mean when he said had we heard about Conrad Wise?"

"He got beaten up—badly. Nose broken, ribs cracked."

"Good. When did that happen?"

"A couple of months ago."

Patrick said, "Oh," then, thoughtfully, "Oh."

Peggy nodded. "Yes, that's when Tom was in town."

"Hmmm. Do they know who did it?"

"Conrad Wise says he has no enemies, and the police say they have no leads."

"Good."

Chapter Thirty

Tom and Samuel travelled to the capital to meet the Minister of Municipalities, Housing and Infrastructure. Cornelia and Gladys accompanied them, representing the island community through their status as the oldest residents.

Gorman Grant greeted the delegation when they arrived at his department on the third floor of the King Square government offices. He was a big, gaunt, grey man, the square mass of his pallid face cadaverous with its tightly drawn skin and sunken eyes, its looming forehead. His thin grey hair was spread in oily tendrils across his pate and his bony hands clasped and unclasped as he spoke, his thick fingers intertwining. He waved aside his receptionist and himself ushered them through an ante room into his office. He fussed over Cornelia and Gladys. He offered coffee and biscuits, which the receptionist brought.

Cornelia murmured, "So kind."

They sat in deep leather chairs, a coffee table between them.

Tom said, "You're from Cape Sable Island, up north—right?"

The minister nodded.

"Then you know what island living is all about."

The minister nodded again.

"So—just where is your government coming from, with this drive to close down the island communities in the province?"

Gorman Grant rose, coffee cup in hand, and crossed to the window. He looked down at the traffic on King Street. Sighed. Sipped his coffee. Returned to the group, closing the door on the way.

"I expect you want me to be honest."

"That'd be nice," said Tom.

"And unusual for a politician—you don't have to say it." He sighed again. "I'll level with you, but I'm speaking in confidence. I trust you never to use anything I say against me."

"How would we do that?" Tom asked.

"I mean politically." He looked at each of them in turn.

Samuel said, "We're not into politics. You know that."

"That's why I'm levelling with you." He added, "I'm talking personally, not politically." He paused. Sipped his coffee again.

Gladys said, "Spill it, Gorman."

"I was brought up on an island, like you, an island I've always loved, that I still love, where my parents and grandparents lived all their lives. I went into politics because I thought I could make conditions better for the rural areas of the province, and especially for the islands. When I looked for a political party to join, this one, governing now—and set to govern for a long time, you know …"

They nodded, knowing the strength of Bernard Appleby's Progressive Democratic Alliance, which had been returned to power with an increased majority a month previously.

Gorman Grant went on, "… When I joined them, some years ago, they made much noise about the rural communities, something that neither of the other parties seemed to care about. They expressed much concern for their future, although, I realize now, that concern was expressed in neither positive nor negative terms, and they were careful not to offer support to back up their concerns. They still make the noise, but I'm afraid it's all negative now. The new leader at the time, now the premier, of course, cared—still cares—very much for the finances of the province, as he has to. But he cares for them to such an extent that everything else becomes secondary."

"Including the rural communities and the islands," Tom added.

Gorman Grant nodded. "Now I have a choice. Do I abandon the party, and my career? Sacrifice both for the sake of my personal ideology?

Or—do I stay, and get myself into a position where I can, at least, do my best to ameliorate some of the consequences of the government's—ah—neglect of the rural areas. That is what I am trying to do, and as Minister of Municipalities, Housing and Infrastructure, I may be able to soften the effects of the premier's drive to … well, to quote him, to rationalize the rural communities of the province."

"Which is double speak for destroy them," said Tom. "By the way, we met your premier on White Rock Island a year or two after he was elected. He didn't impress us."

"I know. I have to say that you didn't impress him, either."

"Good."

Gorman Grant smiled. "I understand." His face grew serious. "I also know what you have accomplished with the Defiant Island plant. It is similar to what they have done on Cape Sable Island, with the tourism and the fish plant there, as you know. You, and they, deserve every success. If I had my way I would pour money into your island and into all the islands …"

"We don't need government money. We just need to be left alone."

"You need government money to run your ferry, your wharfs, your school, your medical services …"

"So does every community."

"But the cost of servicing rural communities is six times that of the urban centers, and of the islands—twenty times." He held up his hand to stop the protests of Tom and Samuel, and repeated, *"Twenty times.* Is it worth it? I say—yes. The rural communities and the islands are an essential part of the maritime culture of our province. For me, they *are* our province. But the premier, and his supporters, they say—no."

Gladys started, "The premier can go and f …. f … f …"

"Now, Gladys," Cornelia cautioned.

"Shit," Gladys finished.

"I've told the premier that, although not quite in those words. But I am in a minority. I risk losing my influence—my position—if I voice my protest too vehemently. So I stay, and I try to fight quietly on your behalf."

He saw them to the door and thanked them for coming. He said sorrowfully, "I am an islander, like you. I know your concerns. I will do my best, but I have to warn you—that may not be enough."

Tom said, "We appreciate your honesty."

Gorman Grant said, "I am so sorry."

*****

Less than a month later, the government announced that all ferry services between the mainland and islands with a population of less than five hundred would be terminated. River ferries would remain only if they daily carried more than a hundred passengers who were on their way to work and whose journey otherwise would take more than an hour.

Gorman Grant agreed with an interviewer, "Yes, essentially we are preserving these as commuter ferries."

Existing river and island ferries, the government said, could be purchased for a nominal amount and could be run as private enterprises.

As soon as he heard the news, Patrick waited for the ferry at the wharf and asked Gladstone if he'd like to run White Rock Island Coastal Services. It would be a subsidiary of Defiant Island.

Chapter Thirty-One

Patrick started his week as shepherd of Morse Cove alone. The Deer Isle airstrip was closed for two days because of fog and by the time Penelope's chartered flight managed to land, and she had come out to White Rock on the ferry, Gladstone serving her coffee with a flourish, it was too late to sail around to the cove. Patrick had arranged for her to come out the next morning. She stayed the night with Cornelia, Gladys and Tom, and early the next morning Tom took her to the wharf, where Samuel and Jeffrey, who were on duty at the aquaculture site that day, waited.

She stood tensely between the fishermen, enclosed and steadied by them as the boat made its way through the swirling waters of the channel.

Just before they made the final turn into the cove, Samuel said, "Close your eyes. Open them when I say."

Penelope closed her eyes. When, on Samuel's instruction, she opened them, as the boat reached the calm waters of the harbour, and the meadows and beach of Morse Cove lay before them, she looked from the scene to Samuel and Jeffrey and back with wide open eyes. Samuel and Jeffrey grinned, sharing her delight, and happy to be reminded anew of their own pride in the beauty and prosperity of the cove.

She breathed, "Am I dreaming this? Is it real?" She laughed aloud. "Is it a movie set?"

"It's real," Samuel assured her, beaming. "Something, isn't it? Look— there's Patrick, on the fish cages."

Penelope leaned out of the cabin. The breeze swept her hair behind her in a translucent, swirling stream. She waved. Patrick untied a rowing boat from the cages and rowed towards them.

"Penelope, you made it. 'Morning, Samuel, Jeffrey."

Samuel called, "Special cargo today." He held Penelope's hand as she climbed down to Patrick's boat, where she sat facing Patrick as he rowed to the beach, while Samuel and Jeffrey went on to the aquaculture site.

"You look like a fisherman—like Samuel and Jeffrey."

He was wearing dirty jeans and a gray roll neck sweater, muddy from rescuing a lamb that had somehow managed to scramble over the rocks to the beach, and carrying it back to its distressed mother.

"You look the same as always … spectacular."

Penelope said, "Oh …," blushing, looking down. She received compliments all over the world as she went about her engagements, fielding them graciously and warmly and without embarrassment. Only when Patrick complimented her did she feel such a jolt of pleasure that she blushed. It was as if they were back in their childhood days, stumbling between the time when compliments between them had been unnecessary and the time when the awareness they revealed heralded friendship giving way awkwardly to love. She'd never quite made the adjustment.

She rushed on, "You look well."

"You, too."

He beached the boat and took her hand as she jumped out. He held it, looking steadily at her. "No cell phone—right?"

She shook her head, her hair floating in the breeze from the water. "Right. You said it wouldn't work here, anyway."

"It won't. And you're staying for the week—right?"

"Right."

"No interruptions. No rushing away."

"No."

He took her other hand.

After a moment, he said, "I have to work."

"I know. Can I help? Tell me what to do."

They spent the day tending the sheep, maintaining and rebuilding the old stone walls that divided the meadows, and helping on the aquaculture site, feeding and culling fish. Samuel and Jeffrey sailed out in the late afternoon, leaving Patrick and Penelope alone in Morse Cove. Patrick cooked supper in the shepherd's cabin. They took their meal outside, eating fast on the beach before the breeze cooled the food. Patrick said he wanted to take a last look at the sheep before it grew dark. They had a habit of getting themselves trapped in a deep gully where rain and snow melt ran from the cliffs. Penelope walked through the meadows with him. When Patrick had finished his check of the sheep, they sat in the upper meadow, under the cliff, watching the last of the light filter from the cove. They wandered down through the meadows, along the beach, and back through the meadows to the cabin under the cliff. Patrick lit the lamps and filled the woodstove. They sat each side of the table, their hands resting on it, clasped together.

"I've given up my career," Penelope said suddenly. "I'm retired."

Patrick realized he hadn't seen her face on a magazine cover or on television for some months. "When?"

"A few months ago. I still have some engagements to do, but I just told Don—no more. He says I'm taking a sabbatical. I say I'm retired."

"Do you mean … Are you here to stay?"

"If you want me to stay."

"Of course I want you to stay. Should we … will we … get married?"

"I hope so."

"Are you sure you won't regret giving up your career? I've never wanted you to do that."

"I'm not giving it up entirely, although I'll have to in a year or two, anyway, simply because I'm getting too old for it. I still have engagements, booked from way back, and I'd like to do the occasional show, if Don can arrange it. But I want to spend more time—*all* the time—here, with you."

"Why?"

"Don't ask silly questions, Patrick."

"I mean—what changed your mind?"

"I think it was seeing you on White Rock Island, with Cornelia and Gladys and Tom, all of you like a family."

"Rather a strange family."

"A family, all the same. I had my career, and that seemed … not enough, somehow."

"The same thing happened to me when I came here. But I don't spend all my time on White Rock Island. I'm still in Ottawa quite often for the company, and I still have my apartment there."

"We could share it. I could work from there. It's not like the old days when I had to be in Toronto."

"Of course. We'll have the apartment, and we'll have the house here on the island."

"But—what about Cornelia and Gladys and Tom? The four of you seem so happy in your house. I'd feel like an intruder."

"You'll be welcomed. Anyway, Cornelia and Gladys couldn't live alone."

"You'd better not tell them that. They'll move out just to prove you're wrong."

*****

At the end of the week, in the early morning, Patrick and Penelope waited on the beach for Samuel's fishing boat to arrive in Morse Cove. He was bringing the shepherd who would replace Patrick, and supplies for the shepherd's cabin, and would take Patrick and Penelope back around the island. Penelope had booked her charter flight for that afternoon. Patrick wanted to fly her to Toronto in the Beechcraft, but when she pressed him about work commitments at the plant, and he confessed he had lots to do after spending the week in Morse Cove, she told him no.

Samuel arrived without Patrick's replacement. He shouted from the fishing boat, "He says he's real sorry. His mother was taken ill and he took her over to the hospital on Deer Isle. He'll be out later today, as soon as he gets back."

Patrick was rowing out to the boat. He told Penelope, "Sorry. I'll have to stay."

"Of course." She reached forwards and squeezed his hand as he leaned towards her with the oars.

"Samuel, can you and Jeffrey take Penelope round and put her on the ferry, and arrange a ride up to the airfield?"

Samuel grinned broadly. "We'll look after her."

Jeffrey tied the skiff to the fishing boat. Penelope climbed aboard, taking Samuel's and Jeffrey's offered hands. They loaded the supplies into the skiff, then Patrick climbed up and hugged Penelope. Jeffrey looked down. Samuel grinned.

"See you soon," Patrick promised.

"Yes. I'll call tonight."

They pulled apart. A chill wind whipped suddenly off the water. Penelope shivered involuntarily.

Patrick said, "You're freezing."

"I'll be all right," Penelope said, releasing his hands and pulling her jacket close around her.

Samuel reached into a corner of the cabin. "Here. I always keep a few in case tourists are around." He pulled a Defiant Island sweater from its plastic wrapping and held it out, shyly. "I think it'll fit."

Penelope held the sweater against her. "This is one of the sweaters you make?"

They all nodded.

"But it's beautiful. I had no idea. I haven't seen one before. I thought ..."

"You thought they were just tourist souvenirs," Patrick finished for her. "They are, in a way. But they're a bit more than that."

"It's beautiful," Penelope repeated, casting her jacket aside and pulling it on. "How does it look?"

Samuel beamed.

Jeffrey glanced quickly at Penelope and looked down.

Patrick said, "Spectacular."

Penelope said, "Oh …," and blushed.

Samuel said, "Now you're our Defiant Island girl."

The wind raced coolly across the water again, riffling it and sending tendrils of spray into the air.

"Wind's picking up," Samuel said. "We'd best get going. It'll be choppy."

Patrick and Penelope hugged again.

"Put yourself between us now," Samuel ordered her.

Penelope stood between Samuel and Jeffrey, warmed and held steady by them. Patrick climbed into the skiff and pulled away. The fishing boat turned towards the channel, Penelope looking over her shoulder, waving.

Chapter Thirty-Two

In Montreal, Penelope wore her Defiant Island sweater for a charity appearance. She wore it to feel closer to her friends on White Rock Island, and especially to Patrick, and because she appreciated and enjoyed the quality of its wool and its working. It was her first appearance since she had announced her retirement and many photographs were taken. Soon after that the pictures started to appear in the fashion magazines. *Paris Elan* contacted Don and begged for one more cover picture. He in turn begged Penelope to accept. She did so, as a favour to the art editor of the magazine, who ten years before had been one of the first to promote her career by featuring her picture on their cover. It was the same art editor who insisted at the shoot that Penelope wear the Defiant Island sweater, which she was glad to do. The day it appeared, the magazine was flooded with calls about the sweater. In the next issue they ran a story about how it had been made on a tiny island in Passamaquoddy Sound, with wool taken from sheep also raised on the island, and knitted by islanders working in a converted fish plant. Readers were enchanted and sent enquiries to the magazine asking how they could buy Defiant Island goods. *Paris Elan* contacted Tom at the plant. They wanted one thousand Defiant Island sweaters to offer in a special promotion through the magazine. When the offer appeared, the magazine immediately received over five thousand requests for sweaters. Tom put on an extra shift and shipped more sweaters.

Meanwhile, in an interview for television, Penelope told the story of how she had acquired her Defiant Island sweater, to ward off the early morning chill on a fishing boat sailing around a remote island through dangerous waters, and how one of the fishermen, Samuel, had christened her their Defiant Island girl.

"Really, I'm no longer a girl, and it's not exactly politically correct," she explained. "But I don't mind. It sounds right to me."

Don was immediately swamped with calls for appearances by the Defiant Island girl.

Penelope called Patrick's cell phone but received no answer. She called the plant and was told that Patrick had gone to Morse Cove for a few days and that Tom was on the mainland. She called Cornelia and Gladys, who listened with heads close together, sharing the phone, taking turns to speak.

Penelope said she was in a predicament. On the one hand, she explained, she wanted to cut down on her appearances and spend more time—most of her time—on White Rock Island, with all her friends there, and with Patrick. She didn't mention that they were to be married, not knowing whether he'd told them, and not wanting to cause them worry about the house. On the other hand, she said, she knew her appearances were helping to sell Defiant Island goods ...

"And how, ducky," Gladys put in.

... And she knew from talking to Patrick and Tom, and to Gladys and Cornelia, how important the success of the plant was to the island. So— should she commit to the appearances, did they think?

Gladys said go for it.

Cornelia said they'd talk to Patrick when he came home and get him to call.

By the time he telephoned, after staying in Morse Cove to help with a twenty four hour watch on a new batch of flounder, Don had accepted a dozen engagements on her behalf. Patrick was philosophical about it, his business self, excited and happy to see the plant such a success, warring with his personal self, afraid that Penelope would slip back into the way of life that had created such distance between them.

Tom was enthusiastic. With orders pouring in from all over the world, he'd set up new distribution methods and had kept the extra shift on at the plant.

Chapter Thirty-Three

At the height of Defiant Island's success, the government announced that White Rock Island School would close at the end of the year. There were not enough pupils, the government argued, to justify keeping it open. The province could not afford it. The per capita cost of educating the island children was thirty times that of educating children in larger centres. The White Rock Island children would have to travel to the school on Deer Isle. The government furthermore regretted that parents would have to bear the cost of the children's daily travel on the recently privatized ferry. It was one of the consequences of choosing to live in an isolated area.

Gladstone promptly announced that the children would travel free, courtesy of Defiant Island and White Rock Island Coastal Services.

The school's parent council invited the premier to their monthly meeting in order to voice their protest. To their surprise, he agreed to attend.

Usually the council met in the home of one of its members, but anticipating a larger than usual crowd, the venue was changed to the community hall. The meeting was set for seven o' clock, coinciding with the premier's arrival on the seven o' clock ferry.

At eight o' clock he still hadn't arrived and the crowd waited restlessly while the members of the parent council, sitting at a table at the front of the hall, conducted their routine business.

Cornelia, in the front row beside Gladys, whispered, "Do you suppose he's forgotten?"

"Not everyone's as barmy as you," said Gladys. "More likely he thinks he's too important to arrive on time. Thinks it's our privilege to wait for him."

The premier arrived on the next ferry, at eight thirty, and was immediately invited to address the meeting.

Bernard Appleby started by apologizing for his late arrival. It was caused, he explained, first by the ferry crew's failure to delay their departure from Deer Isle for just a few minutes until he arrived at the slip, despite knowing he was scheduled to travel on the ferry leaving at six fifteen, then by the failure of Coastal Services to provide another crossing until the one that had eventually brought him to the island. He suggested that the islanders put pressure on Coastal Services to provide more crossings. The residents had the right, he said, to receive efficient and regular ferry service.

Their children also had rights, he went on. Paramount amongst them was the right to a good education. This had traditionally been difficult to provide because of a persistent culture on the island of, not ignorance, he wouldn't say that, but of … call it non-learning. The children of White Rock Island, and of other isolated and rural communities, imbued with this culture from birth, tended to scorn education, leaving school as soon as they could in order to apply themselves to the simple, traditional tasks of fishing, agriculture and forestry, traditional tasks that were fast becoming extinct. What would children raised in such a culture do when the traditional tasks were no longer an option? Theirs was a culture which celebrated simplicity and unsophistication in the name of preserving the rural and island way of life, but which in fact served to stunt opportunity and breed dependence on government support and subsidy. Those days, and this culture, he said, had to end. The province was deeply in debt and could no longer pour money into hopeless and helpless causes, be they single mothers, people who refused to work, artsy organizations catering to their privileged and pretentious friends … or people who chose to live anachronistically in isolated communities. No-one disputed anyone's right to live where he or she liked, but the people who had elected his government, the ordinary people of the province, had clearly stated that they disputed the right of anyone to enjoy a free ride at the tax payers' expense.

A stunned, dismayed silence greeted the premier's speech. When someone in the crowd called out that the island was independent, and had no need of government money, Bernard Appleby quoted from documents provided by his Minister of Finance. The island had indeed received money, he said. The people of White Rock Island had enjoyed free ferry travel for the best part of one hundred years. They had been offered education, even if they had chosen not to take full advantage of it, which was not only free but was also significantly more expensive to provide than anywhere else in the province. Their medical clinic was built and staffed by the government at a per capita cost that was, again, exorbitant compared with costs elsewhere. And what about the supply of power? What about family services and children's services? What about the construction and maintenance of their roads? They were all outrageously expensive.

What about the money brought into the province by the Defiant Island plant, someone called out. White Rock Island was paying its way.

Bernard Appleby grew sorrowful. He lauded the efforts of the islanders to make Defiant Island a success. The cottage industries of the province were a proud legacy of its past. But—pay their way? He was afraid not. Were they aware that the fish plant in which Defiant Island operated, when it was set up in 1920, was built entirely with provincial government money? Did they remember that it had been subsidized for the first five years of its existence? Did they know that the government had pumped millions of dollars into Clinch and Son Fisheries to keep it going for the last ten years before it was taken over by Mr. Given's organization?

"Clinch and *Son* may have needed government *money*," Dale protested. "But Defiant Island hasn't received any and doesn't *need* any."

The premier shook his head sadly. He asked—how much did it cost Defiant Island to build the plant? Nothing. How much did Defiant Island pay for it? He guaranteed that Mr. Given, being an astute businessman, had paid a fraction of what it was worth. Defiant Island, then, far from being independent of government assistance, was operating in a plant in effect built by, and in large part maintained by, the government of the province. He didn't begrudge them using it, he added; he just wanted them to be clear about their indebtedness to the government and to the ordinary people of the province. Moreover, while it was true that the federal government funded wharfs and lighthouses and offshore buoys and air and sea rescue services, nevertheless the provision of all of these impacted the province's finances negatively because a like amount was deducted from the province's equalization payment. So, once again, White Rock Island enjoyed government largesse at the expense of the ordinary people of the province. This was to say nothing of the cost of building and maintaining the island's harbour, and the ferry landings on both sides of the channel, and the inshore buoys and channel markers, all of which benefited the Defiant Island operation.

In sum, Bernard Appleby concluded, the island's annual subsidy presently totaled—he looked around the audience—over five million dollars a year, which represented about fifty thousand dollars per resident. In more prosperous times the ordinary people of the province had been happy to subsidize their rural and isolated neighbours. Now, in these days of fiscal restraint, they expected them to live sensibly and rationally, in larger centres, where services could be more economically provided.

The premier urged them all to take his message to heart and to do their part not only to rehabilitate the financial state of the province, but also to bring the province and its economy and its society into the twenty first century.

When the premier left the hall, he found there were no more ferry trips that day. Gladstone explained that they had engine trouble.

Chapter Thirty-Four

The next provincial minister to visit the island was Gorman Grant. Since the premier's visit, Gladstone had been on the lookout for politicians. He'd enjoyed stranding the premier on the island. After his forced overnight stay, Bernard Appleby had eventually called for a helicopter the next morning when the ferry experienced another inexplicable bout of engine trouble. Gladstone was looking forward to inconveniencing more politicians. He scrutinized Gorman Grant carefully as the minister parked his car at the top of the ferry slip and approached the ramp on foot. He stopped him half way down it.

"I've seen your picture in the newspaper. If you're a politician, you might want to walk back up the ramp, because you're not welcome on this ferry." As he spoke, Gladstone continued to inspect Gorman Grant. His face was familiar in the half remembered way of public faces, as if their reality was greater in transmitted image than in actuality, but his disheveled clothes and haggard face seemed out of place. Gladstone's sympathy superceded his suspicion and he added, "Are you feeling all right? Do you need help?"

"I am a politician. Gorman Grant. I understand how you feel about the provincial government and I don't blame you for it. I've hesitated to come here, but Samuel and Tom, with Ms. Cronk and Mrs. Morse, took the trouble to come and see me, and now I've come to see them. That's if you'll let me on your ferry."

Gladstone waved him on. He radioed Dale. "I've got a Gorman Grant on board. Says he's a politician and he's coming to see Tom and Samuel, and Gladys and Cornelia. I was going to bar politicians from the ferry, but this Gorman seems different."

"Samuel's in Morse Cove. Gladys and Cornelia are here in the store. I'll send them over to the plant and I'll call Tom."

Tom watched from his office window as the ferry came in. He saw Gorman Grant walk up the ramp and stop outside the plant, on the spot where Patrick had been attacked. Tom wondered whether this was another attack, of a different kind. He expected his visitor to enter, but Gorman Grant stayed where he was, gazing around, at the ferry, the fishing boats, the store. Tom noted that Gladstone, from the deck of his ferry, was also watching the politician carefully. He saw Gladstone take a few steps towards him, as if to approach him, then hesitate and stop.

As Cornelia and Gladys crossed the road outside the store and headed for the plant, Gladys said, "There's Gorman."

"Gorman?" said Cornelia.

"Gorman Grant, who we went to see in Fredericton—remember?"

"He gave us coffee and biscuits. Gorman Grant—from Cape Sable Island."

"Right. Well now he's come to see us."

"That's nice of him."

Cornelia and Gladys approached the politician.

Gorman Grant didn't see them coming. His hands were clasped in front of him, his shoulders sagged, and his head hung down.

Tom strode from the plant, saw him, and hesitated. Was he meditating? Praying? He moved forward, into his visitor's field of vision, but received no response.

He said quietly, "Mr. Grant? Gorman?"

Gorman Grant looked up. Tom was shocked by how he had changed since their meeting in Fredericton. Then he had looked tired and tense. Now he looked exhausted, his eyes dull, the skin around them puffy, his face sallow. His right eye fluttered.

Tom asked, "What can I do for you, Gorman?"

Gladys, arriving with Cornelia, echoed Gladstone. "Are you all right, Gorman? Do you need help?"

Gorman Grant shook his head. He sniffed twice. "No. Well, yes, I do need help, but not from you—thank you—or from anyone I can think of."

He fell silent again. Just as Tom was about to prompt him, he drew himself up and spoke, at first as if he was making a statement to the media, but quickly relapsing into a musing tone.

"I am no longer Minister of Municipalities. I am no longer minister of anything. I have resigned. It will come out in the news later today." He smiled bleakly. "I made a bit of a scene in the House this morning. You'll hear about that in the news, too. If I hadn't resigned, I'd have been kicked out."

"What's going on, Gorman?" said Gladys.

"What's going on is this, and I'm sickened by it." He produced a paper from an inner pocket. "This is the announcement that's scheduled for release tonight. The premier may release it earlier after my outburst this morning. It means the end of rural life in the province, and the end of the small islands."

"What do you mean?" Tom asked.

"Read it and you will understand. I came to see you because you've been on my mind since you and your friends came to see me, and I so admire what you're doing here—what you have been doing, because it will have to end, you know. I wish the influence I boasted to you about, the influence to ameliorate what the government was planning, had been greater. In fact it was insignificant. I was in my position as a publicity ploy." He recited bitterly, "See the Minister of Municipalities who's presiding over the destruction of rural and island life. Well he's one of you, he's from an isolated island community, and if he agrees to it, then it must be okay." He thrust the paper at Tom. "Here. I'm truly sorry. I'm on my way back to Cape Sable. I'm going to try and live—survive—there, but I suspect I'll have as little success as you will on White Rock Island."

He turned away, turned back and offered his hand in turn to each of them, hesitantly. As the islanders shook it, Gorman Grant mumbled, "I'm so sorry."

He walked slowly down to the ferry, from where Gladstone still watched.

With Cornelia and Gladys on each side of him, Tom held the paper and read aloud:

For Immediate Release:

Because of the financial state of the Province, which from the start of our mandate has proved to be much worse than this Government had anticipated, after years of profligate spending by former governments, we are forced to take drastic action to avoid the Province being downgraded to the humiliating and financially disastrous I.O.C. (Invest Only with Caution) category on the Briggs and Toombs Index, which would effectively label the Province a bad financial risk, thereby at best inhibiting, at worst prohibiting, future capital investment in it.

Therefore, there will be further cuts in the budgets of the Health and Education departments. The Government has no wish for these cuts to impact directly on patients or on pupils, and expects both Area Health Authorities and School Boards to be creative in the administration of their budgets in order to prevent this. If the cuts do result in the closure of some small rural hospitals and schools, this will be by the decision and the wish of the Area Health Authorities and Local School Boards, and not of this Government, which believes the application of creative budgeting can avoid it, if the will to do so is present.

Rural and island residents of the Province must also do their part, consuming, as they do, a disproportionate amount of the budget through the provision and maintenance of Power, Health, Education, Highways, Seaways, and other Government Services, to and in isolated areas.

Accordingly, we are implementing Policy and Action Paper 15463: Voluntary Resettlement Project. Under this project, your government will create Resettlement Centres in which rural and island residents may take advantage of existing services. It is important for affected residents to understand that there is no coercion involved. They are simply invited to take advantage of new homes which will be offered at generously subsidized prices in the Resettlement Centres, and with financial assistance for removal expenses. This offer will be available for six months only, at the end of which time residents will understand that if they choose to stay in isolated rural or island communities, as of course they have every right to do, they thereby forfeit the right to the financial assistance described herewith, and moreover will agree to live without Power, Health, Education, Highways, Seaways, and all other Government Services, which will be terminated six months from today.

Signed by, and released with the authority of …

Gorman Grant, Minister of Municipalities, Housing and Infrastructure.

Chapter Thirty-Five

The Progressive Democratic Alliance, in its ten year review of the Voluntary Resettlement Project, trumpets it as one of the most ambitious social and financial engineering experiments of the twenty-first century. The party, in power now for sixteen years, proclaims it a huge and lasting success, making full government services available to many people of the province who would otherwise have to do without them, and at the same time enabling the province to develop one of the strongest economies in the country.

The other parties, and some of the more radical social organizations, among them the Basic Human Rights Society and the Poverty Network, continue to denounce the project, calling it variously the wanton destruction of rural life, an unprecedented intrusion into people's lives, and a callous trampling of the right to self-determination.

*****

Gorman Grant paces on the crumbling boardwalk of a Cape Sable Island beach. He is hungry, and hopes the tourists have left behind something to eat. He is checking the garbage cans before they are emptied by the Special Protected Area wardens. He has become a tourist attraction. They call him the Hermit of Cape Sable. He lives in a shack on the beach and speaks to no-one.

*****

Tom Cronk, thrusting papers into his briefcase as he listens to Bernard Appleby proclaim on the news his satisfaction with the Voluntary Resettlement Project, mutters, "Bastards," and hurries from his downtown Saint

John office, on his way to the airport to catch the noon flight to Montreal, where he will represent the Atlantic Fisheries Co-Operative at a national aquaculture conference.

He pauses only once, standing beside his desk to gaze fondly and sadly at two photographs beside the telephone.

One is of an elderly lady. From the glint in her eye and the word forming on her lips, the spectator guesses she is about to do something outrageous—pull a face, or tousle her hair, or give the photographer the finger.

The other picture is of two men who stand beside a small lobster boat, proudly holding their catch at the end of a day's fishing. The boat's name is just visible. It's called *The Millionaire*.

*****

At Resettlement Area 26 (Deer Isle), Recipient 153(M) and Recipient 154(F) wonder whether to have the soup tonight and save the chicken strips for the end of the week, or to splurge on the chicken strips tonight. 154(F) gets lots of part time work, without benefits, as a supply nurse. 153(M) is called in to pack fish, also without benefits, when the International Consolidated plant on the island is shorthanded.

"It's not as if we're *celebrating* tonight," says Dale Morse. "At least *tomorrow* we can look forward to the *weekend*."

Carol-Ann says, "I'm so tired I may not survive until the weekend."

*****

Patrick Given sits in his Ottawa office. His day's work is finished but, with an empty evening stretching before him, he is reluctant to leave. His book, *In Defence of Defiance*, is in its fifth printing. When it first appeared, it was a reminder of his earlier fame as an investigative journalist. It still brings him many invitations to speak and lecture around the world at business and

226

sociological conferences. He idly pulls a draw of his desk open and beneath some papers discovers a small notebook. He opens it and reads, *I'll write this for you, Penelope, although you'll never see it. I'm not even sure what it will turn out to be—a journal of holiday travel, some kind of self-indulgent emotional catharsis, a celebration of our long friendship, or a mourning for the death of love.*

As he reads, his shoulders sag, his lips tighten, his eyes cloud. He looks away for a moment before resuming his reading.

*****

From her desk nearby, Peggy looks up from her computer and watches Patrick covertly.

*****

Penelope Diamant sits at a sidewalk café in London. Her image as the Defiant Island girl has enabled her to continue her career long past the age when she might have retired. She is still devastatingly attractive, is still in demand all over the world, still receives endless eloquent compliments, still blushes only at Patrick's. She has a two hour break between a shoot in Hyde Park and an evening appearance. She fingers her cell phone. Should she call Patrick? She starts to dial. Cancels the call. Puts the cell phone away. She is still upset with him, and she thinks he is still upset with her. Their last meeting—it was in Athens—had been one of their brief and unconsummated encounters. It had left them both burdened with unspoken and unspent passion.

They had lunched together near the Keramikos Museum, escaping from their respective engagements, and had arranged to meet later. But Patrick had been delayed at his conference when the organizers begged for a book signing session. Then Penelope had been whisked away to be photographed at the Parthenon with the moon shining on the ancient buildings behind her. By the time she was finished, Patrick was on his way to Piraeus to catch the ferry to Italy, in response to an urgent call from Peggy warning him that a company in Naples, to which Given and Associates had made a long standing commitment, was in crisis.

No—she won't call. She'll wait a little longer. Perhaps he will call her. One of them always gives in and calls. She wonders where he is; whether they will ever arrange their lives to accommodate their work and their friendship and their love. Her mind drifts to their week in Morse Cove. How ironic it was that that time of peace and satisfaction had brought them at last so close, in undisturbed affection, at the same time as it thrust them apart, launching her as the Defiant Island girl, through Samuel's casual, fond remark. If it were not for that serendipitous change in her career, would she and Patrick have been together now? Did he understand that she accepted all those engagements for him, for Defiant Island; that it was her way of contributing to their efforts to stay on the island; that *that* was why she had not seen Patrick once during that trying time?

As she thinks of Morse Cove, and of her friends no longer on White Rock Island, and of Patrick—where? —she feels the threat of incipient tears. She mustn't cry. Her public face must not betray her unhappiness, which it will do, even hours later, even from a distance, if she cries. Besides, she fears that if she gives way to weeping, she may not stop. She sips her coffee. She avoids the admiring glances of passersby. She bites her lip.

She murmurs to herself, "I mustn't cry."

She cries.

Chapter Thirty-Six

Cornelia is on the ferry, on her way to White Rock Island. She goes once a month to visit Gladys. There is only one car on the scow. It belongs to Gladstone, who picks her up from Sunny Haven. Gladstone drives her to his ferry, which he operates in the summer for the tourists. He gives guided tours of White Rock Island and of the decaying Defiant Island plant. In the winter months, he unhappily collects unemployment, earns a little extra money doing odd jobs for his neighbours in Resettlement Area 26, and operates the ferry, just for Cornelia, once a month.

Cornelia is still hoping to receive a one hundredth birthday telegram from the premier, although her birthday was a week ago. She plans to rip it up and send it back.

Sometimes, on these trips to White Rock Island, she talks to Gladstone. More often she talks to Dale Senior and to Gladys. Gladstone is used to this, and is happy to be there when the shifting veils of time in Cornelia's mind part to reveal him, in the present, on the ferry, or driving on the island, or waiting for her. He thinks her mind is like the revolving stage he saw at the theatre on his one trip to Toronto. He imagines the stage revolving in Cornelia's mind, stopping at different scenes in her past. When the curtains part to reveal a certain time, Cornelia steps onto the stage and joins the action.

Today she has talked with Gladstone about the weather, about her room in the west wing at Sunny Haven, and about her birthday.

Gladstone says, "One hundred. Wow."

"Gladys is one hundred today, a week after me."

"Yes."

"We went to the Wharf Inn for my birthday. I said—Bottoms up. Gladys said …"

"More like bottoms down at our age."

"Is it my birthday?"

"Turn yourself around. Face the harbour."

"She kicked me on the bum."

"Gladys did? Just like her, doing something like that. Why did she kick you on the bum?"

"She said I was losing my marbles."

"Never," says Gladstone, gallantly.

Gladys, hands on hips: "Never mind cogito ergo sum. Let's … let's …"

Cornelia, triumphant: "Voramus."

She repeats, nodding in satisfaction, "Voramus."

Gladstone, smiling, glances at Cornelia. He shakes his head, mystified.

They are at a table overlooking the harbour, studying menus.

Cornelia looks up. "I miss you, Gladys."

"I bloody well miss you, too, Cornelia."

They are on the ferry, returning to White Rock Island after their night at the Wharf Inn. They are standing side by side on the deck. Gladys puts her arm around Cornelia.

It is early morning. Another ferry trip, this one charged with tension and excitement. The deck hand offers coffee.

"You ladies are out early again."

As Gladstone drives carefully up the crumbling ramp, avoiding the seaweed filled potholes, wondering how much longer the wharf will resist the relentless erosion of the tides, Cornelia discovers him.

"You ran the ferry."

"That's right."

"There's the old plant."

The proud lettering is still there, defying the battering of wind, salt and ice, announcing *Defiant Island* to anyone disembarking from the ferry.

Gladstone, reading it, says proudly, "We were defiant, weren't we? For six months, anyway."

He turns on to the Shore Road. They drive past the community hall, its doors hanging open, inviting in the community that no longer exists, past the abandoned store, its display window shattered, the bench outside collapsed at one end, past the decaying houses that dot the Shore Road. A shutter hangs from one hinge here, a front door swings open there. The dwellings stare mournfully at them, like mistreated animals, their glassless windows dark eyes of bewildered abandonment.

Cornelia says, "There's my house."

Gladstone knows the routine. "Do you want to stop?"

"Just for a moment."

Gladstone helps her out of the car and up the path to the front door. She peers through the glass panel.

"Do you want to go in?"

She shakes her head. It is too much, going in, the memories rushing around, crowding and colliding and confusing. "Not today, thank you."

They go around the house, past the kitchen door, and past the extension Patrick built for himself and Penelope, in which they never lived. The meadow has invaded the back garden, strewing a profusion of wild flowers through the tangled grass. Cornelia struggles through the clutching undergrowth, gathering a few last, lingering daisies. Gladstone offers to help.

"No. You rest."

He sits carefully on one of two old garden chairs placed side by side in a rose bower. Satisfied with her bouquet, Cornelia joins him. Gladstone jumps up to help her lower herself into the chair beside his.

He delivers his customary warning. "These chairs are going to collapse under us one of these days."

She is sitting in the rose bower with a cup of tea. Moses Ingalls and Jeremiah Miller arrive silently. They are holding their caps in front of them. They stand before her in silence, their ruddy faces grave.

"Dale Senior?"

"He's gone, m'dear. We're sorry."

"You didn't want to tell me, did you? You just stood there, with your head down."

Gladstone understands that he is his father, bringing the news to Cornelia.

They walk back to the car, Gladstone holding her elbow, ready to support her if she stumbles on the uneven stones of the overgrown path. Cornelia pauses to rest, looking at the front door.

Dale Senior kicks the door open. It's like a romantic movie. They are just married. He is holding her. He carries her upstairs.

"You'll hurt yourself."

"You're just an armful of air."

All the way from the western beach, he carries her. She thrills.

"I feel I'm a burden."

"You couldn't be a burden if you tried."

Gladstone opens the car door and helps her settle in the passenger seat.

"You must be exhausted, carrying me all that way."

He drives to a promontory near where the road ends at the Southern Point. He helps Cornelia from the car.

"It was a stroke," Cornelia says, arranging things in her mind. She always has to.

"Yes," says Gladstone. "A second stroke."

He supports her with his arm around her waist and his hand on her elbow as she picks her way carefully through the overgrown mounds and crumbling headstones.

"Thank you, Gladstone. I'll be all right now."

Gladstone retires to a discreet distance, from where he watches carefully, solicitously.

Cornelia lowers herself cautiously to the ground. "It's your birthday. I've brought you some flowers. It's the end of my week to boss you around. Now we're the same age again. One hundred! Who would have thought the wild things would be one hundred?"

Cornelia Morse and Gladys Cronk.

Wild Things. Private.

The wild things are hiding in the attic.

They are little madams.

They are renegades on the western beach.

"Holy-ee..."

"Holy."

Legs like alabaster. No—like ivory.

Gladys is lying unconscious on the rock.

"I kissed you. I thought you were dead."

Gladstone starts forward, thinking Cornelia might be speaking to him. He stops, understanding, smiles, settles back, waiting.

A swirl of wind out on the water between Deer Isle and White Rock Island stirs a buoy bell. It rings with the arrhythmic two tone monotony of a village church bell, like the buoy bell that Samuel placed to mark the channel into Morse Cove.

Morse Cove is golden in the afternoon light. They are picnicking in the meadows, Cornelia and Gladys among the sheep. Tom is at the aquaculture site. Patrick and Penelope are on the beach. Everything is perfect.

"Morse Cove is the key to the island."

Gladys raises her eyebrows.

"We tried, didn't we? We all tried. We hung on as long as we could."

She is at Sunny Haven, in the west hallway. She doesn't have to try here, where her days are easy and comfortable.

"This place is bloody awful. Watch they don't try and drag you down that west hallway."

"You made me leave. You said—Cornelia, get your arse out here."

All that effort—pretending to say goodbye, climbing out of the window, waiting all night for the ferry, locking myself in my own house, defying Carol-Ann and Dale.

All our efforts ... You, after your stroke ... Tom left alone ...Patrick beaten up ... Penelope crying ...

The wind reaches the shore, riffling the water around the promontory, stirring the unkempt grass. Cornelia breathes in salt and meadow.

She hears the bleating of the sheep and the chug of Samuel's boat and the clang of the buoy bell in the passage.

A weak sun filtering through high cloud casts a long shadow from Gladys's headstone. Still kneeling, Cornelia reaches a hand towards it, strokes it gently, rests her fingers on it.

Bones and veins and mottled skin.

She reads, *Gladys Cronk. 1910-2005. Loved and missed mother of her precious boy.*

The rising tide, quickened by the freshening breeze, laps at the rocks around the promontory.

Bitterness is not in Cornelia's nature, but it rises, unexpectedly and briefly, a healthy counter to retrospective self-assurance, as she reflects on how easy it might have been for Gladys, after her first stroke, and for herself, living peacefully and easily together at Sunny Haven.

"Was it worth it? What did we get from all that ... all that ... defiance?"

Gladys's voice is in the grass and the wind and the salt laden air and the restless rising sea.

"Our independence, old girl. We had our independence."

Gladstone, from his discreet distance, sees Cornelia's head incline. He guesses she is crying. He approaches and lowers a comforting hand to her shoulder.

"Wind's picking up. Time to go, Cornelia."

COLORLAND
by
Robert Rayner

Visit us at www.speakingvolumes.us

www.ingramcontent.com/pod-product-compliance
Lightning Source LLC
Chambersburg PA
CBHW022039240626
47154CB00007B/2479